The Smith

Kindle AISN: B0DRW7WP5S

Paperback ISBN-13: 978-1-0693186-0-2

Cover design by: Éme Stölting

Library of Congress Control Number: 2018675309

Printed in the United States of America

To my great grandmother and her half-sister.

One of whom was a lesbian and the other, a witch, back when neither were acceptable.

Foreword

This book takes place in early medieval France over a stretch of land that was used and abused by a lot of important people with very little thought to the less important people. Or the land itself. It has a rich and fascinating history, and I highly encourage anyone with the means to go and visit and talk and spend as much time as you can in the museums and archives. Having said that, this is also a work of fiction. While I tried to remain faithful to the time period, there are going to be occasional anachronisms. The medieval period is one of my favourites, but it is also a vast expanse of time with vast regional differences. Most of what most people think they know is mostly false and largely informed by movies, books and video games which themselves are wonderful works of fiction and also anachronistic. Please do not make the same mistake with this book. It was also significantly more diverse than most realise. "Whiteness" as a concept is very new and yet we let it infiltrate and taint almost every aspect of how we view the past. Lastly, this is an independently published book for a reason. You can help me and all other independent writers by leaving a review. A huge thank you to the lesbian and queer writing community, as well as my wife, who puts up with my bullshit, and our cat who causes most of it.

This book is written in UK English.

Chapter subheadings are from the 35 subconscious virtues and their vices, *Liber Vitae Meritorum*, St. Hildegarde de Bingen, Public Domain

Map on the back of the paperback edition 2024 is by Leibniz-Institut für Ost- und Südosteuropaforschung (IOS) GeoPortOst, Public Domain

Content Warning

This book contains mature themes, including racism, misogyny, abuse, murder, suicide and graphic descriptions of lesbian sex. It is not intended for minors.

Chapter Playlist

1. Secret – Peach PRC

2. Tell Her – Mia Wray

3. Use Me – PVRIS feat. 070 Shake

4. Supernova (tigers blud) – Kat Cunning

5. A Night to Remember – Girl in Red

6. Red – Gaustad

7. Nothing Hurts Like a Girl – GIRLI

8. Closer – Tegan and Sara

9. Chosen Family – Rita Sawayama

10. Everything – MUNA

11. Gravity – Pale Waves

12. Little Girl Gone – Chinchilla

13. Jealous – The Aces

14. Joyride – Fletcher

15. Burn the Witch – PVRIS, Tommy Genesis & Alice Longyu Gao

16. guillotine dreams – KiNG MALA

17. creep – mxmtoon

18. Hardline – Julien Baker

19. Get Me Outta Here – G Flip

20. What if it Doesn't End Well? – chloe moriondo

21. Boyhood – The Japanese House

22. Demons – Hayley Kiyoko

23. Hypocrite – Lauren Sanderson

24. Knew You – Kailee Morgue

25. Won't Pray for You – Jayden Hammer

26. Bloodstream – Zolita

27. i did this all for you! – Xana

28. Dreamers – K. Flay

29. Cursed – King Princess

30. Wild Heart – Towa Bird

31. Hot and Heavy – Lucy Dacus

The playlist can also be found on YouTube by searching for *The Smith Playlist*. Feel free to leave comments proposing alternate songs.

Dare to declare who you are. It is not far from the shores of silence to the boundaries of speech. The path is not long, but the way is deep. You must not only walk there, you must be prepared to leap.

St. Hildegarde de Bingen

Chapter One

Constantia / Inquietudo

Ama heard the hiss of embers nearby. The slow, seductive dance of light passed in front of her eyes, casting low shadows across the room. She had stared at embers a lot in her chosen path in life, but this was different. She was not standing in front of a forge. She was laying down. That meant, she needed to take in her surroundings and make a decision.

There was that strange silence that happens only in the darkest hours before dawn, when even the night creatures had settled down, but before the magpies had started calling. That was a good sign. There was also an arm around her waist, small and warm. Her fingers found their fingers. Slender, but calloused. An herbalist maybe? Or a wool spinner? Which one might determine where she was.

Her mind wandered to the way those fingers made her feel last night and a small smile crept across her face. It had been fun. She was older than her, but she had no man to worry about. She had said something about being widowed and there had been a somewhat disturbing smile that had accompanied that statement. She hadn't spoken of any children either, nor did she see any evidence of them. If she had said a name, Ama had forgotten it. Names were often false anyway. It was probably safe in this hut, at least for now. Ama suppressed those thoughts and forced herself to concentrate.

Where exactly was she? Was there any danger in being seen leaving? She allowed her eyes to relax and thick hairs of the animal skin she was resting on came into focus. Bear, most likely. She knew bears far too intimately for her own comfort. She must still be in the forested part of the country. Much of that forest had been mowed down when the Romans came and a lot of the land had become sandy, swampy and unproductive. She blinked, trying to clear the sleep.

Large stones formed the square brazier that held those embers, and she could clearly see the mortar. North of the swamplands then, northeast of the mountains. The locals here still used undressed stones that came from tilling the land, but they were uneven and hard to stack. The cleared land to the south meant it would be cold when she mustered the will to rise. The Master winds wouldn't be as bad here as they were to the southeast, but it would still make the morning air uncomfortably cool in late summer.

She craned her neck as gently as she could to avoid waking whomever was next to her. Dried plants hung neatly in bundles from the rafters. An herbalist then. She was likely just outside of any village and unlikely to be spotted if she left at the right moment. Herbs needed to be kept away from domestic animals and children, especially since many of them could easily cause death or illness. Yes, they were needed from time to time, but women who grew plants that caused death, even accidentally, had a way of being accused of witchcraft, even though true witches were rare. She had only ever met one and she had been a nuisance. She would prefer to never meet a witch again.

Herbalists also tended not to have husbands, or if they did, those husbands tended to have accidents. Her malicious smile made sense now. Another stroke of luck for her though. She decided she could afford to sleep for a few more minutes.

The embers had gone completely dark by the time the magpies started loudly protesting the dawn. She rolled over with a start to find her companion missing. Out gathering those mushrooms that only show up in the crepuscular hours maybe? She knew some things about herbs and herbalists, but not enough to trust her judgement when it came down to it. And that knowledge had been acquired a lifetime ago. She stopped herself from reminiscing and looked around for her things. Knee length boots, grey with age, but not leaking yet. Her rondel was still tucked inside the calf and a small pouch of silver pieces were in the toe. The woollen roll laid next to them, wares still inside. She wasn't expecting to be robbed here, but she appreciated that she had left her things unmolested nonetheless. She would make a mental note of this place and plan to return in a few years, hoping things hadn't changed too much by then.

She dressed and prepared to leave. An awful scraping sound announced her exit and she cast her eyes up toward the iron hinge. It was rusted through and a small miracle the door hadn't blown off long before. She unrolled her pack and fished out a new iron hinge, leaving it on the bear skin before striding off into the frosty dawn.

Curls of vapour spilled into the air from her nose as she took in her surroundings. A few buildings with sagging thatch in a rough circle stood below. There was no mill nearby. No river either, which meant they had a well – likely what those houses were built around. There were hundreds of similar villages, groups of families that had banded together to escape some tyrant lord, flee a plague or live out their religious differences.

After the Romans had left, there was no unifying force. Many cities had collapsed, especially those reliant on a large trade network. Some residents stayed and repurposed stones from the once-grand architecture. Others simply left to start over elsewhere. Land once under the control of local governments was now freely settled by whoever had the will to take it and the competence to make it productive. Certainly, there were those who lay claim to it from afar, but enforcement was nigh impossible, especially since any record of ownership had disappeared along with the Romans. These new settlements would send in men with carts to larger settlements to get what they couldn't hunt, gather or raise in a pen, but they otherwise relied on wandering merchants. Merchants with skills like Ama.

Ama knew that places like these survived purely because of their insignificance. They rarely had anything worth stealing and only the most petty lords would bother hunting down stray peasants that had escaped their purview. The occasional bandit raid might occur to gather slaves, which itself was a gamble since no-one who had the money to buy a slave wanted a malnourished teenager whose depth of knowledge covered the difference between cows and pigs and not much else. Girls fared much worse.

Behind her, Ama first heard, and then felt, the hot, moist and grassy breath of a horse. It was Porridge, her faded grey Konik mare that she'd had since she was a yearling.

Ama had bought Porridge for only five silver pieces and a hunting knife because she was considered especially useless. Porridge, like all of her breed, weren't considered fast or graceful, but she didn't exactly take to hard labour either. What Porridge excelled at was being petted, and if you gave her enough attention, Porridge would eventually do pretty much anything. Of course, anyone who had hard labour that needed doing also didn't have the time to indulge their horses, and so Porridge was sold.

The other especially nice trait that Ama had discovered about Porridge was that she was about as loyal as horses could get. Porridge was essentially a large dog. Ama could leave her anywhere and she wouldn't wander too far out of eyesight. Occasionally she would attempt to follow Ama into a building clearly not meant for horses.

She also seemed to take no notice of anything beyond Ama and Ama's affection. Falling rocks, howling wolves, and sudden movements never seemed to phase her. Ama suspected Porridge was either deaf, or she firmly believed she was the most regal beast on the planet and everyone existed only to pet her. Ama wished she had such confidence. She'd learned early that her angular features and limp, fine, sand-coloured hair did not endear her to most, and so she had learned caution when dealing with others. Polite, but standoffish.

This did not seem to hinder her ability to attract women like her, but Ama always attributed it to their lack of available options. If women were what these other women were into, then when Ama passed through a village, she was quite likely, the only one they would see for quite some time. Make hay while the sun shines, and all that.

Porridge did not harbour those thoughts. Ama suspected that Porridge did not harbour much of anything between her ears, but she loved her all the same. Ama straightened the worn leather straps that held her saddlebags. Those would have to be replaced soon. She should probably make her way to the village below for some supplies before she moved on. Porridge didn't notice when Ama climbed into the saddle, or if she did, she didn't make any sign of it. Ama spent several minutes massaging the sinewy muscles in her neck before Porridge decided to start her slow, steady gait down the hill. The sun had barely moved by the time they reached the village and, while no-one was outside, there was smoke from some of the chimneys, indicating that people were awake, at least. Ama slid off of Porridge, who wandered over to a small group of emaciated chickens pecking in the grass for worms while waiting for someone to emerge from a hut and feed them.

Ama picked out the most important looking house and approached cautiously, making sure her hood was down and her thin wool cloak draped behind both shoulders so as not to appear threatening. She knocked on the rough-hewn door planks and took a few steps back. A thin man appeared, brown eyes popping from the gaunt skin of his face. His red-brown hair had clearly been cut by a less than sharp knife. She guessed he had grown it out until he could grab it in hanks and slice or saw his way through it. He blinked the sleep away and focused on the small man in front of him.

"Master blacksmith. What can I do for thee?"

It took Ama moments to assess her situation. These people still used "thee" and "thou" to refer to a single person, which meant they must have been isolated for a while. Or, had some sort of belief system that prohibited more modern language. And she was being perceived as male. It may be dangerous to shatter that illusion. She lowered her voice and willed her tongue to comply.

"I'll thank thee to point me to a baker or food seller before I take my leave". The words felt strange coming out of her mouth, but it must have been adequate because the man pointed toward another, smaller house before he closed the door with no further ado. An innocuous interaction and a few supplies before she disappeared from these people's lives for years was the most she could hope for.

As she crossed the muddy square, Porridge lifted her head to make sure Ama wasn't going too far before returning to the sward of grass her and the chickens had found. Ama approached the door, which was somehow even more roughly hewn than the previous one. Their woodcutter needed a better plane. This time a woman appeared, but only peeked from behind the half-open door. She stared, but said nothing.

"I've come to pay thee for bread or other food you could provide." Ama held out her coin pouch to show that she was serious and not here to waste her time or cause harm.

"Oh! Thou art the blacksmith who arrived yesterday!" The woman's face lit up. Ama could make out a missing tooth from her smile. "I saw thee leave to our cunning woman in the evening" she whispered as though the square were full and someone might overhear. "Fortune smiles upon thee, for I've never seen her take a man before." The woman winked, screwing up her face and highlighting all of her weather-etched lines.

This was very much not the compliment the woman thought it was and now she had to tread even more carefully. For one, she would have to be even more vigilant in the future, but presently, she would have to make damn sure the village kept believing she was male or there might not be a cunning woman the next time she returned. The quicker she made her exit, the surer she was she could avoid disaster.

"I could pay thee silver" Ama offered, "or in goods." She thought to the man in the larger house. "A set of shears perhaps?" she offered. The woman's eyes lit up at the suggestion before squinting back at Ama.

"It seems me thou needst the shears more than we!" Ama took a moment to parse their bizarre grammar. She had forgotten about her hair.

"I'm from the marsh cities" Ama was most definitely not from the marsh cities, but that didn't matter. What did matter is that they were far enough away that these people had likely never been there. "Men fashion their hair thusly," Ama pushed her luck, "and women shear theirs close to their ears" she added. That was definitely too much, she thought. She should have stopped while she was ahead.

The woman's eyes popped wide in amazement. "As do the Moors?" Ama's face slipped in confusion, but she quickly regained control.

"Uh, yes" she stammered, "though the Moorish women also keep theirs longer." Ama knew a few Moorish merchants. This woman had no idea.

"I knew my man was a liar" the woman puffed. She shot out a knobbly hand with well-muscled fingers. "Give me thy satchel and I'll fill it!" the woman demanded. Ama obliged and went to find Porridge and the shears. When she returned, the woman was standing with her satchel mostly full. Ama handed her the shears.

"Keep them oiled in bear grease, or they'll rust." The woman nodded and tucked them into her apron. Ama inspected her satchel and couldn't detect any smell of mould, which was a blessing. "Which way to the next village?" she asked.

"Go south to the river. It's a day's walk. Follow it west." The woman pointed east. Ama made a note of it and nodded. "I thank thee, good woman." She turned to Porridge and headed south.

Chapter Two

Caritas / Invidia

As Porridge settled into a steady, lumbering gait, Ama reflected on her interaction with locals. If you didn't look too closely, of course it was easy to mistake her for a man. Her loose-fitting gambeson hid her hips. She had bought it from a merchant the last time she had been in Narbo Martius and it was old even then as he had accepted it as a trade from someone else against a newer one. It had never fit correctly, but then again, gambesons weren't usually made for women and she hadn't yet found anyone willing to make one for a price she could afford. Nonetheless, it served its purpose, which was to dissuade lone bandits from thinking she was easy prey.

Had she cut her hair shorter, she could probably pass for a man more often, but Ama liked the feeling of it loose around her neck. This confusion had happened previously and was sometimes necessary to avoid unpleasant situations, especially since she always wore trousers. She told herself that doing so made it easier to avoid stray sparks from the forge, but now she could no longer bring herself to wear a skirt without feeling lumpish.

Ama had once entertained the thought of living permanently as a man simply to make things easier for herself but quickly discarded the idea. She could never actually take that step. Her problem was that she simply didn't admire men in any sort of capacity sufficient enough to make that mental leap. If she couldn't *appreciate* one, she couldn't *be* one. This put her at odds with the rest of the world where female babies were abandoned and girls were sold off in marriage as soon as it was socially convenient and sometimes before, depending on the dowry market. Women were livestock that just happened to be made by humans – bred, bought and sold to serve the needs of men.

There were exceptions. Sister Klara. Sera. She had no real idea where the other various women she spent the night with stood. She hadn't asked and it didn't matter. There was only the world she couldn't change and how close you could skirt toward the edge of it before you fell off. That had happened once and she had learned a painful lesson. Her throat began to ache at those memories bubbling up, but she told herself it was because she was forcing herself to pitch her voice down earlier this morning.

The first thing Ama noticed about the next settlement was that it was significantly larger than the previous one. This meant that there was likely a mill and even more likely, a smith already. She may not have much luck selling here, but she could at least resupply before moving on. The rule of thumb was that if a settlement both lasted a year and had a forge and a mill, it would show up on at least one person's map.

Settlements came in three sorts. The most common were the ones who couldn't get along with others for various reasons. Likely that last one, based on how they spoke. Then, there were the farms that were successful enough that they essentially became villages. These were rarer. The rarest were groups of outlaws. Those tended to fail because they were comprised entirely of men, but it wasn't unheard of if they somehow managed to gain a few women, for them to eventually forget their criminal roots. None of them, however, were of any significant size without a forge or a mill.

It was mid-morning by the time Ama and Porridge sauntered into town. She could hear some voices and bustling coming from the square, so she dismounted and lead Porridge toward the commotion. It was a simple market. Bakers selling loaves, spinners selling skeins and brewsters selling ale. She didn't register the ring of a hammer, but there were too many vendors for this town not to have a forge. She decided to take a chance and found herself a spot next to a hempen tarp laid out by an herbalist.

She unfurled her woollen roll and neatly arranged her knives, handles, hinges, nails and other assorted bits of metalwork. She felt her market neighbour's eyes on her and turned to see a pair of deep blue eyes, almost indigo, surrounded by the smoothest cinnamon coloured skin she'd ever seen. The herbalist swept her gaze down and then back up, as though she were sizing up the new arrival like prey.

Her eyes met Ama's stunned silence, shadowed by ink-black eyelashes. She had been caught gawking and Ama felt her cheeks flush. *Goddammit, Ama, what is it with you and herbalists?* she thought. The last woman she had been with was an herbalist. As were three of them last year. The only one she had loved wasn't though, but she did *know* herbs, so maybe that still counted? Ama realised that she was still staring and being stared at and she needed to do something, quickly.

"Y-your skin" Ama managed to stammer. She watched a wrinkle form between her eyebrows and immediately knew she had fucked up. "My mother was a Moor" she huffed.

"Uh, no!" Ama protested. "I mean, it's so smooth. Sorry, I didn't mean…"

The herbalist's lips turned to a playful smirk and she fished a small clay pot with a wide wooden stopper from her apron and handed it to Ama.

"Jenne" she said smiling.

"Oh!" Ama said with surprise. She hadn't expected this. "Uh" she muttered as she tried to find something suitable to repay the gift. She settled on a slender, long handled silver spoon.

"I can't take that" Jenne smiled. Ama felt dejected. "I can only use gold. It doesn't alter the mixtures." Ama's eyebrows nearly reached her hairline.

"This must be expensive ointment!" Ama muttered. Jenne laughed. It was so entirely delightful that Ama immediately wanted to make her laugh again.

"Keep it" she said "And you can bring me a gold spoon later." Ama looked away, focusing on her wares.

"I probably won't be back for a while." The corner of Jenne's lip moved upwards, almost imperceptibly, but Ama caught it. She was sure some plan was afoot. Or Jenne was flirting. Which was remarkably brave considering they had met not five minutes ago and two women openly together had been considered unthinkable at best and lethal at worst since the church had solidified its hold over this area decades ago.

Certainly, there were many who still made secret offerings to the various fey and the old gods, but that was more out of fear that they might take offense and curse harvests, cows or the weather, rather than any love or devotion to them. There were also, of course, "witches" who flouted the laws, but lived further away from settlements. The ones who knew where they were only visited them if strictly necessary and kept that knowledge secret, lest they be found. Ama had only ever met one and that was not a day she would ever like to remember again.

The type of women who were interested in Ama were usually much more subtle - in villages that had no inns, they would offer to put her up for the night, or casually let it be known that their man was away. Then they would dance around the topic for hours alone before something - or occasionally nothing, happened. Dalliances with someone who would leave the next day were about as low risk as was ever possible for women trapped in villages. For her part, Ama tried to avoid ever dropping hints, especially in public. Her manner of dress and the fact that she travelled alone, Porridge notwithstanding, attracted enough attention.

Her thoughts were interrupted by a man who took notice of her wares. Beady eyes and a raised eyebrow over a ruddy and meaty face. Equally meaty hands picked up one of her blades. The man fingered the edge, judging the heft and balance.

"You made this, miss?" This lot were clearly more perceptive than the last.

"I did" she said, weighing her words carefully, listening, watching for hints that the situation could turn confrontational, or worse, aggressive.

"Would you take 30 copper for it?" That was more than she had expected. This definitely wasn't her best work - she hadn't used those sorts of skills in a while. Something was going on, but she couldn't see the whole picture and it bothered her.

"I would." she answered, hoping she wasn't walking blindly into some trap. The man counted out 30 small, round copper pieces and dropped them into her hand.

"Hendrick" he offered. Odd. Clients rarely offered their name. "Are you staying long?" he asked.

"I'm just here for today's market" she said as plainly as she could, trying her best to hide her unease.

"Mm." the man grunted. She thought she saw a quick flick of his eyes toward Jenne, but she couldn't be sure.

"Then you'll have to join me at the inn for an ale after the market is over" Jenne said brightly. Ama's brain screamed at her to flee, but Jenne's face was practically pleading. Ama knew better, but those dark blue eyes twinkling in mischievous delight and her flawless cinnamon skin. Her heart raced so loudly she was afraid everyone in the market would hear. She hadn't been this attracted to anyone in a very long time and it was absolutely demolishing her sense of self-preservation. Had she been a sailor, and Jenne a siren, she could have lashed herself to the mast to prevent her own demise, but alas, there was no rope, no mast and Ama was absolutely helpless.

"Of course!" she found herself saying. God she was stupid. Before she could correct herself, Porridge wandered into the market and nuzzled her head into Ama. She had been ignored for too long and required attention. Right now. "Ohhh, who's this!" Jenne cooed, reaching up to scritch Porridge's ears. From somewhere, she produced an apple, which Porridge accepted and then it was over. There was no way to back out now.

The inn was the largest building in the village, which was unusual for villages of this size. Usually, it was a church. But Ama couldn't recall seeing one. There must be an itinerant priest that stops here regularly to perform various rites and formally marry couples that had been living together since the last time he passed through.

Porridge tried to follow Ama into the inn, but Jenne managed to distract her with another apple as they made their way inside. Jenne ordered two ales for them and laced her slender fingers between Ama's short, scarred and calloused hands, pulling her toward a table at the back. They sat across from each other, Jenne leaning over the oak table so she could be heard above the din. Ama slammed her eyes shut to avoid staring at the dark swell of skin spilling out over the table and then immediately realised how *that* would look and focused her eyes directly on Jenne's. Jenne sucked the corner of her plush bottom lip in between her teeth and it was obvious that Ama had been caught. Again. It was equally obvious that Jenne didn't mind and likely that she had hoped it would happen.

"So, where do you make all of your wares?" Mercifully, Jenne broke the tension this time before Ama made a bigger fool of herself.

"I forge over the winter and then travel after the trails become passable." Ama flexed her fingers as though remembering the hammer. Jenne's eyes lingered a little too long on them.

"But isn't it a lot? The weight of all that metal, I mean? Why travel?" Ama's face turned stony.

"I can't stay. I need to travel." Jenne's expression softened. She nodded, solemnly as though she understood.

"If you're an outlaw, you'd fit in with about half of this village," she whispered.

"I'm not an outlaw" Ama said tersely. She caught herself. She didn't need to bring additional trouble by acting unnecessarily rude. "I'm sorry. It's just a very long story." Jenne brightened a bit and she reached across the table to place her hand warmly on Ama's.

"I have time." Ama cast her eyes toward their hands.

"It's also a painful story."

"I can wait" Jenne smiled. *What the hell did that mean? It's obvious I don't want to talk about it. Also, where does she get the audacity?* Ama's forehead twitched. She was not used to women being this friendly or forward, especially in public. And it was doing *things* to her. Things she had mixed feelings about, but before she could untangle it, a matronly woman with thick curls who carried herself as though she had seen and overcome any and all nonsense humanly possible within these walls, placed two heavy-walled tankards of cellar-cooled ale on the table.

As she turned to walk back to the kitchen, she revealed a giant of a man standing behind her. The same man who had overpaid for her knife. He sidled on to the bench next to her, trapping her beside the wall. Ama flexed her calf, assuring herself that her rondel was where she remembered. The man nodded, acknowledging Jenne. Ama withdrew her hand and slipped it below the table to finger the top of her boot.

"No need to be alarmed," Hendrick said. *This is a strange way to avoid alarming someone.* Ama swept her eyes over Hendrick. He appeared relaxed, but then again, he probably expected that his size and *maleness* would be intimidating enough. He was right.

"Speak plainly then" Ama said. She cast her eyes toward Jenne who lowered hers. "You've been strange all day." Hendrick raised his hands, meaty palms out in an attempt to appear non-threatening. It didn't work.

"Alright" he said. "I'll be brief. We need a smith. I don't know what crimes you've committed, or which lord you've offended. I don't care. You've clearly forged in a castle and we need someone with those skills." He continued quietly, "If you refuse, this village will die, just like all the others."

"I'm not an outlaw" Ama protested. "And where is your smith? A village doesn't get to this size without one."

"Exactly. Which is why it won't stick around if we don't get another. He passed last winter."

Ama raised an eyebrow toward Jenne.

"I didn't learn about his illness until it was too late" she spoke, eyes fixed on the tankard. Ama hated her expression and wished she could make those eyes never look sad again. *Stop it!* she chastised herself.

"Did he not take an apprentice?" Ama asked. "His skills might not be up to castle standards, but surely it would do for a village this size."

"His boy had only eleven summers" Hendrick said quietly. "His mother passed the year previous. The bakers took him in."

Ama sat quietly, watching the foam slowly disappear on her ale. None of this was her problem and she doubted they understood what they were asking.

"Jenne, why don't you order us some food?" Hendrick offered, breaking the awkward silence. Ama watched as Jenne rose and left the table. "Jenne's mother was a Moor. None of us had any issue with it" Hendrick spoke toward where Jenne sat, as though not looking at Ama would lend some sort of authority to his words. Ama wasn't sure what Jenne's parentage had to do with her. "No-one here would mind a woman smith." *And there it was. We don't mind Moors, so we won't mind you either.* Ama snorted derisively.

"You think you know, don't you?" Ama looked straight at Hendrick, who continued to avoid her gaze. "None of us mind that Jenne's never taken a lover either" he said. "Well, some of the lads do" Hendrick breathed a weak laugh at his own joke.

So, they knew she thought. *That's why she felt no fear. How many merchants has she seduced? But he said she'd never taken a lover? That can't be right, can it?*

Ama decided it was time to stop dancing around and be blunt. "If I stay, I'll be a danger to you all. And not just because of Jenne. As I said, I'm not an outlaw. I *am* wanted though. The knife you liked? It's not half of what I can make." Ama reached into the calf of her boot and withdrew her rondel. Hendrick flinched thinking she was going to stab him, and then relaxed when she placed it on the table instead.

The steel was dark, with even darker bands running through it. The bands appeared to move like water as the candle light of the inn flickered over them. Soft polished rowan wood made up the grip and a flattened oval pommel with a cutout so it would fit neatly against a limb made of the same dark metal as the blade. Hendrick's eyes grew wide. He had never seen metal like that before. Not many had. He reached out to inspect it, but Ama picked it up.

"That's very dear metal to use for a rondel" Hendrick said, attempting to regain his composure.

"That metal is why I can't stay" Ama replied as she placed the rondel back in the calf of her boot.

"The village would hide you from the church if you're worried about witchery. We already hide Jenne." Hendrick offered.

"What makes you think this is witchery?" Ama scoffed. "And it's not the church that wants me, they don't care about witches anyway. It's peasant superstition." she added. They sat in uncomfortable silence. Jenne was taking her time.

She took a long drink from her tankard. "Tell me about Jenne" she said in an attempt to change the subject. "You said you hide her from the church. How often do they come around?"

"She and her father showed up about eight, maybe ten years past," he said sombrely. "They were rope makers, but they stayed. Jenne took a liking to plants and our herbalist had her as an apprentice. I never met the mother. I knew she was a Moor, but her father never spoke of her to me. He was always away making business deals. He left us permanently when Jenne was sixteen. Sold the house and left her in the care of the herbalist."

"Where is your old herbalist?" Ama asked, taking another sip.

"Gone a while back" Hendrick waved it off. "She gave everything to Jenne and left with a brick layer she found in the woods and nursed back to health one winter. Still don't know what he was doing out there" he scoffed.

Jenne returned with a bowl of thick stew and a stack of flat oat bread. Long dark twists spilled from her shoulders as she leaned over to place the food on the table. Ama averted her eyes in time, having learned her lesson earlier. Jenne smiled at the two of them as she slid into her chair and began spooning stew onto a piece of oat bread. Ama felt her rondel whisper against her leg. There was something familiar about Jenne. The way she moved? The way her full lips parted when she smiled maybe? She caught herself staring in thought and quickly began spooning stew onto her own bread, but it was too late and Jenne smiled wider, candle light dancing across those indigo eyes. *Goddammit Ama.*

Chapter Three

Abstinentiae / Convivii

Hendrick rose to leave. "Stop and see me before you leave tomorrow. I think I have an idea that might be suitable for you. I need to check something first." Ama was about to mutter *not likely* but Hendrick hadn't been rude, so she shouldn't be either. The effort of being polite had drained her mind of words, so she just nodded and thankfully, that was enough for Hendrick. Which left her alone with Jenne.

"So" she said between bites, keeping her eyes on her stew "do you have somewhere to stay?" *She really had no fear of being caught.* Ama thought. *Is this how people who weren't like her acted all the time?* Ama tore a piece of bread and scooped up some of the thick brown sauce.

"This is an inn. I was planning on staying here. I'm used to the woods as well, if the price isn't reasonable." Jenne's visage fell. Ama smirked. She had the upper hand now. "You were going to offer your bed, weren't you?" Ama asked, a slight teasing edge in her voice. Jenne did not appreciate the humour.

"I'm not your type?" she asked with an exaggerated pout.

"So, you're *not* just offering out of hospitality?" Ama watched as a litany of expressions passed over Jenne's face. *That might have been too far,* she thought. "What makes you believe women are *my* type?" Ama cocked an eyebrow. Jenne's eyes swept over Ama and she cocked her eyebrow in return. Ama nodded, the corner of her lip twisting upward. It probably wasn't wise to be so obvious, even if Jenne was. She caught the disapproving eye of a man covered in flour, leaning unsteadily over his ale.

Men tended not to be attracted to her hair, hazel eyes and splotchy complexion anyway, so most of the time it didn't matter. If she ever became a threat or competition, that was a different situation - one which she normally avoided carefully. Jenne spotted the change in her demeanour

"I'm sorry, I've never done this before." Jenne whispered and then reached across the table and put her hand on Ama's again. Was her confidence false bravado then? Or was she simply trying a different strategy to see what Ama would fall for?

Ama pointed a hunk of bread at her, but didn't withdraw her hand. "An even better reason why I should stay here." She pinched a bit of stew and placed it in her mouth.

"Why?" There was that pout again, with a hint of anger. "The other girls take whatever travellers they want."

Ama pinched the bridge of her nose. She had been others' firsts before. She had regularly loved and left. It was dangerous not to leave. But she couldn't understand why she felt conflicted about this. Why did she care? She felt the rondel grow hot against her calf again. Jenne looked up at her through her eyelashes, a spark of electricity causing Ama's pupils to dilate. "How old are you?" Ama asked, trying to fight the fluttering sensations trickling down toward her legs.

"Old enough" Jenne smirked, trying to inflect her voice to sound more flirtatious. There was that confidence again. Or was it simply the euphoria of finally getting what she wanted? Jenne knew she was winning this exchange. Ama knew it too. She couldn't come up with a reason not to – at least, not one that didn't sound ridiculous.

Ama pinched herself harder. "A number please."

"Twenty-two. That's plenty. More than most girls." Ama really couldn't argue with that. She couldn't be certain of her exact birthdate, but she was roughly twenty-six.

"Fine" she sighed. "I'll save some silver on the inn anyway." Jenne grinned. Ama pointed some more bread at her "I'm not promising anything though. We're just sharing a bed."

Jenne dragged Ama away from the village like she'd won a prize. Porridge dutifully followed. Ama watched as those black twists bounced across her back from beneath her kerchief, sloping inward to where her apron tied and swelled back out again, hips swaying with each step across the hill toward the house, like a pendulum she had seen once in a city. She felt her ears heat against the chill night air and worried at her bottom lip. Her previous hesitation about this was quickly vanishing under the spell of Jenne's body. It bothered her, but not enough for her to stop following.

As they approached the door, Jenne reached out toward Porridge to pet her good night. Ama paused, admiring the display of affection as though it was familial and then quickly shooed those thoughts away. Jenne was not family. Jenne was a girl – one she would perhaps spend a pleasant evening with and then leave tomorrow. If she ever returned to this place, she would likely have a husband and children. That wouldn't necessarily preclude spending another pleasant evening together, but any feelings of attachment should be nipped in the bud, not just with this girl, but with all others as well.

Jenne held the door open and Ama slipped inside. It was more of a smallish hut with no other doors, but herbs hanging from the rafters and coils of hempen rope from the walls. Almost every square inch of space was covered in something useful. Jenne certainly knew how to maximise the space she had. In the corner, next to dying embers, was a small bed. It was not unusual to share beds with strangers when traveling, which she did often if she ran across other female travellers, but a bed this small would be impossible for anyone to share but lovers. She heard the door shut behind her and Jenne place the bar.

Jenne approached Ama like a stray cat, cautious and eyes unblinking. Ama remained where she was, her gaze sweeping Jenne slowly, lingering over her hips. God, Ama loved hips. She could happily stare at a woman's hips endlessly. There were times she wished she had been born a painter, and she would spend her days pouring herself into each brushstroke, recreating how she felt about hips for the world to marvel at. She was not a painter though. She was a stocky, calloused ironsmith, covered in soot, rather than paint and would never be able to afford a place to paint, let alone the paints themselves.

Ama was pulled from her reverie seeing Jenne's skirt ripple. Her legs were tense and fidgety. Fingers played nervously at the edge of her apron. Her breath was quick and shallow. Ama felt a sudden wave of pity and lowered her head to appear non-threatening and looking at her with as much compassion as she could muster.

"This was your idea," she said. "We don't have to do anything. I can still go back to the inn."

"I know" Jenne stammered. "I just don't know what to do now that you're here." That wasn't surprising. The other *firsts* Ama had encountered had all had some degree of nervousness. Some hid it better than others. Some hadn't told her until after. And depending on how tolerant of differences a place might be, that nervousness could easily have more than one source.

"I…" Jenne started, continuing to play with the hem of her apron and staring at the floor, "…don't want you to go." She flicked her eyes quickly to Ama's. "I want to," she added quietly.

Ama understood. "Would it make you feel better if I moved first?" she offered. Jenne locked her gaze to Ama's, head still bowed. She nodded enthusiastically, doe-eyed and relieved.

Ama gingerly stepped forward, like she was approaching a frightened animal. "Alright, but I'm going to ask you a lot of questions, is that okay?" Jenne nodded again. Ama placed a reassuring hand on her arm. "I'm going to need to hear you say yes. Your fire is fading and I won't be able to see you nod for much longer."

Jenne took a deep breath. "Yes," she said, nodding emphatically. Ama gingerly closed the gap, slipping her arm from her shoulder to her chest. Ama could feel her racing heartbeat. Deep thuds hammered against her palm. Ama paused, taking deep breaths until Jenne did the same and her panic subsided.

"Is this okay?" she asked. Jenne nodded again, before remembering to say "yes." Ama lifted her palm, leaving her fingers, skating them up to her collarbone. Her other hand slid to Jenne's, still clutching the hem of her apron. She laced their fingers. Jenne squeezed and her breathing relaxed further. It was the sign Ama had been looking for. She ghosted her finger tips across the hollow of her neck, and then returned to stroke the length of her throat with the backs of her fingers.

Jenne closed her eyes and sighed, letting herself melt into Ama's gentle touch. Ama pulled her closer, placing a kiss behind her ear. "You have," she whispered against her neck, "the most." *Kiss*, "Beautiful." *Kiss*, "Skin." Ama raked teeth across her earlobe, eliciting a small whimper. She drew back to check in. Jenne's eyes were heavy-lidded with want. *Good*, Ama thought.

Her fingers rose to Jenne's cheek and she nuzzled against the back of Ama's hand. Her fingers wrapped around black twists, tugging gently as soft whines left Jenne's barely parted lips. Ama traced her jaw, slow and certain. She knew what came next as she'd done it a hundred times before. Her fingers would leave, one by one, until just her index remained. If she didn't stop moving, her fingers would leave her face entirely.

But that never happened. As her last finger would be about to leave their chins, women would always lean forward to stop it, as though a spell had been cast, and Jenne was no different. Ama drew her finger directly to her waiting lips. Their foreheads rested against one another, stopping Jenne from following her finger. They shared a breath between them. Two breaths. Three. Jenne's eyes, now too dark to tell the colour opened lethargic as though she had taken dwale.

"Yes," she whispered.

Ama closed the gap, flicking the tip of her tongue upward, skipping against Jenne's top lip. A small inhale of surprise parted Jennes lips and Ama seized the opportunity to catch her lower lip, releasing it slowly from between her teeth. Jenne drew her head back in shock, but then, as if she had just understood the rules of the game, she perched like a viper ready to strike.

Ama paused, watching the flood of adrenaline and unadulterated desire cloud over Jenne's eyes. She unlaced her fingers and pushed Ama back onto the tiny bed, tearing off her apron, lifting her shift over her head before straddling Ama. Ama wanted nothing more than to take each dark nipple perfectly placed on each sublime breast by the loving hand of whatever deity had created women between her lips but managed to regain enough composure to refrain. For now.

"Whoa" she said, immediately reprimanding herself for sounding like she was talking to Porridge. Thankfully, Jenne didn't seem to notice. She placed her hand, splayed across Jenne's heart again, feeling it hammering faster than before, speeding lust through her veins.

"Did I do something wrong?" Jenne panted. There was worry in her eyes, but behind them, a fervent hunger that would make her do *anything* if she could only continue.

"No, but you need to slow down. At least for now," Ama cautioned. "Now that you've felt it – that... feeling," Ama was no poet, but she needed her to understand. "We're going to let it simmer. Let it take you places. If you don't, especially your first time, it's easy to ignore your body and hurt yourself. Or someone else." Jenne didn't understand, but she nodded anyway.

"Tell me then," Ama continued. "Why did you remove your shift? What is it you want me to do?"

"I don't know. I thought that's what you did" Jenne felt like she was being scolded. "Is that not what you wanted?" Her face was a mixture of surprise and desire.

"Oh, I cannot tell you how much I appreciate this" Ama grinned, "but what do you want from me? What do you want me to do?"

"Touch me again" Jenne whispered. "Here." She draped an arm across her breasts. Ama smiled, lacing her fingers up over her sides.

"I will" Ama answered quietly in the light of dying embers, "and the next time that feeling comes over you, I want you to tell me what you want." Jenne nodded and then whispered "okay".

Ama adjusted herself to sit upright under Jenne, skating her finger tips across each rib. She pressed firmly, digging short nails into the soft skin along the sides of her breasts. She listened for the soft gasp and pulled Jenne's body to her mouth. Ama felt her own blood rush between her legs, pasting lingering kisses across Jenne's collarbone, across the swell of a breast. Lifting a stiffened nub to her lips. Ama swirled her tongue, sucking gently and then harder, listening for the sighs of delight or any sign that she might be moving too fast. She could no longer see Jenne's eyes, but she could tell she was close to losing herself again. Ama buried her head into Jenne's breasts and felt arms drape around her shoulders. "Tell me what you want," Ama reminded her. "I want," Jenne whispered, "this off". She plucked at Ama's own shift under her gambeson. Ama smiled and leaned back.

Jenne's deft fingers made quick work of the laces of Ama's gambeson. Being overly large, it was a simple task to slip free of the heavy quilted garment. It fell stiffly behind her against the wall and Jenne slid Ama's linen shift over her head. Her straight sand hair was both stuck to her face and pointing in every other direction. It tangled easily, but Ama couldn't bear to cut it any shorter. Jenne laughed and ran her fingernails delicately up Ama's now-naked torso. Ama slipped her arms around Jenne's neck and allowed her to explore.

Ama had always thought herself unappealing. Her muscles were too prominent. Her shoulders too wide. Her breasts too small. Her underarms too hairy. Other women were more rounded. More delicate. More graceful. Their hair wasn't fine and straight like hers. Their necks were more slender. Over time, however, she had come to accept that other women liked the way she looked, even if she didn't. She rationalised it by telling herself that other women simply had few options and that was what allowed her to indulge them when they wanted to touch her.

Jenne knew what she wanted and she wasn't going to pass up this opportunity, having waited twenty-two years for it. Her hands dove straight for Ama's breasts, a bit roughly for Ama's taste, but bearable. She leaned back into her gambeson as a makeshift pillow and allowed Jenne to explore with her mouth. Jenne took a nipple, sucking hard enough to cause Ama to yelp. She drew back in surprise.

"It's okay," Ama said, tucking a loose twist behind her ear. "Just a little softer next time." Jenne nodded and continued her admiration. There was something about being appreciated by a beautiful woman, even if you didn't appreciate yourself, that caused her confidence to soar and heat pool between her legs.

Bodies pressed together, the liquid flow and heat of skin on skin, breast against breast. Ama peppered kisses along Jenne's neck. She tested her teeth against the delicate skin of her throat and the delightful noises Jenne made encouraged her to continue. Jenne bit the thick muscle of Ama's shoulder and her eyes blinked open. That would leave a mark and was probably harder than Jenne realised. She didn't mind. The heat in her core told her she more than didn't mind.

Ama fingered the hem of Jenne's skirt, which she immediately wanted to remove. Ama would have preferred to tease for a while before moving on, but Jenne was clearly in a hurry and she *did* tell her to make her wants known. Jenne stood, naked in the meagre moonlight now that the embers had completely died, a silhouette of every shape and curve that Ama could ever want. Her desires had been revealed long ago, but every time a woman stood before her, it made her realize just how far outside of *normal* she was.

Jenne stared darkly. "Now you," she encouraged. Ama disrobed, untying the top of her trousers. Slipping free from her boots. Peeling the stockings from her feet. She did not feel nearly as confident in her appearance. She knew she was not attractive. Her legs were muscled and scarred. The curve of her wide hips was marred by protrusions of bone instead of softness. Jenne was a goddess in comparison, but the way her breath caught as Ama slid her trousers off her legs, you would have thought it was her instead. Ama slunk back down on the bed, pushing self-conscious thoughts away. Jenne straddled her, looking down from above, eyes shining in the moonlight like an angel had descended to bestow her grace.

Ama skimmed her lips across Jenne's in her act of worship, fingertips trailing the slope of her back. Jenne kissed greedily, pressing into her stomach. Ama let her control the rhythm, cupping, squeezing, gently scratching, following Jenne's sighs as a guide. Ama leaned back and slid her hand between Jenne's legs, absorbing the heat, arousal pooling generously around her fingers. "Is this what you want?" Ama stared at Jenne's moonlit eyes. Jenne nodded with a little less control than she thought she had. "Yes" she whispered, remembering.

Ama drew her fingers together, cupping, teasing as the glorious sounds from Jenne's throat intensified. She ground harder against Ama's hand. Ama slipped a finger between her. Jenne rocked forward putting more pressure on her clit against the heel of her hand. She found the spot, a small patch of rougher texture against the flood of Jenne's arousal. Stroking as gently as she could against Jenne's lack of control. Jenne's eyes flew wide. Ama had no idea if Jenne had ever touched herself before, but it was obvious this particular sensation was new to her.

"Look at me" Ama said and Jenne obeyed, heavy breaths dripping from her lips. Ama slipped another finger into her and Jenne threw her head back closing her eyes. "Keep looking at me" Ama ordered. Jenne bucked against Ama's hand.

There's a point where your arousal becomes so high that you either become so overstimulated that you stop and forever wonder why everyone makes such a big deal about sex, or you tip into a cascade that forever alters your perception of relationships. Many of us discover this ourselves. Others never do. Still others need to be guided there by someone else. If you've never felt it before, things just feel more *good*. And so, you either stop there, or you keep going, unaware of what is about to happen.

Ama saw it in Jenne's reactions, the way the muscles in her fingers gripped against her shoulders. The way her panting breaths turned into full throated moans. The way her eyes locked onto Ama's searching for the answer to what was happening. Ama couldn't tell her. She could only show her. And then it happened. The damn burst, her eyes popped wide in surprise and she screamed as she fell apart. Her fingernails bit into the meat of Ama's back and Ama remained motionless, fingers locked inside Jenne until she was able to unclench.

And then Jenne began to sob.

Ama wrapped herself around Jenne's quaking body, raking gently her fingers though her beautiful thick hair. Once Jenne had stopped crying and had quieted herself, she turned to face Ama. Heads against the single pillow Jenne owned, she asked "is that supposed to happen?"

"Which part?" Ama asked.

"I don't know," Jenne said earnestly. "All of it. I didn't know my body would do that. I felt like I lost all control. And then I was embarrassed."

"Did you like it?" Ama said, stroking the backs of her fingers against Jenne's tearstained cheek.

"It was the most amazing thing I've ever felt," she said, "but it was also so…" she searched for the right word.

"Exposed?" Ama offered.

"Yes," Jenne sniffed. "I was terrified."

"Then yes, that's supposed to happen." Ama slipped her fingers from Jenne's hair to hold her tighter. "That's usually why people don't do that unless there's some level of trust there."

"And do you…" Jenne started

"Not tonight."

"You don't trust me?" she seemed worried about that. The women Ama slept with always had at least a base level of trust that neither would expose the other. The consequences could vary in severity, but they were always more for the other woman. Ama could always leave, assuming an angry husband wasn't stopping her. The other woman, not so much.

"It's not that," she said reassuringly. "It's just that you've had a very big night. You can make it up to me the next time I visit this place." Ama moved her hair out of the way and kissed the back of her neck. Jenne wriggled in closer and neither said anything more until they drifted off to sleep.

Chapter Four

Misericordia / Crudelitas

Rain beat down so hard that it drilled into the earth and ricocheted upwards, soaking the woman a second time from below. The pattern of her Iberian cloak had faded with age and what hadn't been was now hidden by mud. She ran, stumbling toward the light in the distance, clutching her swollen belly, blood tingeing her vision a dangerous shade of red. The trees had grown sparser and younger, slowly reclaiming the sandy swamp. Through them, she could see an old fortress. It appeared to be crumbling and abandoned, but she might be able to find refuge under a wall for the night. As she approached, she could see light peeking through the doors of one of the buildings. Whether this made it more or less dangerous for her, she did not know. Nor did she have a choice.

Sister Klara was the one who heard the uneven knocking on the door and then the sound of a body collapsing against it. She raced to the heavy oak door and threw it open. The woman fell into the hall as she did. She was a Moor. They weren't uncommon here; most were merchants and most others were happy to trade with them. Things had only turned sour later when some dispossessed Goth nobles invited the Moors to aid them in reclaiming some throne. Religion had been the unifying banner to rally the dispossessed and now all of them paid the price, even though few could name who sat on a faraway throne. Fewer still could describe how a particular ruler had any effect on their lives. The result was always the same; hate and division based on colours, accents or anything identifiably *different.*

Sister Klara knelt to examine the woman, seeing a horrifying gash across her left eye. Blood pooled in its remainder and joined the rivulets of rainwater streaming across her face. And then she noticed the woman was heavily pregnant. She ran to rouse her Sisters. They carefully carried her inside, her consciousness waning. A wet stain, tinged with blood began to spread over her legs. Sister Hildegaarde called for water to be boiled and towels to be fetched. Acolytes swarmed like bees around their queen, appearing instantly to deliver what was required and disappearing before they faced the stern visage of Sister Hildegaarde.

Screams echoed off of the old stone walls, keeping the orphans awake and terrified, huddled in their beds. They were shushed and consoled by the Sisters who were not attending. This part of life rarely happened here. People disposed of children here when a famine or plague struck, or a poor family had a girl for whom they could never afford a dowry. They were usually the youngest and so the cries and wails that brought life were not something that they had ever heard.

A girl took her first breath, deep brown eyes like her mother and perfect in every way. Sister Hildegaarde lifted her to show the mother the beautiful fruit of her labour, but her one eye had shut. The bleeding had stopped, but exhaustion had taken root.

Her tiny mouth contorted in a cry, but no sound passed her lips. Sister Hildegaarde quickly placed her weathered fingers on the child's throat to judge her pulse. It was strong. She searched frantically for an obstruction in the throat, but there was none. It was as though the child had taken a vow of silence in this holy place. Whether it was holy due to a man in sackcloth sprinkling water and burning incense or due to the women who brought forth, protected and nurtured life was harder to say.

That night she slept in the cradle placed in Sister Klara's cell. The mother had remained unconscious and the Sisters had done all they could. Time and rest were her only salves now. Sister Klara woke repeatedly in a panic, afraid that the child had died since she heard no noise. And when she did, it would rouse the child, who would fuss noiselessly. She ran her iron-stained fingertips across her tiny black curls until she remained motionless, the air passing through her perfect miniature nostrils being the only sound in the night.

Sister Klara was by the forge when Sister Hildegaarde approached to tell her that their visitor was awake. She padded quietly into the bare room, a single chestnut coloured eye following her as she sat next to the woman. Sister Klara was old enough to have learned that in almost all situations, patience and keeping your mouth shut were the only solution. Though it would never truly heal and may leave an ugly scar, the pain would diminish with time, both her eye and the trauma that had caused it.

She placed her hand on top of the other woman's and remained. She sat in silence until the bells rang and then she rose to attend her duties. As she reached for the door, she heard a strained whisper. "My child?" Sister Klara turned and spoke, willing her eyes to communicate as much compassion as she could. "She is in a cradle with the orphans. Would you like to see her?" The woman closed her one eye and settled back into the bed to sleep. She was alive and cared for and that was all the woman could handle right now.

Morning arrived and the woman awoke. Sister Klara was by her side. Sister Maria appeared in the doorway with a piece of bread and boiled oats. Tears welled up in her eye and spilled across her brown cheeks as she ate. Sister Klara ate with her. "You can tell me what happened if you are able. I understand if you are not."

The woman finished her mouthful and took a deep breath. Her eye, a deep brown focused on Sister Klara and then on some ghost only she could see. "My husband" she exhaled. Sister Klara leaned in closer so she wouldn't have to strain her voice. "Murdered. Bandits. I ran and hid." Sister Klara slid an arm around the woman's shoulders and held her as she shook and wept. Her great howls echoed off the stone walls, making it appear as though the room were mourning with her. When she had finished, Sister Klara spoke through her own tears "you are welcome to stay as long as you need." The woman shook her head, staring at the piece of bread in her fingers. "I will return to my family when I am able."

Days passed. Sister Klara was working at the forge when she spotted the woman hobbling slowly across the courtyard. She locked eyes with Sister Klara, focussing as though they were the only thing keeping her upright. She sat next to the hot embers. Sister Klara smiled sympathetically. She received a weak smile in return. "Do you want to see your child?" Sister Klara asked again. The woman closed her eyes, tired, and slowly shook her head. Sister Klara understood. "Do you have a name then?" she asked. The woman did not answer.

Sister Klara could see what was happening. What care would this woman be able to provide? Alone and with few marriage prospects being as scarred as she was. Many believed a mother with a physical ailment would pass it on to her child. But she was here, with Sister Klara, having made a great effort to walk all the way over here. Clearly, she needed human comfort.

Sister Klara hammered the glowing metal. She made it seem effortless. Her robes flowed almost as though they were imbued with magic that enhanced her strength. The woman watched, transfixed on the fluid waves of cloth, ending in sparks flying, like the glittering of the sun upon the sea.

"Will you tell me about your eye?" Sister Klara asked, hoping to take the woman's mind off of what she was about to do.

The woman sighed, but she was relieved to distract herself with a pain only marginally less horrible. And that was only because it was in the past. "A man held a knife to my throat. He told my husband he would murder me if he did not give him our gold." She took a deep breath to steady herself.

"You don't have to continue," Sister Klara said.

She shook her head. "I ran. His knife caught my eye. They killed him. It was my fault." She said it almost matter-of-factly. She had no more tears to shed. She had accepted her fate and its consequences.

Sister Klara continued to hammer. "I'm sorry," she said after a long pause.

"Will you teach my daughter?" she asked. "Women do not do that where I am from."

Sister Klara let out a low laugh. "They don't do it here either, unless there is no-one else."

The woman nodded.

"I will teach her anything I am able, if that's what she wants. If not, there are many other women here who can teach her their crafts."

The woman made to wipe a tear away, but none had fallen. "Thank you," she whispered.

A few days later, Sister Klara went to check on the orphans. The midsummer sun had finally set and they often had trouble sleeping after the longest day. Some of the locals still lit bonfires and wakefires to ward away the evil spirits and their revelries could be heard over the hills. Even those who had repurposed the day to honour St. John the Baptist could not do away with the late-night festivities, and so the children would often wake hearing noises in the dark.

She was surprised to find an adult silhouette there, kneeling in the dark. Sister Klara was not trained to fight, but she was strong enough to delay the attacker and give the children time to flee if needed. She approached cautiously, knowing the candle she held would cast a flickering light a little too long and eventually the intruder would notice her. The amount of time she had before she was noticed would be up to God.

But it was only the woman. She knelt over the cradle of her daughter. Their newest arrival. Her lips found the child's forehead and she bequeathed a silent blessing. She rose stiffly and her eye met Sister Klara's, a shining iridescent, earthy brown illuminated in the candlelight.

When holy men speak of the spirit or the soul and its everlasting nature, they also speak of its pollution by earthly filth. The soul, they reason, yearns to be free from these mortal vessels, these corruptible bones that will ultimately die and rot and return to the dust and ash from whence they came. And so, we must all live by their reasoning in order to also exist as souls. To do otherwise, is to live as beasts and to then be treated as such.

And oh, they hate that the soul requires its earthly container. They hate that the container is only borne from women, who are too weak and frail to understand their reasoning about the soul. Who bother them with their insistence on caring about insignificant things. Insignificant things are what the body requires, not the soul.

These earthly cares resonated in the woman's eye. And Sister Klara knew that look. She had seen it every time a woman saw their child for the last time. She understood the heartbreak of knowing that this cherished daughter would never be able to thrive if she left with her. Insignificant earthly things always, in the end, outweigh the needs of the soul. The woman nodded slowly and pressed a coin into Sister Klara's palm. "Her dowry," she whispered and then turned to leave, walking more upright than she had in days back toward her cell.

The next morning, Sister Klara went to find the woman, but she was gone. Sister Hildegaarde informed her that she had left earlier with a family of rope makers passing through, but heading in the direction she needed. She had hoped they might catch up with her family on the road. No-one had seen any reason to disallow it, so she had gone.

"And the child?" Sister Klara asked, though she already knew the answer.

"She is still with us." Sister Hildegaarde answered with no small amount of scorn.

"You and I made the same choice to take our vows, and for the same reason. We had every comfort and spurned it because we could not bear the price," Sister Klara reproached. "Do not judge the choices of women who did not have even that. The poor are guided by the hand of God."

"Even the Moors?" Sister Hildegaarde asked incredulously.

"Stop it. Monségnor Rachid isn't here. You know you don't care about that." Sister Klara grasped Sister Hildegaarde's hand and then returned to her duties.

"And you break too many rules." Sister Hildegaarde called after her.

Sister Klara only laughed, but it was mirthless. She said a silent prayer for the woman and promised she would care for her daughter as best as she could.

Chapter Five

Desiderium cælestium / anxietas de terrenis

A sunbeam illuminated the dust in the house. She didn't normally sleep this long. She would normally have taken stock of her surroundings and made a decision about gathering supplies or moving on quickly under the cover of darkness. Something about Jenne had distracted her from her usual vigilance and it disturbed her.

Yes, Jenne was attractive. Incredibly attractive, but she had been attracted to many other women before. Something about Jenne was *infectious*. It nagged at her. She did not like the feeling of someone being able to pierce through those defences she had put up. Especially someone she had just met. Those defences were there for a very good reason.

Ama slipped out from under the linen blanket, careful not to disturb Jenne. She fetched her things and stole out the door. Porridge sauntered over to greet her, but Ama noticed a slight lilt in her gait. She petted Porridge until she would allow her to inspect her hooves. As suspected, she was missing a shoe. She had spares and she had brought her stump anvil, but it would take her at least a day to build an appropriate fire, shape the horseshoe perfectly, and re-shoe Porridge. It would be faster if she had a proper forge. Ama squinted at her Konik. "You did this on purpose, didn't you?" Porridge huffed and nuzzled in closer for more pets. "I suppose we had better go see Hendrick then and see what he wants."

As they made their way toward the rest of the village, Hendrick spotted them on the path, raising his hand in an easy, silent greeting. Ama twisted her mouth in distaste.

"You thought we would leave without stopping."

Hendrick laughed. "You never promised you wouldn't."

"Fair," Ama responded. "Now, what's this proposal?"

Hendrick turned to walk toward the village. "It's better if I show you," he said.

In a few minutes they had crossed the town square and made their way toward the abandoned forge. A thin layer of rust had accumulated on the top of the anvil, but it was still one of the largest she had ever seen. Ama inspected it for cracks or divots and found none. The forge itself was dressed stone with a pit of charcoal two ells wide. A massive bellows, with some sort of gear and crank system, now covered in spiderwebs and dust, fed air underneath. With this, one could get their forge up to temperature within half an hour. Ama ran her finger through the dust.

"How long did it take him to put this all together?"

"I have no idea. Karl arrived here before I did" Hendrick said, drawing patterns in the dirt with his foot. "He had plans to move the whole thing to the river, next to the mill and power the bellows with water, but he took ill before he could start."

Ama nodded sombrely. "So, your proposal?"

"Right." Hendrick's meaty hand massaged the back of his neck. "Stay a year. Just one."

Ama rolled her eyes. "Why would I do that?"

"Take on Karl's boy as an apprentice," he said.

"This proposal is becoming worse," Ama pinched the bridge of her nose. "Also, there's no way he'll be ready to take over the forge in a year. You said he was eleven." Hendrick placed his giant palm on her shoulder.

"Let me finish. If after a year, you still chose to leave, you can take whatever you want from here. It won't matter, because the village will die. If you stay, the forge is still yours."

"Look" she said, removing his hand, "you have no idea what kind of danger you're in if I stay."

"Half a year then," he pleaded. "Summer is over and whoever is pursuing you won't be looking during the winter. You can be on your way in the spring. With whatever you can carry."

Ama looked over the forge. The anvil was definitely better than anything she had or could afford. She could probably figure out how the bellows worked and recreate it if she spent enough time with it. Her spot was near a river and a constant flow of air would make forging a lot faster, which would mean more pieces and more time to peddle her wares before she would have to return to her own forge. She would be able to travel farther and would be even less likely to be discovered.

"Fine" she said. "I'll give you until the end of winter. Hendrick beamed and clapped her back. "I'll go fetch the boy." Ama shook her head and turned to find a tinder box so she could shoe Porridge. Working with this forge was even better than she had imagined. Within ten minutes, the new shoe was a glowing cherry red and the shop was blistering hot. She set the shoe to the side and removed her gambeson, exchanging it for a leather apron she found hanging on the wall. It was ridiculously large, but with a few well-placed knots on the neck-tie, she could make it work for now. Ama tied the sleeves of her linen shift at her elbows and got to work.

Ama rang the hammer a few times on the anvil to measure the bounce. The hammer was unfamiliar - too large for her comfort, so she retrieved her own from Porridge's saddlebags. It wasn't her best hammer - that was at her own shop, but it was small enough for her hands. Ama checked the bounce again and the hammer nearly ricocheted into her forehead. This would do nicely. She reheated the shoe and placed it against the horn. Ama's muscled forearms moved the glowing metal like butter against this anvil. She doubted she would ever find a better forge, even in a castle. Wherever Karl had come from, he knew how to set up a shop, though by his name, she suspected he was from northeast of here. She regretted not being able to meet him.

Lost in thought and now slick with sweat and her linen shift soaked, she caught Jenne out of the corner of her eye staring, her cheeks flushed. She hadn't even seen her approach.

"So, this is where you ended up. I was afraid you had left already," she said, resting her elbows against the wooden counter that separated the forge from the square. Jenne's black twists spilled from her kerchief, her skin glistening in the early fall sunlight. Ama could feel the energy radiating from her beaming smile, even if she refused to look. She knew that if she did, she would only feed that gnawing pit in her stomach crying *danger* at the same time as it insisted that she rush headlong into it. Her own body wanted to self-destruct into her oblivion and she hated it. She hated even more that Jenne somehow seemed to know this about her. If she didn't know, some mischievous force kept placing her in her path.

Ama didn't take the bait this time. Instead, she placed the glowing shoe in a barrel of water, swishing it around as it hissed and sputtered angrily. She found a brush of some unknown oil and coated the shoe liberally so it wouldn't rust right away.

"You talked with Hendrick, I assume" she said, her eyes fixed on the shoe.

"I did," she said tersely

"You'll stay a year?" It was more of a statement than a question.

"Half a year" she said. "But this doesn't change anything." Jenne's smooth forehead twisted into a confused frown.

"You don't like me?" she pouted. Jenne was trying to manipulate her again. On purpose. Ama had not had to deal with this sort of thing in a very long time. Usually, she was gone before any *feelings* could take root. The women she had been with were equally glad that she wasn't sticking around to cause problems. To them, Ama was a rare dalliance, a spot of pleasure against the backdrop of a miserable and dreary life. Lives that often came with a jealous man or spurned suitor. But she was only a taste. Staying would have been a problem and both women would never have believed otherwise. Like being foolish enough to believe a sailor's promises of love in a port city.

"No," she said, petting Porridge so she would acquiesce to the shoeing, "I barely know you. And you barely know me. Last night was fun, but we did that with the assumption that I would be leaving in the morning."

"You said you'd still visit. And tonight could be fun too," Jenne teased.

Good Lord, this woman was tormenting her. Ama knew this would happen and now she was dealing with the consequences of giving in last night. Jenne needed to understand that being her first lover did not mean Ama was her first *love*. Those were different things. But a flush of heat betrayed her. Ama tried to convince herself it was the heat of the forge, but she knew she was lying.

"You don't know what you're asking," Ama said, still petting Porridge. "If you're hurt now, it's going to be a hundredfold worse in the spring."

"Tell me why you have to leave." Jenne demanded petulantly.

Ama took Porridge's leg and bent it upwards. "I said it was a painful story." Ama fitted the shoe and gathered some nails. Satisfied that it would fit, she pinched the hoof between her knees and picked up a hammer.

"I don't care what you've done," Jenne protested.

"I keep telling you, I'm not an outlaw. I haven't *done* anything. It's what other people will do." Ama tapped in the first nail. Porridge shook her head.

"You know the people here don't care." Jenne reached out to distract Porridge with some ear scritches.

"It's not the people here that I'm worried about. Well, I am, but not in the way you think." Ama hammered in another nail. Two more should do it and then she could be away from this maddening woman.

"You could just tell me. That would save everyone some time, don't you think?" Jenne said.

Ama had genuinely considered this. She hadn't been around people for months at a time in at least two years and even then, it was because she had been prevented from leaving due to the weather. She had divulged a little too much about herself with some friendly merchants and been told that there were more of her people in Chamonix. All she found was a monastery and some snow. And she had already had about enough of monks for one lifetime. It was a waste of time and she vowed never to do that again, but at least the monks had bought all the iron she carried.

But then again, if she were going to stay overlong and be the cause of all of their deaths, shouldn't they be entitled to know why? Or if they knew, would they seek out her pursuers for a reward? If she did tell them, it would have to be with enough time for her to be on her way before the fort could be informed. Ama did some quick calculating. From here, it would be a good three days ride in good weather with a good horse, if you could camp. If you couldn't, you would need to make it to a village within a day. She didn't know of any villages that fit those criteria from here, but given how often they sprang up and disappeared, she couldn't be sure.

"How far to the nearest village?" Ama asked.

"Three days northwest. But it's smaller than ours" Jenne said. "That doesn't answer my question."

Dammit she thought. That was the village she had just come from. If she continued to stall, would Jenne get bored of chasing her? Half a year might be long, but who else would she chase? The poor girl had waited until she was twenty-two for her first lover. It might have been romantic, even, if it weren't so absurd.

"How do you get supplies in the winter?" Ama continued to probe.

"No-one really leaves in the winter." Jenne said. "That would be stupid. Some go out hunting and there are always fish in the river, but you can't pass carts through the trails in the mud."

"And single riders?" Ama asked.

"I've never seen anyone do that." Jenne answered.

Ama finished tapping in the last nail. Porridge shook her head again and turned to Ama for her treat. "Look," she said, turning to Jenne, "I think that you are stunningly beautiful and equally naïve." Jenne blushed, but Ama continued, "If I tell you, one of three things is going to happen. One," Ama lifted a finger, "you'll ask me to leave immediately. Two", she continued, "you'll decide it's worth the risk just to keep a blacksmith around, but someone in this village will seek out a reward for finding me. Or three, they'll find me anyway and burn the village to the ground. Which one of those options can you live with?"

"Or four," Jenne took Ama's callused hand and forced a finger up, "no-one says anything and you stay."

There was that foolish optimism that vexed her so much, but at the same time made her stomach flutter. How could she be so stupid as to believe that was even a possibility? Ama was not prepared to risk everyone she cared about again. But she didn't care about Jenne, did she? Ama wanted to slap that thought out of her head, but Jenne was standing right there. Why was she doing this to her?

"Jenne," Ama started, looking into those wide indigo eyes, nearly losing her resolve. "This is that naïve part that I was talking about. You've found someone like you after waiting your whole life. But the sort of life you think could happen doesn't get to happen for people like us. Sooner or later, they will come along and ruin it. And so, you take what happiness you can, while you can and then you let it go and you move on."

Jenne kicked at the dirt and took a few forceful breaths. Ama waited for the outburst. "Fine" she spat. Jenne reached out and grabbed the strings of Ama's leather apron, pulling her into a forceful kiss. Ama's eyes popped wide in surprise. "If I can only take what happiness I can, I'll take it while I can." She wheeled on her feet and stormed off.

Good, she thought. *That's what should happen. She should be angry with me. It will make leaving easier.* Ama pulled her fingers away from her lips. She hadn't been aware that she had been touching them. *You are so fucked.*

Chapter Six

Modestia / Jocularitas

Sister Klara's soot-stained hands grabbed a pair of tongs and pulled a bar of glowing iron from the forge. Ama sat, mesmerised at her robes flowing like water as she beat the metal into shape. Scale split and flew off, like Sister Klara was hitting a dragon's egg. Ama had touched it once and learned very quickly that just because it wasn't glowing red, didn't mean it wouldn't burn you.

"If you're going to watch me, at least be useful" Sister Klara said, between blows. Ama slid off her stool and began pumping the bellows. The coals roared and sweat began to bead on her face.

"How come you don't add bones to your iron?" Ama asked, wiping her brow.

Sister Klara stopped hammering. "Why would I do that?"

"I don't know." Ama eyebrows furrowed. "I read it in a book."

"Which book?" Sister Klara asked.

"I can't remember," Ama lied. "We found it in the library".

"We?"

"Sera showed me."

Sister Klara grunted and returned to hammering. "How old was this book you found *in the library*?"

"I don't know. It looked old, I guess." Ama shrugged. "Why does it matter?"

"Well, some say that the closer you get to creation, the closer to truth you get." Sister Klara started. "That's why the Romans knew more than we do. And the great civilizations before them knew even more."

"Why are they no longer here, then?" Ama's eyes were wide. She loved it when Sister Klara told her stories. Sister Klara was the oldest woman in the orphanage and seemed to always know the answer to everything.

"They knew too much. Remember the tower of Babel?" Sister Klara said between blows.

"Why teach us to read then? Won't we know too much" Ama asked.

"Maybe one day. That's why you must be careful with what you learn. But it is hard to say how much is too much. Understanding that is the difference between knowledge and wisdom. And what tree did Eve eat from?"

"The tree of knowledge, Ama dutifully recited.

Sister Klara placed her work back into the coals and raked them. "Pump," she ordered. Ama worked the bellows and the coals glowed. Sister Klara shuffled over to the counter to rest against it

"Where were these people adding bones to their iron? Do you remember?"

"Somewhere from the North"

"Heathens then," Sister Klara huffed.

"Like Sera?"

"Sera's not a heathen. She was born here. I was there. I was there when you were brought to us as well. The man who brought you was from the North. Does that make you a heathen as well?"

"Maybe?" Ama wiped her brow again. She noticed the small twist in Sister Klara's mouth toward her eyes.

"Maybe indeed. Keep that to yourself, or you'll get beaten and be saying *Hail Mary's* until your knees bleed."

"Is your family heathen?" Ama asked, pressing her luck. She couldn't help it when Sister Klara was in a mood to tell stories.

"No, I came here when I was twenty." Sister Klara put the iron back into the fire and raked some coals over it.

"Why? Did your husband die?" Ama asked.

Sister Klara laughed. "Sister Magali may have taken her vows because her husband died, but no. I was told to marry or come here. I chose to come here."

"Who did you have to marry?" Ama asked.

Sister Klara waved her hand dismissively. "I don't even remember what he looked like. My father presented him and I said no. So, he gave my dowry money to a convent and they took me instead."

"What's a dowry?" Ama's giant brown eyes were fixed on Sister Klara now.

"A dowry is money that gets paid to your husband for taking you."

"You have to pay to be taken away?" Ama's face screwed up in confusion.

Sister Klara laughed. "Usually, it's used to build a new house. Your husband will also give you something like gold or a jewel so you can sell it if he dies. Then you have something to live off of." Sister Klara touched her finger to Ama's nose. It left a grey stain of iron dust. "You have a dowry too. When you're old enough, we'll give it to you."

"Why can't I just live off of my dowry?"

"You're full of questions today."

"You always say that."

"That's true, I do." Sister Klara pulled the iron out again and began hammering. "Most people find they *want* to live with someone else. And have children."

"You don't want children?"

"No. Children are work. If they weren't, no-one would leave you here." Sister Klara removed the iron from the fire and began hammering again. "Besides, I have you."

Ama beamed with pride. She wrapped her chubby fingers around the handle of the bellows and pumped to stoke the charcoal.

"I still don't understand why I can't just live off of my dowry. What's the point if he gives me something and I give him something?"

Sister Klara put the piece back in the fire. "Where did you get this?" she pointed to the bag of dried chamomile tied around her neck with a piece of jute.

"Sera gave it to me." Ama thought she might be in trouble.

"And did you give anything to Sera?"

"I made her some rosemary oil for her hair."

"Do you think she could have made that herself?"
Ama nodded.

"And could you have made this bag by yourself?"
Ama nodded again.

"Then what's the point?"

"Oh. I get it. So, you marry your friend then?"

"If you're lucky." Sister Klara removed the piece and began tapping more gently on it. It was almost finished.

"Who taught you to forge?" Ama asked.

Sister Klara quenched the new stable door handle and brushed it liberally with leftover kitchen grease. "My father's blacksmith."

"Your father had a blacksmith?"

Sister Klara nodded. "My father had a lot of land. And he wanted me to learn to read. But I didn't like reading. So, I would run away from my tutor and hide in his shop."

Sister Klara wiped her hands on her leather apron before removing it and hanging it up for the day. It hung like silk, well-loved and stained so that the outline of Sister Klara could clearly be seen in it. She quenched the coals with a ladle from the water barrel and held out her hand to Ama. Ama took it and she led her across the wide courtyard to the hall for prayers and the evening meal.

Most of the cobblestones placed by whoever had built this place had long since disappeared. Either they had been dug up and repurposed or simply buried by sand and rotted leaves. Along the north wall, Sisters had cleared them away and created a bed for grapes and even a few apple trees. Both were heavily pruned and tied to espalier against the stones. The amount of space for food production was limited by most of the surrounding area being forested and so the courtyard had become their kitchen garden.

No-one truly knew what this place had been before the Sisters had taken it over, but it was on the main road and so, they assumed, the trees had grown up around it after it had been abandoned. Ama could not imagine their absence. The shade of their enveloping branches made her feel like this was their little secret, even though merchants and priests stopped by regularly. It was like the forest was giving them a hug.

Ama knew, but had not seen, that to the south was a wide expanse of scrubby grass and that if you went to the east or west too far, it would become a briny marsh. If you kept going south, you would find more forest and then the mountains. Over the mountains, were the Moors that some people were upset over. She could not understand why anyone would be upset over Sera. Sera always obeyed the rules. She was kind and quick and pretty. She didn't bother anyone because she never spoke, but some of the merchants would keep their distance or say mean things under their breath.

Ama was six when she had heard a merchant mutter something about Sera being *dirty* under his breath. It was before she had learned that adults are sometimes allowed to say things that children are not. She had marched up to him, secure in her authority, and scolded him as she had seen the Sisters do when children had made similar remarks, finishing her tirade with a slap to his leg with the willow stick she was carrying.

This ended with Ama getting sent to kneel in the chapel for an entire day, the merchant refusing to sell them anything and Sister Klara laughing the entire time. Sera had snuck her food from the kitchen and gave her a big hug before slipping silently into the shadows, undermining the entire point of the punishment.

Ama had not quite made the connection between skin tone and treatment. She was teased because her skin was splotchy and freckled. Sera's was smooth and brown and most everyone else was a tanned olive. To her mind, she was *more* different. It did not make sense to her why Sera was singled out more than she was, no matter how many times Sister Klara had tried to explain it, and so Ama had just accepted that this is the way they would be treated and she would not be allowed to hit people no matter what they said.

Sister Klara led Ama between the garden beds, holding fast to her hand so she didn't go running off to jump over the cabbages again. "You're eight now," Sister Laia had said. "You must work. You can no longer play. And if you disturb my cabbages, you'll be working harder to pay for it!" But Sister Klara knew that Ama still wanted to.

"But you *did* learn to read," Ama said.

Sister Klara nodded. "I did. My mother was very cross about letting me get dirty in the forge, but my father thought it was funny and he allowed his blacksmith to teach me whatever I wanted. He didn't believe that girls needed to know how to read anyway."

"How would we learn anything then?" Ama asked.

Sister Klara laughed "Now you're asking questions that will get you into *real* trouble!" She wiped a tear from her eye. "He later regretted letting me when I refused to marry," Sister Klara continued. "Not that I had many suitors anyway. The dowry market had gone up after the last war."

"I would marry you!" Ama exclaimed. Sister Klara laughed.

"You've had eight summers and I've had over sixty. And you have to marry a boy, or you can marry God."

"God has had a lot more than sixty summers." Ama pouted.

"True," she said. "But God doesn't make you bear his children."

"What about Mary?" Ama asked.

"Most of the time" Sister Klara answered. "But I'm not as sinless as Mary, so I don't think that will happen."

"So, I should be naughty if I don't want to have children?" Ama scrunched her entire forehead in thought. Sister Klara laughed even louder.

"Don't let the other Sisters hear you say that. You're going to get *both* of us in trouble and then they will make you work somewhere else."

"I could go to the kitchens!"

"They wouldn't put you in the kitchens. You and Sera would cause too much trouble together. They would make you tend to the pigs."

Ama stuck her tongue out in disgust, but resumed her questions. "What if I don't want to marry a boy or God?"

"Then you can live by yourself in the woods like a witch, but that is a very hard life. It's hard for one person to live by themselves."

"Sister Maria says that witches don't exist."

"That's true, they don't anymore. Like a cunning woman then. But even they have to live close to villages."

Sister Klara shooed Ama into the children's dining hall. She ran in and threw her arms around Sera, nearly causing her to drop her oat cake on the floor, but with a silent giggle on her lips. Sister Klara shut the door but did not hear Sister Hildegaarde behind her. She yelped in surprise when she turned.

"Time for prayers, Elke. Or are you seeking to take on Sister Irati's job tonight?" Sister Hildegaarde teased.

Sister Klara shook her head and started off toward the chapel, Sister Hildegaarde keeping pace.

"You're overfond of those two."

"I'm not the only one," Sister Klara said tersely.

"I just don't want you to do something rash if someone comes looking for a wife and we have to separate them."

Sister Klara cocked an eyebrow. "No one wants orphan girls right now. Certainly not a Moor or a girl who acts more like a boy. They'll be with us for a while yet."

Sister Hildegaarde sighed. "I hope you're right."

Chapter Seven

Benevolentiam / Malignitas

Jenne turned to leave and marched angrily back toward the woods to collect more herbs before the weather turned. She would need much more feverfew and tansy to help the village make it through the winter. Before she reached the edge of the village, however, she heard a man on horseback call.

"Are you Jenne?" he yelled. Jenne did not recognise him, but it was unlikely someone would be looking to cause her harm in the middle of the village during the day.

"I am. And you are?" she asked, sceptical.

"Just a silk merchant, but your father paid me to pass on a message when I told him I'd be traveling this way." The merchant pulled out an intricately folded piece of parchment and handed it to Jenne.

"Do you know where Hendrik is? I'm to see him next." Jenne pointed him in the right direction and turned away as he rode off. She unfolded the parchment and immediately blanched. She stuffed it into her apron pocket and walked faster toward the woods.

Jenne fell brusquely to her knees in front of a patch of feverfew, ignoring the bruising that would surely follow and withdrew her harvesting knife. Twenty-two years she had spent, being the ideal daughter, being useful, earning her keep. She had kept her father's house while he was away, selling his wares -

wares that she made that still hung in her house after he sold his. She had spurned love until only yesterday and then, like a fool, had fallen for someone who didn't even want her. She had thought herself grown, responsible, but mere hours had revealed her to be nothing more than a stupid girl.

Jenne hacked at the plants in a rage, tears brimming and then spilling over her face, contorted in anguish. Her eyes screwed shut, as if she could keep out the hurt. Her life was about to irrevocably change and there was nothing she could do about it.

Ama was hanging up her leather apron when Hendrick appeared, a blonde boy covered in flour dust in tow. "This here's Karl's boy, Karlson." *Original* Ama thought. Karlson's hair stuck up and appeared to tangle easily, like Ama's. Either that or he hadn't washed it in a while. He was on the tall side, for eleven, coming up to her shoulder already. Thin and wispy, like a hay stalk, she thought. Apt, for someone who worked with bakers. He would need more muscle to work the forge though.

"Hendrick said you're going to teach me to smith." Karlson said, not looking at Ama. He wandered around the forge as though he owned it, which, Ama supposed, he would, once she left. He'd surely spent more hours here than she had.

"I'm done for today, and I need to make a trip to gather my own tools. It should only take a few days. Once I get back, I'll teach you what I can."

"Can I come with you?" Karlson asked.

Ama looked at him quizzically. "Have you ever travelled before? You wouldn't rather wait for me at the bakers?"

"No," he said with the abrupt honesty that children have. Ama looked at Hendrick, who just shrugged. Karlson added "It's too crowded." Karlson seemed like he wanted to say more, but he didn't and Ama didn't push him. It wasn't her business.

She turned back to Hendrick. "There's another thing. I'm going to need to stay somewhere when I get back. I don't think Pèire wants to keep me at his inn the whole time."

Hendrick looked confused. "I thought you were staying with Jenne."

Ama ran a hand through her hair. It stuck, like it always did. She needed to stop doing that. "Look, you know as well as I do that if I stay with Jenne, she's going to be crushed when I leave." Hendrick was about to speak but Ama cut him off. "And I *have* to leave."

"Jenne really, *really* wants you to stay with her," Hendrick said.

"Yes, I know that. But do you want to be picking up the pieces when I'm gone?"

"You don't know the whole story," Hendrick protested.

"Of course I don't! I just got here! That's what nobody seems to understand! None of you actually know me!" Ama finished her tirade and Hendrick puffed his cheeks.

"I guess you can stay at Karlson's house," he said.

"Karlson has a house?"

"Yeah, but it needs to be fixed up," Karlson yelled from the back of the forge.

"Fine. I'll add that to the pile of things I'm going to be doing, I guess. Can you deliver some planks? I'll start on it when I get back."

Hendrick nodded.

"You can take Karlson back to the bakers then. I should only be a couple of..." They heard a high-pitched shriek and when Ama turned, she could see a shocked and whimpering Karlson holding his hand, tears bubbling and his lips quivering. She knew immediately that he had touched some of the black, but not cool, iron resting on the edge of the forge. Perhaps he hadn't spent as much time here as she had thought.

Ama grabbed his arm and plunged it into the quenching bucket. That would do for now, but she needed to get him to the herbalist who had just stormed off. She scooped him up and ordered Hendrick to find Jenne and let her know they were coming.

Hendrick ran toward Jenne's house at the edge of the woods and then stopped abruptly. Jenne was slumped in front of a patch of hacked herbs that appeared to have borne the brunt of every grievance she'd ever had since she was a child. Her head lolled forward and her back heaved with great sobs and then he noticed the blood. Jenne appeared to have cut her arm, which was now red and dripping.

"God have mercy!" he yelled as he picked Jenne up and moved her inside. Jenne sat on the bed while Hendrick wiped the wound clean. It didn't appear to be too deep or that severe. He stood and asked her where she kept her water. Jenne pointed with one arm to a corner while she wiped her face with the other, smearing more blood in the process.

"Now, tell me what's going on?" Hendrick asked. "Your wound isn't that bad. Not enough to cause this." Hendrick gestured broadly.

Jenne muttered a *thank you* and dipped a rag in the water bucket. "I received word from my father." Hendrick waited, but Jenne didn't continue. After a few moments, Hendrick nodded. He suspected he knew anyway. "Ama and Karlson are on their way here," he said. "Karlson burned himself at the forge. He'll need an ointment of some sort."

Jenne laughed bitterly. "You're going to need to get me an apprentice, then." Hendrick nodded sadly and stood, trying to decide what more he could do. "There was a silk merchant looking for you," Jenne muttered. "I pointed him toward the inn. I thought you were there." A conflicted look took over his face. "Go," she said. "You've done all you can." Hendrick quickly left.

Ama passed Hendrick on the hill up toward Jenne's house, but he kept his eyes toward his feet and refused to look at her. *Strange* Ama thought. A few minutes later, she backed herself into the door, pushing it open, careful not to hit the whimpering boy's head on the doorframe. She placed him on the small bed while Jenne busied herself preparing an ointment. Everyone in the room seemed aware of an odd tension and so no-one spoke, Karlson's sniffling occasionally breaking the silence. Ama stared at the bandage around Jenne's arm while she dressed the burn. Once finished, Ama escorted Karlson outside. She was about to walk him home when she realised she didn't know where he lived. She was the stranger here, yet somehow responsible for both a forge and now a boy. Karlson turned to her.

"So can I come with you tomorrow?"

"You're not going to be much use with a burnt hand. You should probably stay here and heal for a bit. I'll collect you when I return." Karlson was clearly disappointed.

"Please?" he whined. It was then Ama noticed a faint colouring just beneath the collar of his shift. That explained it. She sighed. Just how much more involved was she going to get in these people's lives? But she couldn't just ignore it either.

"Fine," Ama said, already scolding herself for getting further entangled. "Meet me at the forge at midmorning." Karlson grinned and ran off, his burned hand apparently forgotten. Ama decided that she should probably ask Jenne how long this burn would take to heal. She turned to open the door, but paused. She knew full well that it would be best to just disappear. Picking at wounds just delays healing. She might have a tenuous agreement, but no-one but her knew the danger they all were in.

And then the door opened. Jenne stood before her, arm bandaged and a frown marring her beautiful face. And behind the frown was hurt. Hurt she had caused. Ama scrunched her eyes shut and sighed deeply. "What happened to your arm?" Ama decided that was a safe question. Jenne just turned away and walked back inside. It was clearly not a safe question. Ama followed. Jenne stooped to poke at the hearth, back turned to Ama.

"If I tell you what I can, will you tell me what happened?" Ama asked. "I suspect Karlson's going to need your help a few more times before I leave and I'd rather not have the village herbalist hate me."

"Are you always this condescending?" Jenne spat. Ama snorted a small laugh.

"Probably. Also, bitter. Jaded. Aloof as well. It's kept me alive this long," she said. "And you are sweet and full of energy and," she blew out her cheeks, "so beautiful. Any woman would be so lucky to have you."

"But not you," Jenne interjected.

"No, it's...I would be so unbelievably happy to stay and see where this goes, but I just can't." Ama lowered her voice. "I didn't mean to hurt you. I'm really not used to this. Not in a long time. I'm always gone the next day."

This was true, Ama thought. If she could just be free of everything hunting her, she could picture herself staying. *Being* with Jenne. Which was not something she had pictured for herself in a very long time.

"There was someone else then?" Jenne asked, a slight hint of jealousy in her voice. Ama felt the rondel dig into her calf.

"A long time ago. I've been running ever since. It's safer that way."

"From her? Or him? I'm sorry, I don't know how this works." Jenne looked up at her with a bit more compassion this time, firelight playing across her face.

"Her. But she isn't the one after me." Ama wasn't going to bring those memories up. Not tonight. "I was held captive by someone," she started. "I escaped and they've been trying to get me back ever since. They'll hurt people to do it. Including you, and the village."

"Who?" Jenne asked, eyes contorted in worry and confusion. "Why you? You're just a smith. There are smiths everywhere."

Ama started pacing. "I said that I would tell you what I could. If I say more, someone might find and tell the people hunting me, hoping for a reward." She stopped, hands hanging limply by her side. "If I'm going to stay here for half a year, I can't risk that. *You* can't risk that," she added. *I can't risk you*, she had almost said, before pushing that thought out of her head. Even though this was an avenue she would have liked to explore, it wasn't available to her. Believing that it was would only make things more dangerous and harder for both of them.

Jenne nodded pitifully. "I received a message from my father," she said. "He has promised me to a sail maker. He hopes to make a business alliance. I can't imagine him getting her before spring, so I'm just as stuck as you are."

Ama's heart sunk. She didn't understand why. Most of the women she had been with had had husbands or some sort of companion. Why did this cause her so much distress? Why was she *feeling* so much? This was the best-case scenario, wasn't it? Both of them would be obliged to walk away by the spring and, while it would hurt to leave, neither of them would be the ones causing hurt to the other.

Ama nodded slowly and then closed the gap and knelt to hold Jenne close, rocking together on the floor in front of the hearth; the solidarity of womanhood in a world that only saw them as pieces to be owned and traded as men saw fit. They stayed and mourned their lives until the sun grew red in twilight.

After the tears had fallen and Ama's arms ached from holding Jenne so tightly, she brushed a twist of black hair behind her ear. Indigo eyes looked up at her expectantly. "I have half a year." Jenne whispered. "Let me take happiness where I can. Please?"

Ama could feel her resolve slipping. *No,* she thought. *This is not how these things go. This is not how you survive.* But she knew she was lying to herself. It wasn't about survival. She had been presented a perfect opportunity and she knew that if she took it, it was her who would find it too difficult to let go. It was anger at choices being made for them. It was anger at the thought of Jenne being taken from her, even though Jenne wasn't hers. Even though she would have to leave anyway. It was anger that her façade of being detached and walled off wouldn't work this time. She was being forced to confront and admit that she *wanted* this. That she *wanted* Jenne.

And for the past eight years, Ama had been able to want and have for one night only, like a carefully regimented diet. She had allowed herself to satiate her body by walling off her heart. Ama was afraid that if she allowed this, her heart would become gluttonous. She would not be prepared for the consequences when it ended. And it *would* end.

But Jenne's eyes were wreaking havoc on the walls she had built up over years and Ama never was very good at resisting temptation. She hadn't had to be because she was always gone the next morning. *No!* she tried to tell herself again, but it was quieter, more resigned, and that's when she knew she would give in, no matter the consequences in the future because her heart only saw the present. And the present was glorious.

Chapter Eight

Libertas / Cupiditas

A ma slipped away from Jenne and gathered a few more logs before returning to rebuild the fire. She rose and turned to face Jenne, who had removed her apron and shift without Ama noticing. The movement of the firelight highlighted every curve and Ama felt the pang in her stomach turn to warmth between her thighs. Once her brain reset itself, Ama realised that Jenne was waiting for her to do the same. She crossed her arms to grab the bottom of her shift and pulled it over her head. Jenne blushed as the linen flowed like water over Ama's bicep. Ama kicked off her boots and wriggled awkwardly out of her trousers while Jenne bit her lip staring at her leg muscles flexing and unflexing. She could tell Ama was self-conscious about her body, but Jenne thought it was beautiful, so she kept her mouth shut, lest it sound insincere, or worse, mocking, and hoped her eyes would convey her appreciation instead.

Jenne approached her lover and draped her arms around Ama's neck. Last night had been a blur of emotions and new experiences and she was determined this time to savour what she had, while she had it. Ama was only slightly taller than she was, but Ama's body was so much more powerful. Her muscles flowed effortlessly under her skin like the well-kept steeds some of the Moorish merchants proudly displayed in the city.

Jenne had seen some of the village boys running around shirtless and, occasionally, naked. They would fight and wrestle, trying to prove which one of them was the strongest and therefore, presumably, who got to claim one of the admiring girls as a prize. Jenne did not understand the appeal. Their muscles looked stringy and mean, like starving badgers. Inevitably though, the contest would end and they would pair off. At first, they had tried to convince Jenne of their beauty. They had even acted threatening when their entreaties failed. Their muscles had flexed angry and violent. They gave up after Markel.

Ama's muscles though, Jenne felt like she could get lost in them for days. These muscles were earned through work, not by grace of her sex. They were comforting and capable. They built things. They promised safety. They enveloped her with the scent of chamomile and linen and the tang of iron dust.

Jenne's lithe fingers traced them as they poured into one another underneath her soft skin. She leaned forward, angling her head to skim her lips over Ama's who arched her neck to accept the invitation. Her tongue skirted along teeth, lips, gentle at first and then diving, hungry for more of her.

Ama's fingers skirted across Jenne's back, ghosting over dimples, just above the base of her spine before pressing short nails deep into her skin. Jenne squealed and laughed as their tongues fought hotly, consuming and consumed, grinning like fools into one another.

Ama reeled. This did not feel like the others. She felt herself falling into a space that had been closed off and empty for years. Locked away, like a forbidden crypt. At first, she worried that it would feel disrespectful to have someone else there. But all she felt was *happy*. She would worry about the other emotions after.

Jenne felt Ama's hands drift lower across the curve of her hips and the rush of arousal blossomed molten in her centre. Jenne thought she was prepared this time, but Ama scooped her up and she wrapped her legs around Ama's waist before thinking. Ama deposited her brusquely on the bed, dark twists fanned against the covers. In the reflected red twilight, Jenne saw the wicked hunger on Ama's face and she desperately wanted to satisfy it.

Ama knelt forward to kiss her again, roughly, like a starved wolf. Jenne had a moment of fright at the thought, but remembered last night and tried to calm her ragged breathing. It didn't help. The fear of the unknown only amplified her desire to find out.

Ama traced the soft skin of her throat with her tongue and then sat upright again, observing like a general scanning a battlefield and planning their attack. Lust dripped from Ama's eyes and the dying sun only made them appear like she had been enchanted by some fae. How many women had Ama seen? How many had she looked at like this? But she found she didn't care. Tonight, Ama was looking at her.

She splayed her fingers across Jenne's chest. Jenne worried at her lip in anticipation. She could feel her heart slamming against her ribcage and was certain Ama could too. Ama lowered herself forward slowly, seductively with a slight curve on her swollen lips. She was doing this on purpose. She had to know what this was doing to her. The weight of her pressed Jenne further into the mattress the closer Ama came, as though Ama were pushing her into the earth, a grave of her carnal delights and Jenne was going willingly.

Ama burrowed her face into Jenne's neck, the down standing at attention to her breath. Chamomile. Linen. Sex. How had these moments only just come to her? How had she languished here for so long when she could have been with Ama? She determined that she would do anything to avoid her fate and she would write a new one. For both of them.

Ama planted her hands on either side of her. Jenne's back arched upward, missing Ama's weight only for her nipple to meet Ama's waiting mouth. Her tongue swirled, savouring, like a cherished fruit she had been eyeing all summer waiting to ripen. A cry escaped her lips, hands grasping at Ama's ridiculous mop of sand-coloured hair. She somehow knew exactly where Jenne wanted to go and led her there as though she were giving her a tour of her own body.

It was all too much. She had never felt so aroused, so *willing* to do anything to satiate the desires she so recently realised she had. Jenne wrapped her legs around Ama again, pressing herself against her, seeking relief from the pressure building in her core. She could feel Ama's smile against her breast as she ground back before she untangled herself from Jenne's grip.

Jenne whined in protest, but Ama only smirked and snaked lower, leaving a trail of sinful kisses in places she didn't know needed to be kissed in her wake. Jenne felt Ama's body flow between her fingers, her ribs, her breasts, the underhair of her arms and finally her head resting in her hands, between her thighs. Ama turned to kiss the valley where her leg joined her body, her fingers combing through the short tangle of hair between them. It pulled against her in the most delightful way and Jenne could feel the rush of blood pulse between her lips. She had never imagined this was a thing, but now couldn't fathom wanting anything more than Ama's mouth on her.

As if her thoughts could be read, Ama obliged. A long, languid lap of her tongue upward toward Jenne's clit. Ama placed a kiss, chaste, if it had been anywhere else, against her bud and then devoured her. The tip of her tongue lashed at her entrance, the flat cradled her clit. She drank deeply the rush of arousal that followed and slipped her finger inside finding the spot Jenne had only discovered existed yesterday.

Ama was appreciative of all women, even if she could not understand why they desired her. To Ama, women were ethereal beings who walked the earth, bestowing grace upon unappreciative fools. Ama was determined to rectify that by worshipping appropriately. The way women smelled, sounded, tasted, all of it was nothing short of divine.

But Jenne was something *more.* Her optimism that Ama had discounted as foolishness had somehow infected her. This person who had just carved out six months of her life for her and was bound to enjoy it to the fullest *with her,* even though it was doomed to end in heartbreak had chipped through her walls. Ama had already lost herself, like an insect drowning deliciously in honey. It was dangerous and she couldn't find it in herself to stop.

Moaning is normally the word we use when describing noises one makes during sex, but this was not that. Jenne burst into full-throated song as Ama ravished her, praising whichever of the old gods had created women, for it was not the austere sackcloth-wearing fools that paraded around, pretending to know and justify why men ruled over them. Whoever she was, Jenne believed Ama must be her most cherished disciple. Ama loved women and therefore, Ama must love her.

Jenne lay on her side, nestled into Ama's embrace. She hadn't been ashamed this time, just very exposed. She didn't understand how Ama could do this and then leave in the morning. She realised she didn't want to understand, for that meant life could be unimaginably crueller than she thought. Ama lazily dragged the curtain of black twists away from Jenne's face, placing a soft kiss at the back of her neck.

Jenne sighed. "Tell me about where you're from." She felt Ama's hot breath grow slightly quicker against her back. Another kiss.

"I don't know" Ama muttered against her skin.

"You just appeared out of nowhere?" Jenne laughed.

"I mean, I grew up in an orphanage. They told me I was from the North. That's all I know." Ama traced her fingers across Jenne's ribs.

"Oh," she said. "My father is from Italia," she offered. "I already told you my mother was a Moor."

"Hendrick said she passed before you got here. What kind of Moor was she? I haven't met many, but I know they aren't just from one place," Ama said.

"She said her family was from Al-Andalus," Jenne said with a hint of sadness. "I never met any of her family. Or his. She met my father at a market. They were both merchants. She died in childbirth that came upon her suddenly as we were on the road. Twins. One died. The other was a girl and my father left her with a church. He said I was too young to take care of her. I cried for a long time, for both my mother and my sister, but he threatened to turn back and give me to the church as well."

Ama slipped her arm around her waist and they let the silence embrace them.

After a moment, Jenne added, "I've never forgiven him for that."

Jenne turned to face Ama. "I wonder if she ended up in your orphanage."

"How long ago was this?" Ama asked.

"She would be ten now."

"The churches only brought them to us if they didn't have room and they couldn't find families in the area. And the orphanage was only built because of how many people died during the last plague, and then the famine right after the war."

"Maybe she was brought there after you left?" Jenne sounded hopeful, but she could feel Ama shake her head.

"It burned down. She would have been two when it did."

"Oh. I'm sorry," she whispered. "Did you lose anyone?"

Ama closed her eyes so she wouldn't see tears welling up and laced her fingers through Jenne's. "I lost everyone."

Chapter Nine

Humilitas / Superbia

Ama slid out of bed, heart aching at how beautiful Jenne was in the morning light and yet, how doomed this... she didn't know what *this* was. She had only loved once and had she known how that was going to turn out, she would have never gone down that road. Ama felt the rondel chafe against her calf. *Wouldn't she?*

She sighed and fingered the grip, adjusting her boot. *If she'd known, would she have really never started?* Maybe not. Different decisions maybe, but she was lying to herself if she thought she could have *not* loved. This, at least, had a definite ending. They would be heartbroken and unhappy, but alive.

Ama put those thoughts to the side and straightened herself. Today was for gathering tools. She stepped outside to find Porridge waiting for her. She was certain she hadn't brought her, but Porridge always knew where she was. "Silly Konik," she said, scritching her ears. A few minutes later, Ama was at the forge, emptying her saddlebags and tool belts to make room for the things she would be picking up. If she was bringing the boy, they would need to travel at walking speed. It would be at least three days then. Ama led Porridge to a patch of grass and stopped at the inn to gather provisions.

When she returned, she found Karlson petting Porridge.

"I thought I told you to meet me at the forge," she said.

"Yeah, but I saw your horse and knew you would be here." Karlson jumped to reach Porridge's ears.

"Don't do that. You're lucky she doesn't kick." Karlson looked away, sheepish. "What did you bring for the trip?" Ama asked. All she received in return was a confused look. "Well, it's not that cold. We'll have to hope it stays dry so we can make a fire. She thought about a few spots they could stop along the way and made a mental note to stop at Hendrick's to borrow an extra blanket. It was his fault she was doing this at all and she didn't trust the bakers.

In moments, they were off. Karlson pointing out good places to catch frogs and the rules to a game called *stick*. Ama only half listened, but it was a good distraction from her thoughts earlier in the day. It was noon by the time they had reached the woods.

Karlson took a break from the very important gossip about the village kids, and a few adults, to tell Ama he was hungry. She plucked an apple out of her saddle bag and threw it to him. He jumped enthusiastically and caught it, but it was clear this was not what he wanted.

"Also, my feet hurt," he said.

"I guess we can take a break for a few minutes," she said, looking around at a suitable place to stop. "We'll have to move off the trail so we don't block anyone else."

Karlson looked around. "There is no-one else," he said.

Ama rolled her eyes. "That you can see."

"What about over there?" Karlson pointed at a small clump of alder trees with an inviting nook.

"Absolutely not," Ama said definitively.

"Why?" Karlson asked.

"Alders are trees of death. You can't stop under them."

"Oh," Karlson said. "I've never heard that."

"That's because it's something old people know. And travellers." Ama looked around for a better place to stop.

"Then how come you know it?" he asked.

"Because I'm old. And I travel," she paused. "A lot." Ama added.

"You're not that old. You just dress like a boy," he said, as though those two things had anything to do with each other. Ama frowned at him. She was about to respond but then he pointed.

"What are those trees?"

"Those are ash trees." Ama walked over to the ash. "You can tell by the way the leaves are separate." Ama pulled a branch and showed Karlson the leaves. "We can stop here."

Karlson ignored her and pointed to another group of trees. "Are those ash?"

"No, those are rowans. Some people call them *mountain ash* though. Old people say the first woman was made from a rowan."

"So, they *are* the same?" Karlson said with an impish grin.

"No, they're not. Some people just got confused because of the leaves," Ama said with annoyance.

"What tree was the first man made from?" Karlson asked.

"An ash," she answered.

"So, they're the same," Karlson said with finality.

Ama wasn't going to keep arguing with an eleven-year-old. "Let's keep going. I don't want to be making a fire in the middle of the woods or walking in the dark"

Karlson skipped ahead, feet apparently no longer hurting.

By the time the sun had fallen, they had made it to the clearing Ama was hoping to reach. Karlson had stopped pointing out every squirrel, grouse and magpie he spotted about an hour ago and Ama was grateful for the silence. It was short-lived, though, as the crickets, frogs and owls started their nightly chorus. Ama stopped and turned to Karlson.

"Until we stop, I want you to pick up every fallen branch you can carry." This was now a game and Karlson ran off with a burst of energy from some hidden reserve only children seem to know about. Ama and Porridge continued down the trail until they reached a large hill with a stony outcropping and a circle of stones used regularly by travellers. No-one else was on the road tonight so they wouldn't have to share. Not that sharing was a burden, but one did have to use judgment. She felt the rondel again.

Karlson came huffing behind with an armful of sticks and branches and then gracelessly deposited them in front of her. Ama led Porridge to some taller grass and then dug out her flint from the saddlebag.

"If you're going to learn to forge, you're going to have to know how to start fires. Later, I'll show you how to make charcoal." Ama showed Karlson how to stack the wood so that it would burn from the top down and make a lot of heat. Karlson squatted nearby and leaned forward, exposing the bruise beneath his shift. Ama knew hitting children was common, especially those who were not your own. She also knew she shouldn't intervene. *Just keep your nose out of it for once, Ama* she thought. *The world isn't fair. There's abuse and death everywhere. You're not a hero, you can't solve every problem.*

Remember what happened last time.

And still, as if some other force took over her tongue, she found herself asking, "What happened here?" Ama pointed a stick at his collar. He turned away. *Good,* she thought. *This is not your problem. Let it go. You tried. You're a good person.* But it was too late. Karlson started shifting uncomfortably. His face screwed and unscrewed, mouth twisting in thought, trying to find the words.

"I couldn't fill a sack of flour as fast as the other kids and I spilled it." The words came tumbling out, several thoughts mixed together in a poorly-constructed sentence that nonetheless, explained everything to anyone who knew angry men. Of course he couldn't keep up with the other kids; he wasn't one of them. He hadn't grown up in a mill. And rather than teach him or let him learn to work faster through practice, a beating was all he got, as though knowledge or proficiency could be gained through blows.

Karlson was hyperventilating and she was the cause. *Fuck,* she thought. Now she would have to do something.

Ama sidled up next to him. "How many kids live with the bakers?"

"Markel is the oldest, then Danel, Enest, Xelene, and Jokim is the baby, so he doesn't help." Karlson enumerated the kids on his fingers. "Enest is nice to me and Xelene helps make bread, but Markel and Danel are mean." *That sounds about right.* Ama thought. *When you aren't in control, you take it out on someone else. Someone weaker.*

Karlson's breathing slowed with the distraction, but he continued. Ama should have known that once she got him talking, he wouldn't stop.

"Markel got meaner after Jenne refused to marry him and now Txomin refuses to let her help us when we get sick."

"Who's Txomin?" she asked

"The baker. Nerea is his wife. She's nice and tries to meet with Jenne in secret if we really need medicines."

That makes sense, she thought. *I suppose you can't just keep calling someone "the baker" if you live with them.* "That's a lot of kids," Ama said, "but not as many as I grew up with."

"How many did you grow up with?" he asked.

"I never counted them. Also, the number kept changing because it was an orphanage," she said. "Kids, even babies would show up. The boys would go with Monségnor Rachid every time he came by. Some would leave with merchants who came through. But," she continued, "no-one ever hit me hard enough to leave a bruise like that." Karl poked at the fire with a stick.

Ama let him poke, watching his expression soften. "Hey" she prodded. Karlson stopped poking and looked at her. "If that ever happens again, I want you to tell me and I'll deal with Txomin." Karlson gave her a half-hearted smile and returned to poking the fire. Ama wasn't actually sure how she would deal with him. She hadn't even met the man. But it made Karlson feel better and that's what counted right now.

Porridge sauntered over, having finished her grazing and Ama stood to unfasten a couple of woollen blankets. She passed one to Karlson, who wrapped it around his shoulders and huddled into Ama. It wasn't something she had expected and she wasn't sure how to process her feelings. It was like a jolt in the pit of her stomach that now something had changed and she didn't know what it was. It felt like danger, but not the kind you ran away from. Ama felt like she should do *something*, so she tentatively reached her arm to place it loosely around Karlson's shoulder. What would that convey? Would it be any worse than promising to protect him from a man she didn't know? Ama had no idea. Karlson moved in closer, blonde tufts of hair grazing her chin. He smelled like flour and mud.

Ama had been around children for most of her life. They would get older and new ones would just keep showing up. She had been left in charge of them for short periods of time when another Sister had asked and even when she was a Sister herself, but she had never been *solely* responsible. Yet here, under a bit of limestone next to a wide-open field where anyone could come along, anything could happen, she was the only one who would be responsible for this boy.

That was overwhelming. There was no training for it, no apprenticeship. No-one was supervising her work or judging its value. She was responsible for him simply because he *trusted* her to be. And he had no *reason* to trust her. She hadn't done anything to prove that she was trustworthy to him, he had just decided it. Just as Jenne had.

This was all too confusing for her. Ama could not understand how you could trust someone you had just met like that. Perhaps if she had children of her own, she could understand why Karlson would trust her, but she did not. She was just a lone merchant with a silly horse. She had no idea what she was doing or why anyone would think she did.

The amount of panic this was causing her felt surprising. It's not as though anyone was expecting her to be Karlson's *mother*. That concept had been removed from her list of options a long time ago and she wasn't about to revisit it. Ama took a deep breath. She could do this.

Think of Sister Klara, she told herself. At one point, Sister Klara had been exactly who she had wanted to be as an adult. She was useful. She broke the occasional rule. She simply *was* and people loved her. Even the orphans.

Would anyone have felt differently if Sister Klara was alone though? she wondered. Ama didn't feel like they would. She had the confidence to do what she wanted and everyone just went along with it. Or maybe that's just what everyone assumed about her. Is that what people were doing with her? Did they just assume she knew what she was doing? Did Sister Klara ever feel like this?

Ama sighed. Clearly her thoughts were just spiralling before sleep. This would best be dealt with in the morning. She flexed her calf to reassure herself that her rondel was still there in case she needed it. Porridge huffed nearby.

"I guess I've taken care of you so far." Ama said into the darkness. "Or you've taken care of me." Porridge snorted.

"Good night to you too, Porridge."

Karlson was already asleep.

Chapter Ten

Discretionis / Excess

It was almost evening when Ama and Karlson arrived. Though it was practically a ruin before, it was even more so now. Cracked and blackened stones sat atop each other to form walls and even rooms if you squinted hard enough. At the back stood the only building with a roof, though it looked to have been newly constructed - at least, newer than the rest of it. Behind that, flowed a river, overgrown with weeds and willows, half fallen into the river themselves.

Ama let Porridge loose to find some edible grasses and made her way among the ruins to the small hut at the back. Karlson, for his part, climbed and clambered over every obstacle he came across. The hut contained a forge, an anvil and several tools small enough for Ama's hands. Ama began gathering up her favourite tools and some stock iron. She called out to Karlson, who was attempting to scale the charcoal kiln to get Porridge so she could see how much room they had to bring back materials. Karlson didn't respond.

Ama stepped outside and found him staring at the ruins in the twilight. Red and orange hues filtered over the ruins, black dust still hanging in the air. He was silent. There was only one reason why he would be staring like that.

"You can see them, can't you?"

Karlson nodded. "Who are they?" he whispered, not breaking eye contact.

"The Sisters. And many of the orphans," she said with heavy regret. "It was my fault."

"You did this?" Karlson turned to her wide-eyed.

"No," Ama protested. She heaved a sigh. "But I was the cause."

Karlson took her hand, as though he was supposed to be the one to comfort her with the strange audacity of children who repay kindness with no regard to their place. Ama bit the inside of her cheek as she considered what she could possibly tell a child who was currently staring at the very real ghosts of her past.

"They're why I can't stay," she said vaguely.

"You can't stay here?" Karlson asked and Ama realised that he didn't know she was talking about his village. No-one had told him she wasn't staying.

"No, I can stay here as long as I want," she started. "The Sisters make sure no-one else comes here."

"Your house is protected by ghosts?" Karlson's eyes popped.

Ama sighed. "Kind of. I'd hardly call it a house. Also, I can't live by myself. I need food and supplies and other things that aren't iron and charcoal."

"So that's why you're coming to live with us?"

Ama pinched the bridge of her nose. "No. I can't stay with you either. I only promised to stay until the end of winter."

"Why leave if you need other people?" Karlson was very confused.

"Because I'll bring danger."

"You'll bring the ghosts?"

"No, the people who did this."

"Who did this?"

And there it was. The real question that put all their lives in danger and had forced Ama to travel place to place, peddling steel, taking joy where she could and moving on before anyone found her. Ama turned back into the hut and brought out two stools. "Sit," she said. Ama looked toward the fading sunset, directly into the eyes of Sister Hildegaarde's ghost.

"Ama smells like rotten frogs!" A more mature version of herself would have brushed this off. An even more mature version of herself would have recognised the insult as an invitation to play. She would make up her own insult and they would trade made-up witticisms until they both fell down laughing and became inseparable best friends. Ama was most definitely not a more mature version of herself and so she launched her tiny body furiously at Ella, scratching tiny fingernails across her face.

This was a mistake as Ama was not built for fighting and Ella was much larger. She also had a lot of friends; friends who viciously fought back and left Ama bleeding from her nose and more bruises on her body than she had ever had in her short life. The beatings only stopped once Sera dragged Sister Klara away from the forge to scatter the others and gather Ama into her large arms and deposit her into a cell where Sister Ruth would dress her wounds and keep Ella's angry friends away from her for the night.

Sera was not Ella's friend, she was Ama's. In fact, she was Ama's *only* friend. She was one of the few children who were actually born here instead of being dropped off as a baby or a child, and the only Moor - at least, until conversion. One of these years, they were told, a priest would come and baptise them all and they would all take a name after a saint, rather than the names they had now.

The ones who had arrived before they could speak were given names after the first few repetitive sounds they had made. The Sisters told them that they had been angels before and those sounds were their angelic names - which made the children question why they would be given the names of a saint if angels were above saints, but they were always told to pray about it, and so they stopped asking.

Sometimes, the sounds resembled actual names, like Ella or Anna. Most of the time, like Ama, their names were meaningless nonsense. The exception, again, was Sera. Sera had never spoken, and so the Sisters named her after the Seraphim, who spoke only to God himself.

Sera was very good at not making any sounds, including when she padded into Ama's temporary room, slipping easily past Sister Ruth, who was already asleep. She pulled a small piece of bread out from her apron pocket and gave it to Ama who smiled and tore off thick hunks greedily. She learned quickly that she would have to eat carefully, given her very swollen lip and Sera's white smile gleamed in the moonlight.

Once she had finished, Sera motioned for Ama to follow her. Nighttime excursions were not uncommon for them, but it was usually Ama leading Sera to some new discovery. The orphanage was at one time, and old fort, now abandoned. At some point, a local lord had decided to set up a defensive position here, but given these lands consisted mostly of forests and sandy swamps, few nobles wanted them and warlords ignored them altogether.

A new, proper castle had been proposed to be built further away on better land and closer to the mountains, but it still lacked interest and the local lord cared little for stray peasant villages, which then proliferated. Of course, once they gained a certain size and stability, the men would come and demand taxation for defending a piece of territory no-one else wanted to rule, with only moderate success. The *duchy* just like the *kingdom of France* was really only an idea on parchment, and as long as you didn't style yourself a king, they were content to let you ignore them, as long as you pretended that they were the rulers.

As for the original fort, it was left to rot until the churches from nearby cities required somewhere to house the influx of orphans left on their doorsteps after waves of plague, war and famine. Sisters from the northwest had agreed to set up the orphanage and they had remained ever since. All of this meant that Ama and Sera had plenty of undiscovered places and treasures to find.

Tonight though, Sera seemed unusually eager to explore. Her tiny brown feet raced along the worn wooden floor toward the cool stone of the kitchen where she helped the Sisters prepare meals. She beamed as she stood next to the giant iron stove, eyes shining with mischief before she suddenly disappeared. Ama quickly clapped her hands over her mouth to avoid shrieking in surprise and she scurried over to the stove to see what had happened. Sure enough, behind the stove was a missing brick. Ama got down on her hands and knees to see further in and found even more missing bricks. Sera was smaller than her and so Ama had to squeeze herself into the hole and found the most glorious treasure she could have ever imagined.

Sera stood in the middle of a beam of moonlight shining from a hole high in the wall as though the finger of God had burst through it to highlight just her. All around her were piles and piles of old scrolls and sheaves of parchment. Suddenly, the reading lessons the Sisters had been giving them didn't seem quite so pointless.

Ama threw herself at the nearest shelf and began to flip through the dust covered pages. Many were in languages she did not understand, but many more were written in Latin. Whatever steward had been here before had clearly valued learning, or at least one of his higher advisers had. There were folios on great cities, scrolls on strategy and warfare, an illuminated manuscript just on herbs and plants. One volume though, was more special than the rest. It was an account of a voyage the writer had taken to the northern lands and included diagrams and methods on forging. Ama couldn't wait to show Sister Klara.

Ama leapt toward her friend, hugging her so tightly she couldn't breathe. Sera squirmed and her eyes lit up in an exaggerated giggle, but no sound was made. They hurried back, wriggling through the hole behind the oven and racing as quickly and as quietly as they could, back to their mattress on the floor with the other orphans.

The next morning, Sera and Ama excitedly told the Sisters what they had found and work began on moving the precious parchment out from behind the blocked wall to somewhere more accessible and without a hole in the wall so as to protect it from the elements. Sister Ulphia volunteered to catalogue the books since she had come from a convent that had a library. She noted, with much derision, that before she had arrived there, none of the Sisters knew how to read and they were using the parchment as kindling.

A fierce debate broke out between Sister Greta and Sister Maria whether any of the books should be forbidden. Sister Greta argued that all truth is from God and Sister Maria argued that the tree of knowledge was what led to man's downfall in the first place. Biblical passages were thrown back and forth with no consensus reached, but delayed until they received word from the Pope himself, as though he would actually intervene in a dispute between two Sisters from an orphanage in one of the poorest regions of Gascony. Until then, the makeshift library would remain off limits to the children, but the Sisters would be permitted to use their discretion.

This, of course, stopped none of the children from sneaking into the new library and, after a brief attempt at disciplining the ones who stole books, the Sisters quickly realised they had neither the numbers nor sufficient desire to put a halt to it. For many of the children, the novelty of the whole thing wore off after a couple of weeks, but for others, including Sera and Ama, it most certainly did not and soon, parchments and scrolls, at least the ones in languages they could read, piled up beside their mattresses.

Sera found herself interested in all manner of plants and trees. She and Ama spent countless hours scrounging the surrounding meadows and forests for species of mushrooms and herbs to make various dishes taste slightly better and make various ointments and curatives. After one incident that had almost the entire population of the orphanage vomiting, however, she was forbidden from collecting any more mushrooms.

And while Ama took to the books on metallurgy, most of what she wanted to try was brushed off by Sister Klara. For some things, there was a definite reason; gold and silver were too precious and had to be forged extremely carefully -- something that Sister Klara believed she didn't possess the skills to do. Casting was dangerous and required moulds she didn't have and crucibles that needed a higher temperature than she could make. Copper was almost as rare as gold in these parts and they didn't have enough of it. Also, it was too soft to be useful. Other things she simply grunted at and refused to elaborate on. These were, of course, the things Ama wanted to try most.

It was late summer when Sister Klara died. Sera had turned fifteen that year and since Ama did not know her birthday, she assumed that she was fifteen as well.

Their hands clasped and huddled together, they wept as her linen-wrapped body was lowered into the ground. Though Sera could make no sound, Ama was loud enough for the both of them. She placed Sister Klara's favourite hammer and tongs on her body and then stood back while others covered her with earth.

"Sister Aurea, would you say the eulogy?" Sister Hildegaarde asked. Ama had a new name since Monségnor Rachid had heard her vows two years ago. She had chosen Saint Aurea, who had been martyred by the Romans. She and Sera had thought it hilarious when they had reenacted the scene in the courtyard after the ceremony. Sister Klara had barely contained her laugher. Monségnor Rachid was significantly less amused and while it was too late for Ama, he refused to take Sera's vows until he returned. It took a year and many hours of testimony from the Sisters since Sera was unable to communicate her contrition to anyone but Ama, but she was then renamed Sister Philomena, after the virgin saint of youth and beauty - and also babies, which conflicted with her virginity. Sera found it funny, but she had learned her lesson and waited until Monségnor Rachid had gone before pretending to be pregnant.

Sister Hildegaarde knew that Sister Klara would have appreciated an irreverent joke at her funeral and had passed on that sense of humour to her protégée and had therefore prepared the eulogy in advance. She handed the parchment to Ama with a stern look that told her not to deviate from it *as written*. For once, she did as she was told and then returned to stand next to Sera, her now calloused hands finding her fingers and clasping tightly.

Once it was all over, Sera signed to Ama to gather herbs with her. The days were still long and they would have plenty of time to go about their tasks in a comfortable silence. Sera produced two baskets and they left the old fort by the east trail with the sun at their backs. Sera laced her arm through Ama's and pulled her along, clearly in a hurry.

Ama inhaled deeply the warm, moist air of the woods and waited for Sera to point out what she wanted. Ama knew some herbs, but not enough to trust herself not to kill anyone by accident. Herbs and plants were Sera's domain. Sera devoured the herbariums, poring over them late into the evenings. Ama would regularly wake up in the middle of the night only to find Sera asleep, sitting cross legged on her mattress with a folio and some plants she had found and tried to identify falling out of her hands. Ama had always thought Sera was the most beautiful person in the world when she found her like this and never had the heart to rouse her enough to return to her own mattress. Instead, she would close her book, carefully take the precious plant and set it on the floor while she eased her under the thin blankets. Sera would always be gone in the morning to the kitchens, likely taking the same care so as not to wake Ama.

Ama was interrupted from her reverie, hunched over a sward of anise by a brusque tap on her shoulder. She turned to see Sera grinning. Ama made a face and stuck out her tongue.

Will you make me a knife? Sera signed.

Ama frowned. "Don't you have one in the kitchen?"

Sera rolled her eyes. *They're all dull,* she signed again. *Sister Klara said she'd make me one but then she got sick.*

"Fine," Ama muttered, sighing at the memory of this morning. "For Sister Klara."

Sera raised her eyebrow. Ama scrabbled to her feet and pushed Sera who threw her head back in silent laughter.

"For you then," Ama laughed. "What do I get in return?"

Sera pursed her lips in thought and then launched herself forward to kiss Ama. Her eyes bolted open in shock and Sera bounded off toward the fort without glancing back. Ama's heart thudded so loudly in her chest that she was afraid Sera could hear it.

When raised in an orphanage, particularly an orphanage that only received girls, since boys could more easily be given to families requiring labour, there are only two outcomes available to you. The first is that when you are old enough, you disappear with a group of merchants, one of whom has caught your eye, or you are sought out by some widower who requires a wife to raise his children. The second, is that you take your vows and remain.

In both cases there is no need for anyone to teach you about sex. Either your husband will do it, or it is irrelevant. Menstruation is explained as punishment for Eve's sin and children are *given* to you by a husband, but inasmuch as possible, sex is decoupled from procreation. It's not that the Sisters were particularly prudish either – ribald jokes about various body parts were often heard in their midst.

But unless one grows up surrounded by people who are attracted to one another and fall in love and have sex and then have children, as far-fetched as it might seem (unless you yourself have experienced this,) it is entirely possible to misunderstand feelings of attraction, love and yes, even sex.

And given that a not-insignificant number of the current Sisters were orphans themselves, it is entirely likely that a large portion of them had no idea what they would be talking about, even if someone had deemed it a topic of great import.

Or at the very least, no-one had bothered to tell Ama.

Which meant that Ama was left, bewildered at the actions of her incredibly beautiful best friend who she loved more than anyone or anything in the whole world. And more bewildered still at the reaction her body produced because of said actions. Upon introspection, Ama had found confusion, embarrassment and joy, but most importantly *want*, which was not something she had expected. *Desire* was too delicate a word for something Ama didn't understand yet. She simply *wanted* for Sera to do that again and perhaps to let Ama do that to her.

The emotion missing, however, was *shame*. Had Ama known what sex was and understood that sex was something that was reserved for *men and women*, in particular, *husband and wife*, and not for *women and women*, she may have felt differently. The rest of their time together may have progressed differently, though upon much later reflection, Ama doubted it. For while the awkwardness of two teenagers discovering each other for the first time is unforgettable, so is the intensity of the memories it creates. And from the moment they had met, Ama and Sera were like two stars, circling each other faster and faster until they collided and became inseparable. Their love was inevitable, as if God himself had ordained it.

However, like all foolish teenagers discovering themselves for the first time, they were never as clever nor careful as they had thought. It was Sister Hildegaarde who had caught them and demanded they join her in the chapel. Hearts sinking as they sat across from her, terrified that they were about to be sent away, Sister Hildegaarde peered at them from beneath her kerchief with her icy blue eyes, surrounded by lines carved with age.

"You two are incredibly fortunate," she croaked at them quietly. Confusion spread across their faces. Perhaps their punishment would be less severe since they had been ignorant? And then Ama caught the tear start to form in Sister Hildegaarde's eye. She suddenly felt the pangs of shame for causing this woman enough distress that she cried. It was rare that she had seen a Sister cry, and *never* Sister Hildegaarde.

"Sisters," she started once she had regained her composure. She searched for what to say next, mouth opening and closing, hands gesturing aimlessly before finally settling, clasped in front. She inhaled deeply. "Sister Klara and I were like you," she said at last. Shock spread across their faces.

"You were friends?" Ama said, tentatively. "We thought you didn't like Sister Klara because she always broke rules."

"Well, yes, she definitely did that," Sister Hildegaarde fussed with her hands. "But we were friends. More than friends."

Ama exchanged glances with Sera who seemed equally confused. "What is more than friends?"

"We were," Sister Hildegaarde huffed, unsure what to reveal to these two fools, "like husband and wife."

"Sister Klara was a boy?" Ama blurted out.

"No!"

"Are you a boy?" Ama was very confused and Sera was shaking with laughter.

"Stop talking and listen," Sister Hildegaarde hissed. "Not all girls will fall in love with boys. Some girls will fall in love with girls." Ama blinked, stupefied. Sera blushed. "Like you two," she concluded.

"Is that allowed?" Ama asked.

"It doesn't matter if it's *allowed*. What matters is that it *is* and that it's what you two have been doing. You don't kiss your friends like *that*," she flustered about. "At least not more than once," she added under her breath.

"We never knew!" Ama exclaimed.

"Quiet Sister," Sister Hildegaarde reprimanded. "Of course, you never knew. That's the point!" Sera and Ama glanced at each other, again, confused. "Whereas I've known about you two fools since you were children! You *must* be more careful!"

"But our vows?" Ama started before she was cut off by Sister Hildegaarde waving her hand.

"Our vows say nothing about this," she dismissed. "However, Monségnor Rachid's interpretation of our vows may differ from mine, so you mustn't be fools and flaunt yourselves. Discretion, Sisters."

"How many others?" Ama had so many questions.

"Discretion!" Sister Hildegaarde hissed before giving them a sideways glance and leaving them alone in the chapel.

Ama made Sera's knife, but she did it her way. Standing over the forge, book propped open on the thick, oak bench opposite, she carefully wrapped some char from chicken bones in leather together with a length of iron in clay. If the book was right, this would take all day, but she would do it for Sera. The book did not have a diagram for a kitchen knife - only axes and swords, so Ama skipped carving the strange markings on the clay since the piece wasn't big enough to hold them. She hoped it would work anyway.

When the clay was chipped away, the char and leather had all but disappeared. Ama placed the glowing iron on the anvil and started working it. The iron did not move at all like she was used to and her forearms soon began screaming. This iron was significantly harder. She hoped that it meant it would hold a better edge as well.

When Ama failed to show up for the evening meal, Sera brought her a bowl. She pulled up a stool and sat, the corner of her lips upturned as she admired Ama's arms, looking up at her from under her dark eyelashes. Unlike Sister Klara, Ama got too hot in the forge and had to tie her shift at her elbows to keep cool. Ama blushed.

"This is your fault, you know," Ama teased. "This knife of yours is taking me all day."

Sera stuck out her tongue and held out the bowl of pottage. Ama finished bevelling the edge and plunged the roughly knife-shaped object into the quenching bucket; her forearms grateful to be finished for the day. The book had mentioned using the blood of the animal that the bone was from, but there wasn't any of that around, so water would have to do. Ama glanced around to make sure no-one was near and took her bowl of pottage, kissing Sera deeply. Sera could not moan, but she sighed and sunk into her love, revelling in her chamomile and linen scent mixed with hot iron before Ama stepped back and stirred her meal. She ate in silence, the two of them exchanging wistful glances as the sun set and the dying embers of the forge cast the only light.

When Ama finally visited the kitchen to present her new knife to Sera, the entire room circled her, clucking like hens. The knife had darker bands running through it and none of the Sisters had ever seen anything like it before, nor had Ama ever produced anything like it previously. All of them took turns dicing turnips and skirret, finely mincing chives and shallots and trimming the toughest cuts of pork as though it were butter. Sera threw her arms around her neck, overjoyed. The Sisters then immediately demanded kitchen knives of their own. Ama laughed and told them she would need a lot more bones, which were promptly delivered the next morning.

As the months went by and everyone had gotten what they wanted, Ama finally had a chance to slow down. A week before the first snows, a hunter had visited and Ama was able to bargain for some bear bones. The hunter hadn't saved any blood, but she could at least experiment a bit more. Her excitement was palpable as she hauled her supplies to the forge. She had been waiting to do this for years. Even though she had no use for a sword, but she could finally follow the diagram she wanted with enough room to carve those strange markings into the clay.

As the piece heated up, Ama busied herself about the shop, sweeping the iron filings when out of nowhere, a deafening roar snapped her to attention. Ama spun around toward the fire and saw the ghastly figure of a bear made of flame. It roared again and Ama backed into the wall, terrified and weeping, her heart racing faster than she had ever felt it before. She was about to scream when the flame disappeared along with a rush of air and icy gusts drifting across the floor.

Ama approached the forge and felt no heat from the now dead embers. Only the metal, glowing through cracks in the clay was hot. Every ounce of her being told her not to, but curiosity still won out. She found herself placing the strange iron on the anvil. She brought down her hammer, fashioning a point as the diagrams instructed. The blows fell and Ama swore she could hear the roar of a bear in her ears instead of the familiar ring, but she kept going. Ama relit the forge. Scale flew and skittered across the floor as she rained down blow after blow. By evening, Ama had a rough blade the length of an ell, just as the diagram had said.

It was dark when Ama slipped beneath her thin blankets, only to find Sera already hiding under the covers. She didn't usually find Sera in her bed, only when she missed the evening meal. It seemed like a bit of harmless fun, if not as discreet as Sister Hildegaarde would have preferred. They were Sisters themselves now and they had their own cells rather than sharing a large room with mattresses strewn about the floor and orphans huddled together for warmth more often than not. They could get away with it out of habit before one of them returned to their cells for the rest of the night.

Ama traced Sera's face in the dark, smile wide and eyes squinted shut. She ran her fingertips along her jaw and found that Sera refused to let them leave. Her face followed her fingertips wherever she moved. Ama giggled and moved her fingertips to her lips. Sera kissed her deeply, as though she were trying to memorise her mouth.

Ama told Sera about the forge and the strange iron that she had made. Sera listened intently, splaying her fingers across Ama's chest. She couldn't sign in the dark, so she tapped Ama twice on the shoulder. *Be careful.*

"Should I tell the Sisters?" Ama asked. She felt Sera shrug.

"Do you think it's witchcraft?" she asked. One of Sera's eyebrows raised against Ama's fingers.

"Even Saul went to see the witch of Endor," Ama laughed. "Though Saul wasn't the hero in that story. No-one cares what you do, as long as you're useful, I guess?"

Sera rested her head on the crook of Ama's arm and soon fell asleep against the rhythmic rise and fall of her chest. Ama did not have the heart to wake her.

Chapter Eleven

Disciplinae / Abundantia

Ama ground and polished her strange blade, dark bands flowing along its length like wood grain. She chose a simple hilt and handle and then hung it in the forge and promptly forgot about it until the next summer when a small group of soldiers and the same priest who had baptised them arrived. Sister Hildegaarde was the one to greet them.

"Monségnor Rachid, we weren't expecting you so soon after your last visit. And with an escort! Are the roads truly so dangerous now?" Sister Hildegaarde flustered, even though she had nothing to hide. Unexpected visitors always made her nervous.

"Ah, no, Sister," Monségnor Rachid waved his hand in dismissal. "I have been asked to remain in Saint-Béat for the time being. There is a fortress to be built for fear the conflicts in Iberia might spill over the mountains. Our brave men require guidance and spiritual comfort and as villages so often disappear without warning, I was asked to show these sentries some of our allies nearby should they require refuge while in the area."

"I suppose you are correct, Monségnor," Sister Hildegaarde put on a grave tone, though she actually cared very little about the various conflicts happening all around. "There are Arians to the east of us, Moors to the south and pagans all around. You know where the guest quarters are. Shall I escort you or would you prefer to guide these men yourself?"

"It is so, Sister, the devil does not rest, nor shall we and the good Lord shall deliver us unto victory in all things. I shall keep my men away from your Sisters and leave you to your duties. We shall depart in the morning."

As Monségnor Rachid said this, he turned to the three soldiers wearing mismatched pieces of armour, only to find that the group of three was now a group of two. Antòni had wandered off. Monségnor Rachid rolled his eyes and ordered the men to "find the buffoon," which they did, staring at Ama forging a horseshoe. Ama was ignoring him, but this was irrelevant as Antòni was staring at the sword she had made last fall. As the men approached, Antòni pointed.

"Do you know what that is, lads?"

"It's a sword, you beefwit. How in the blessed fuck did you get picked for this job?" Ponç asked. Antòni smirked, ignoring Ponç's unfortunate choice of words.

"That's ghost iron. My grandad brought one from his fights with the Norse. He told me only witches make them, but they're terrorful blades and if they're first blooded in battle, it's as if the dead fight alongside you."

Sergi spat. "Your grandad also told you that if you stuck your dick in a beehive, you'd piss bees. How'd that work out for you?"

Ponç laughed and then pointed at Ama. "You! Are you a witch?" Ama stopped pounding and stared at the three men. They might have been older than her, but not by much. Only boys, really – boys that hadn't yet seen much of the world and she doubted they could read well enough to make up for it. She placed her hammer and tongs down neatly on the anvil and turned to pick up the sword hanging on the wall. She hadn't the faintest idea how to use it, but she suspected she'd spent more time holding a sword just by making one than the three of them had spent practicing with one. Ama stepped out from behind the counter that separated the forge from the courtyard and gave the sword a twirl. Pretend confidence was enough for these fools because they all turned and ran to find Monségnor Rachid.

Over supper Ama told Sera what she had heard Antòni say about her sword.

What does your book say? Sera signed. Ama shrugged.

"There are still parts I can't read. But it's probably just tales anyway." Ama shoved a piece of bread into her mouth. "Even if I could read those parts and the book agreed with the boy, I've never seen a ghost. Have you?" Sera shrugged back.

Ama poked at the dregs of her meal and said quietly "Do you think I'm a witch?" Sera nodded and Ama's eyes popped wide before Sera threw her head back in a soundless laugh.

Even if you were, I would still love you.

"I love you too," she said as she rocked her shoulders into Sera. Sera slipped her arm around Ama's waist and stole the rest of her bread.

"I was a fool to intimidate those boys," Ama said, turning to face Karlson. She could barely see him now that the sun had set. The ghosts had all but disappeared. "It felt good at the time, but they came back later, with more men."

"Why?" he asked. "Just because you scared them?"

"Not just," she continued. "Because of what I had made. That sword. That metal. It's how the Norsemen were able to take so much land. But it comes at a cost. And in my foolishness, I had made more."

"What does it cost?" Karlson asked quietly.

"A lot of pain. A lot of blood. Maybe a soul" Ama breathed deeply, shaking the horror from her head. "We should get some rest. I don't want you staying here longer than you have to."

"Why not?"

"Because I've seen what the ghosts can do."

Ama tucked Karlson into the mattress in the room she kept behind the forge and went to sit under the stars. Sister Hildegaarde sat with her. "I'm sorry," she whispered. "Every day, I'm sorry."

Ama and Karlson loaded up Porridge as soon as the sun had risen. The ghosts were visible again in the morning light. Karlson, not knowing better, waved at one of them. It slowly raised its hand and waved back. Karlson had not expected this and he ran to Ama's side in fright. But as some children are, his curiosity got the better of him and as they made their way through the ruins of the orphanage, Karlson waved at another ghost. And then another. Soon, he was waving at every one of them he saw, delighting in watching them wave back. Ama was about to get annoyed when she reminded herself that this was probably the most interaction her Sisters had had in a long time. This brought a fresh wave of guilt and she walked faster.

Once they had found the trail, Ama decided it was her turn to ask the questions.

"Did the bakers take you in after your mother died?"

"Sort of." Karlson kicked a rock and watched it skitter across the trail. "My father left me with them while he was at the forge. He would repay them by fixing their tools."

"But you would return to him in the evening?"

"Yeah. Most nights. Sometimes he would be at the inn."

Ama sided-eyed Karlson. "How many nights a week did you spend at the bakers?"

Karlson paused and thought. "Four?" he asked, as though Ama knew the answer. She just nodded.

"Where was your house? There isn't one attached to the forge."

"On the other side of the village. It's still there."

"Hendrick told me about it. He says it needs to be fixed."

"I guess." Karlson caught up to his rock and sent it skittering again.

They walked for a bit longer. Though at the time, Karlson was not an orphan, for all intents and purposes, he might as well have been. Orphanages, as in, dedicated places where orphans were housed and fed and sometimes, if you were lucky, taught something useful, were rare. More often, kids with parents missing were left with other families. If you were a woman who had recently given birth, you were expected to breastfeed them as well. *Yet more work,* Ama thought. *A man's work is from sun to sun, but a woman's work is never done is how the poem went.* But the result is never to remove work or to share work more equally. It's to laugh at the beast of burden you've acquired.

The more Ama thought about it, the more confused she got. Her brain just refused to understand how most women could find a man so appealing that they would marry and bear children. It was no wonder her and Sister Klara got along so well. But they were still the outliers. That was the part she couldn't comprehend.

She decided that it must be something about *love* itself. Something about it that made you willingly walk into a cage. Which took over your body and made you *feel* and *do* things you said you would never do. Which she was doing right now.

Here she was, with a boy that wasn't hers, walking back to a village she shouldn't be staying at due to a woman she shouldn't have spent the night with. Ama was just as stupid as every other woman. The question was only whether or not the cage had been shut.

Ama blew out her cheeks. Karlson turned to her expectant, as though she were about to say something. Ama realised that she had spent the last several minutes in her head, deriding foolish women only to realise she was one herself.

"So, I have an idea," she said, more to break the silence than anything else.

Karlson waited.

"I asked Hendrick to deliver supplies to fix your house before we left. I'll help you fix it if I can stay there until the end of winter."

"I thought you were staying with Jenne?" Karlson frowned.

"Who told you that?"

Karlson shrugged. "Everyone knows that."

Ama was exasperated. This is not how these things were supposed to go. Everyone is supposed to be discreet and pretend nothing is going on. "Did Jenne say that?" she asked.

Karlson shook his head.

"She's going to get us killed before *I* do," Ama muttered.

"What?"

"Never mind. Let's focus on the house."

"Okay."

Ama ruffled the boy's hair. She immediately regretted it, pulling away her hand, covered in grease. "When was the last time you washed?"

An impish grin was all she got as a reply.

"I'm serious. You're dirtier than Porridge."

"When was the last time Porridge washed?"

"I hope this house of yours has a bathing tub."

"I don't think so."

"You don't think so, or you hope not?" Ama teased.

"I don't remember one," he said. "Really!" he protested when Ama gave him a look.

"Damn. I never was any good at making anything that could hold water," she cursed. "Is there a cooper in the village?"

"A what?"

"I guess not. A cold wash bucket for us, then. Unless I can find a piece of iron big enough to make a large pot."

Ama continued to talk through her plans to build something that would be able to pour hot water over her head. Maybe with a pump that could be operated by foot. She was so lost in thought that she didn't notice Karlson grinning at her the entire time. Or that she had built her cage and was locking herself in.

Chapter Twelve

Oboedientia/ Inoboedientia

Jenne woke to find Ama gone. She stretched and pulled the covers tighter, trying to absorb as much of Ama's scent as she could before she faced the day. Ama would be gone for a few days and Jenne already felt her absence as a gnawing pit in her stomach. She couldn't help but smile against the pillow remembering last night, but then quickly scolded herself for getting too attached.

An older version of herself, or perhaps a version born in a different time would have known that lovers come and go, especially when you're young and just learning what that even means. Jenne knew in her mind that Ama would leave at the end of winter and that she would be married off to some unknown man, their lives all but over because of the decisions and actions of men. She knew this. Her heart, though, refused to accept it as reality. Allowing herself to take joy where she could had only whetted its appetite and now it hungered, insatiable for a woman she had met only days prior. She knew almost nothing about her and yet, she felt herself falling hopelessly in love. This version of Jenne was unaware of the intensity of the heartbreak that followed love or that *love* was not a word one should use too quickly in a relationship because Jenne had never *been* in a relationship before, if that was even what this was.

And so Jenne broke her fast, washed herself and put on her apron and left to collect herbs, head full of thoughts of Ama and pushing her bleak future away. Upon returning, she found Hendrick, leaning against the wall of her house, his bulky form at odds with the childish way he drew circles nervously in the dirt with his toe. Jenne sped her pace toward him.

"What is it?" she asked, skipping pleasantries.

"He's here." Hendrick muttered, delivering the unfortunate news.

"Who's here?" Jenne was growing impatient.

"Your husband."

Instantly the colour drained from Jenne's face, adrenaline flooding her stomach and she vomited its contents directly onto Hendrick's shoes.

"I'm so sorry!" she blurted out, wiping her mouth with the corner of her apron.

Hendrick, understanding the situation more than he probably should have, simply winced and shook off his shoes. "We need a cobbler in this village," he muttered.

Jenne looked up at him like a kicked puppy. "So, what does this mean?"

"Well," he started, "first you're going to have to meet him. He's at the inn right now, waiting for you."

"And Ama?" she asked.

"Ama is still away with Karlson."

"I thought he wasn't coming until spring," Jenne whined quietly. Hendrick shrugged.

"He seems wealthy enough," he said, trying to make her future sound brighter than it actually was.

"We both know that's not..." Jenne couldn't finish. Her body deflated.

"Look," Hendrick said. "We all love you. This village has been your family ever since your father left." Hendrick clasped his meaty hands around Jenne's face and stared into her indigo eyes. "We will do anything we can to make this situation as easy as possible for you until spring."

Jenne blinked away the tears forming in her eyes and willed herself to stand up straighter. "Keep him at the inn."

It was midafternoon by the time Jenne's willowy frame graced the threshold of the inn. A tall, bronze skinned man stood, robes flowing as he did so. Next to him sat another, this one shorter, stockier with a sturdy leather jerkin and a maille of chain peeking out from beneath. His sheathed sword leaned against the table. The tall man removed his wide-brimmed and feathered hat, tipping it toward Jenne. Jenne hesitated. In any faerie tale, this would be a girl's dream come true; a gallant, handsome gentleman of means arrives suddenly to whisk you away from your poverty. Jenne felt nothing but bilious.

"Alfonso of Barshiluna" he announced, taking Jenne's hesitation as modesty. "Your father did not lie about your beauty." Where other girls might have blushed, Jenne felt only disgust. She straightened her face into a slight smile and held out her hand, which Alfonso kissed. Jenne flinched. Alfonso's face changed into a query.

"My apologies, I find it cold." Jenne tried her best to sound fancy and nonchalant.

"Ah, indeed it is colder to the north," Alfonso proclaimed as though he were educating the patrons of the inn. "I promise you that Barshiluna is much warmer and will suit my bride's temperament better." Alfonso gestured for Jenne to take a seat next to him.

She did, crossing her arms over her chest. This felt much different than when she had sat across from Ama.

But what did it matter? she thought. Even if she wasn't getting married, Ama would be leaving anyway. There was some unspecified danger she refused to talk about. Or was it just an excuse for her to leave? She might be in love with Ama, but Ama was not in love with her. She refused to be. Could she force herself to make the best of the situation?

Jenne sat up straighter and put on her prettiest smile.

"This is my associate," Alfonso introduced the man across from them. "He was generous enough to guide me here and provide protection from bandits along the way."

The man rolled his eyes as he gulped his ale. "I was paid to do so."

Alfonso chuckled and lifted his ale toward the man. "Antòni here has not had much time to learn how to speak like a gentleman, but his sword has proved more than adequate."

Antòni grunted and took another gulp of ale.

"I'll teach him yet." Alfonso smiled and sipped his delicately.

Jenne steeled herself and swallowed her emotions. "Tell me about your business with my father."

"Ah, yes!" Alfonso's face lit up. Clearly trade and business was where he derived his self-worth. "My family started as humble hemp cloth merchants, but now, with the conflicts going on, every ship on either side requires constant repair to their sails." His eyes gleamed at the prospect. "Your father's dealings in quality rope have aided us greatly, as have our acquisition of several hemp farms on this side of the mountains." Alfonso finished his ale and called loudly for another.

"To be truthful, however," he said, lowering his voice, "your father was not our first choice of supplier." Jenne's eyebrows pressed together. "But when he mentioned that he had a Moorish daughter, we knew that we were more likely to curry favour with the other side when needed."

Jenne blanched and Alfonso winked, which Jenne was certain other girls felt was charming. She didn't even understand *sides*. Which side was she on?

"Your father talked a lot when he was in his cups. He told me a great deal about your mother, you know," Alfonso continued. "A one-eyed merchant girl who left before the fighting started again. Quite a few of them saw the writing on the wall and made it over the mountains before the current conflict. She died in childbirth, am I correct?"

Jenne barely registered a nod, her eyes wide in shock. Alfonso did not miss it. Jenne realised that she had been playing the wrong game. This was not some exchange of pleasantries before courting. This was a fencing match and she hadn't brought a sword.

"Did you know she had another before you?"

If Jenne's eyes could have gone any wider, they would have.

"Your father said she left your sister at an orphanage." He waved it off, laughing. "This was before they met, but he said when he learned of it, it became a thorn in his side that would never go away. He came to despise her."

"Are you always so cruel?" Jenne spat.

Antòni chuckled while Alfonso took another mug of ale from the servant girl. "I can assure you that I am not." He took a sip and continued. "I have no illusions that we will be a love story for the ages, and neither should you. But I will not be cruel to you. Bear my heirs and keep my house. I can and will find other lovers as needed. This is a business arrangement." Alfonso lowered his voice. "You, however, will not take other lovers," he added. "Of either sex."

Jenne lowered her head and sat in silence thinking over her new reality. There would be no joy for her. Certainly, no love. She would be taken, against her will and forced to breed.

"And you will use your given name. We want them to believe you are a proud Moorish woman."

Jenne hadn't used that name in years. Nor did she have any idea what being a *proud Moorish woman* even meant. She hadn't been south of the mountains. She hadn't even *seen* the mountains. The only Moors she knew were her mother and the few merchants she had met travelling. And they all spoke some dialect of Occitan. She hadn't even learned her mother's language. How *Moorish* could she be?

Her thoughts were interrupted by the innkeeper approaching. Pèire had known Jenne since she had arrived here as a child with her father and noticed immediately that something was wrong.

"Masters, your lodgings are ready for you to inspect" he said, bowing low. Alfonso finished his ale and stood, robes flowing richly.

"Very good. I'll take my leave and call you if anything more is needed." Alfonso patted Pèire on the shoulder patronisingly before they left Jenne sitting, sullen. Pèire sat down across from her and waited. Waiting was all you needed to do when you served alcohol and needed people to talk.

"Did my father come here often?" Jenne spoke quietly into her lap.

Pèire chewed the inside of his cheek. "He did."

"And he drank. A lot?" Jenne asked, realising just how little she had paid attention to what her father actually did once they had arrived here. Her life had really only begun once they had settled.

Pèire nodded.

"And my mother?"

"He spoke of her."

"Did he speak *well* of her?"

Pèire didn't answer. Jenne raised her head to see that he was staring at the table. He felt her eyes boring into him.

"No. He did not."

"Why did you never tell me?"

Pèire sighed. "What would that have done, Jenne? You already hated him. We could all see it."

Jenne stood and shuffled toward the door. "Then goodbye, I suppose," she said without turning around. She should have listened to Ama and never brought her home. She knew she would leave and she had come to terms with that, but now that her impending marriage was staring her in the face, it was unbearable. How could she even be expected to bear it now? The torment of hell is bearable if you've never tasted heaven and Jenne had drunk it deeply. Jenne closed the door and walked slowly up the hill toward her home.

Hendrick bounded in about ten minutes later to find Pèire still sitting at the table.

"Where's Jenne?" he demanded. "I need to make sure this husband of hers treats her right." Pèire just stared at him. "What?" he asked. "Also, where's the husband?"

"Him and his hired guard are upstairs inspecting their accommodations." Pèire said. "Jenne left."

"Did she say where?"

"I didn't ask." Pèire looked confused.

"I swear to God, Pèire, for someone who listens to the entire village in their cups, you've the wit of a barrel of mouldered apples."

"What?" Pèire's confusion deepened, his face contorted.

"And if I'm too late," Hendrick shouted as he ran as fast as his lumbering frame could carry him out of the inn, "I'm coming back to beat your bones."

Chapter Thirteen

Veritas / Erroris

Hendrick burst through the door and found Jenne throwing a loop of rope around a rafter. Startled, she stared at him wide-eyed, but then, just as quickly, her face turned into a frown. "I'm not going to marry him," she protested angrily, continuing to fuss with the rope.

"No," Hendrick said quietly, "but you're not going to do this either." He walked softly as was possible for a man his size over to the bed and sat. Jenne let go of the rope.

"You know that I don't have a wife," he started. Jenne blinked away the hot moisture forming at the corners of her eyes.

"This is a strange way of asking me to marry you." Jenne spat. *Also, he's got a guard and I've never seen you hold a sword, so he would probably win if it came down to it.*

Hendrick laughed. "No, but that might be a plan if the one I'm thinking of doesn't work out." Jenne frowned again. "You've never really thought to question why?" he asked.

"I just thought it was because you're ugly," she said. She was still angry, but now curious as to where this was going.

"No need to be mean," he said. "Besides, not everyone finds me ugly." Hendrick let that sit for a while, watching it simmer in Jenne's brain. Her face screwed in confusion, then disbelief and finally, lit up in realisation.

"The silk merchant?!"

"Did you never wonder why a silk merchant would travel all the way out here? Every year?" Hendrick smirked. "Also, the hat seller," he added.

Jenne smiled slyly and was about to say something before remembering this did not solve her predicament. "No-one is forcing you to marry, though."

"No," Hendrick said quietly. "They aren't. I do have an idea though."

Ama and Karlson made it back into town the next day. Porridge was heavy laden with tools and Ama thought she deserved a treat. "Take her to the forge and I'll get some apples from the inn," she told Karlson. "We'll deal with Txomin after and figure out living arrangements then." Karlson nodded and wearily led Porridge away.

She nearly ran into Hendrick as she opened the door, but even his bulk couldn't shield her view. In the corner, sitting next to a man she had never seen, was Jenne, laughing and clearly flirting with him. Ama blanched, feeling her heart sink but then she made eye contact with someone she had definitely seen before. An all-consuming rage came over her, blood roaring in her ears.

"You!" she screamed. "I'm going to kill you!' Ama reached for the rondel in her boot, now burning hot against her calf, but before she could, she felt herself lifted up by the giant man who promptly carried her outside.

Ama kept struggling, beating her fists impotently against Hendrick's back and the more she beat, the further away he carried her. Hendrick spied Jenne's house in the distance and got an idea. Within minutes, he was shouldering the door. Ama saw the rope and stopped her assault. "What's this?" she croaked out, lungs crushed against Hendrick's shoulder. Hendrick put her down.

"What do you think?"

Ama blinked. "But why?"

"Because, you selfish fool," he blurted out, "how do you not see that she loves you! Has soot so clouded your eyes? The entire village knows!"

"She's infatuated!" Ama yelled back. "She barely knows me! Nor does she understand the danger she's in! None of you do!" Ama stood, breathing ragged as the adrenaline flooded her stomach finding tears streaming down her face.

"Maybe," Hendrick half-whispered. "But you're not. I've never met a girl who threatened murder over someone they barely know."

"It's the other man I was threatening," she said, violence dripping from her voice.

"Was it now?" Hendrick paced the floor, moving behind her. "You know I saw your face when you first walked in. And you weren't looking at the other man."

"I see no reason not to kill both of them," Ama muttered. And then suddenly she cried out "Hey!"

Hendrick had grabbed her hands and was lacing rope around them. When he was finished, he turned her to face him. Ama's eyes were seething. Hendrick pointed his ruddy finger in her face. "You're a fool," he reiterated. "And you're not killing anyone. We have a plan. Do you trust us?"

"No," Ama spat.

"Fine. Are you going to interfere then?"

"How could I?"

Hendrick sat with that for a moment, staring at the hatred in Ama's eyes. It wasn't the malicious kind, more *frustration*. Like she had been thwarted. "How was your trip with Karlson?"

"*That's* what you want to talk about?" she yelled in disbelief.

Hendrick shrugged. "You're not going to fuck up our plans now, so I thought I'd make conversation."

"You're very odd," she hissed.

"Maybe, but so are you," Hendrick cocked his head. "A travelling iron merchant who refuses the best forge in the area, takes children under her wing and rescues lovelorn young maidens."

"Jenne doesn't need rescuing," she spat, thinking of Jenne with Alfonso.

"No," he chuckled. "Jenne can definitely take care of herself. Karlson, though," he suddenly turned serious. "That one needs some help."

"Why haven't you helped him then?" Ama narrowed her eyes.

Hendrick picked at his fingernails. "Txomin has a big mouth," he muttered.

"I'll deal with Txomin. You can help if you just bring some planks to his house."

"That's good enough for me." Hendrick turned to leave. "And Ama?" he started, "she really does love you. Even if she's naïve. I know you have your reasons, but maybe if you peek from behind that stone wall you've put up, you'd see it." He added. "You don't have to protect everyone. You couldn't even if you wanted to."

Ama watched Hendrick shut the door behind him and stood, bound and helpless. Even though she hated to admit it, he was right. She couldn't protect Jenne. She couldn't protect this village. She hadn't been able to protect her orphanage, the Sisters, or Sera either. And yet, Jenne thought she was worth obsessing over. Worth loving even?

Ama felt tears welling up again. She shook her head and squeezed her eyes shut. It was because she didn't know. She didn't truly understand. If she did; if they did, they would run from her in horror. The rondel in her boot burned against her calf. They didn't understand that they would all die.

And yet, here she was, bound by proof that she would have died anyway. Because of her. But the way she was acting at the inn? Something wasn't adding up.

Just then Karlson walked in. He looked at Ama and then headed toward a counter with several glass vials on it.

"Are you not going to untie me?" Ama asked, incredulously.

"Hendrick said not to."

"What?" she sputtered. Karlson shrugged and picked up the vial he needed.

"He said they had a plan."

Karlson closed the door and Ama was left alone again with her thoughts, until she noticed Porridge's head in the window. "You found me," she laughed mirthlessly. "Do you maybe want to explain what's going on?" Porridge snuffed and tried to reach some herb hanging from the ceiling. "Of course not," she continued. "You weren't there when they burned everything to the ground either." Ama leaned against the wall. The knot was too high up for her to reach, but at least she could kind of relax her body here, if not her mind.

"I don't know why it hurts," she whined quietly. "I've seen my lovers with their husbands before. But I didn't feel like this." Porridge huffed, annoyed that she couldn't reach the herbs. "You probably can't untie me, can you?" she joked. "Don't tell Hendrick this, but I probably would have killed them both."

Jenne drew lazy circles over Alfonso's arm, tracing the embroidery on the lush fabric of his coat. "Tell me more about Barshiluna," she cooed. Antòni rolled his eyes and swirled the dregs of his ale in the heavy ceramic mug. Pèire arrived with a maple bowl full to the brim and a few flat slabs of stale oat cake, along with a small finer loaf. He flicked his eyes to Jenne before lowering his head and scurrying away. Alfonso scooped some of the heavy stew onto his oat cake and used a chunk of the finer bread to pinch and place it into his mouth.

"I'm overjoyed that you've come to a reasonable conclusion, my dear. I had so hoped to not make this a difficult process and your cooperation will mean riches for us both." Alfonso leaned over to place a chaste and patronising kiss on her forehead. Antòni served himself and scanned the room for signs of danger. Something felt off, but he couldn't place a finger on it. Alfonso continued.

"Barshiluna is a beautiful city! Your people are building incredible things. The buildings are unlike anything you've ever seen, I'm certain. And the ocean! As blue as your eyes and almost as deep! We advance, of course, and I doubt your people will hold it for long, but neutrality is best in times of conflict - and immensely profitable."

Jenne tried her best not to wince whenever Alfonso said *your people*. Of course, her mother was a Moor, but this was making her feel like an imposter. She knew nothing of Moorish culture, art, or buildings. And to hear him dismiss its destruction as a situation from which to profit only made her decision that much clearer.

Alfonso continued shovelling stew into his mouth, bloviating about how inferior it was to the finer delights of Barshiluna. Antòni, despite his brusqueness, took more time with his. Jenne gazed lovingly as he spoke, rapt as she noticed the flush come over him. Alfonso emitted a gurgled burp.

"You must excuse me my dear," he tried to laugh it off, but suddenly turned and vomited. Antòni's eyes popped wide and he pushed his oat cake away. Alfonso clutched at his chest as his heart raced and then stopped. He doubled over the table, sending mugs of ale careening, soaking both Jenne and Antòni in the process. Jenne backed into the wall as Antòni made for his sword. He unsheathed it, throwing the scabbard to the ground, only to find that the muscles in his fingers wouldn't obey him. The sword clattered as adrenaline sped the poison quicker through his body until he too, collapsed on his knees.

Jenne skirted around him and ran to Hendrick, who had been standing by the door. "We'll take care of this," he said. "She's at your house and not going anywhere." Jenne nodded and sped out the door. Hendrick turned to Pèire. "I'll haul them out to the woods, but you're digging the holes."

"Why me?" Pèire whined.

"Because you're the lackwit," Hendrick countered. "If I hadn't come along when I did, she'd be the one you'd be digging a hole for."

Chapter Fourteen

Vires / Topor

J enne ran. She wasn't sure if she had ever run so fast in her life. Even though she knew that Ama had refused to tell her why she was so hesitant about staying, keeping her in the dark felt like a betrayal. She chastised herself despite the fact that now they were even. Kind of. She still didn't understand why Ama was being so vague about everything. And maybe Ama didn't love her the way she loved Ama, but she would show her. She would convince her.

Our more mature selves are jaded when it comes to love. We have unwritten rules about when to say it, how much of ourselves to reveal, and how to cope when it's unreciprocated. We use words like *infatuation* or *limerence* to refer to the feeling of being hopelessly in love while our minds frantically try to harmonise the evidence, we see with our eyes with the feelings bursting from our hearts. In reality, we use these tools to protect ourselves from the pain of heartache. We have learned that such feelings often spur us to make unwise decisions, to ignore the evidence that the object of our affection is not worthy of it.

What often fails to be learned, however, is that while they may distort those objects of our affections, the feelings themselves are very real. The reactions of your body are very real. The ache in your heart is very real. And while your mature self may decide a course of action based on those reactions, only a fool refuses to listen to their body. Ignoring it comes at a cost. And sometimes that cost is love itself.

Jenne listened to her body, even if Ama wouldn't. She did not know the horrors she had faced or the lingering trauma, but her body *needed* Ama. And so, she continued to run toward her house as if every part of her was being pulled by a strand of invisible spidersilk toward her. She felt the rush of blood pounding through her, hot in her ears, impervious to the cool breezes of late autumn. She pushed her legs, burning with exhaustion from the sudden fury of effort. For her.

Jenne ignored the ludicrous sight of a grey Konik with its head stuck through her window. She ploughed through the door, startling Ama awake, who had been slumped over against the wall. She slammed into Ama, pushing her back against the wall, causing several coils of rope to fall from their nails and kissed her with such ferocity that she tasted iron. And Ama liked iron. Ama barely had time to mutter a surprised *what?* before Jenne's lips were on hers again. She tried to push her away, but her hands were still bound. Jenne laughed and pulled the rope and Ama closer to the centre of the room so her arms could fall below her chest at least.

"Can you explain what's going on now?" Ama sputtered.

"You first."

"Well, I got here with Karlson and my tools, stopped at the inn and saw you flirting with some man" Ama retorted bitterly.

"Why do you care?" Jenne yelled. "Also, you left out the part about threatening to kill him."

"I don't know!" Ama yelled back. "I don't know why I *feel* like this!" Tears started streaming down her face. She couldn't remember the last time she had cried. Or been so angry. "I can't stay!" She yelled between sobs, but even to her own ears, it sounded like a feeble excuse.

Jenne stood there, looking at her beautiful smith with pity. "I'm sorry," she said quietly. "I don't know your reasons and you don't want to tell me." She took a step forward. "But I can take care of myself. I've been doing it since my father left. So can you maybe, just give me a chance."

Ama knew it was a bad idea, but at this moment, vulnerable and coming apart at the seams, she really, *really* wanted to. She nodded, almost imperceptibly, but it was enough for Jenne.

Jenne placed a reassuring hand in the middle of Ama's chest. Ama felt warmth radiate through her, mind reeling at the juxtaposition of the comforting gesture along with still being bound. It made her feel like prey that a hunter was toying with. Worse still was that she wasn't experiencing the panic she thought she should. This was something entirely different.

Jenne leaned forward, her hand still on Ama's chest. Ama thought she was going to kiss her again and ignore her questions, but she moved her head to the side and softly grazed her teeth along her earlobe before whispering.

"I killed them."

"What?" Ama sputtered. She jumped back, stumbling and falling against the wall. The action yanked her hands above her waist again.

Jenne remained standing and cocked her hip, a sly grin forming on her face. "I killed them," she repeated. Ama blinked in confusion. She attempted to sputter a reply, but was only able to form nonsense syllables. "That's what I thought," Jenne said, pressing her hand into Ama's chest again, keeping her pinned against the wall. Ama's heart sped up, thudding so hard she thought it was going to burst through her ribcage. Jenne could feel it and a smile slid across her face. "What?" Jenne asked sweetly. "You thought that because I was new at this," her eyes swept across Ama's body, "that I was naïve when it came to everything else?" Ama swallowed hard. The rush of fear she felt wasn't entirely unpleasant. She was right. Ama had been entirely wrong about her. "I'm a survivor." Jenne walked her fingers slowly up toward Ama's neck.

"I said I survived my father." She placed a kiss on her collarbone.

"I said I survived him abandoning me," she whispered against her skin.

"I also survived the first boy that tried to take me," she raked her teeth, causing Ama to yelp, "though I didn't kill him. I just gave him diarrhoea for a few days. He was afraid to speak to me for a year," she laughed.

"And," she continued, "I'm a very quick learner."

Jenne leaned back and jerked on the rope holding Ama's hands, causing her to collide into her. She laughed and sunk her teeth into Ama's bottom lip. This was the Jenne she had been wary about when they had first met. Their power imbalance had only been temporary and imagined. How had she fallen into this trap? Jenne gazed into Ama's wide eyes, lip still between her teeth. She dug fingernails into her neck and Ama gasped. Jenne took the moment to slip her tongue into her as far as she could reach. Ama was helpless and she turned liquid against Jenne's hunger.

Jenne's fingers slid to the front of Ama's gambeson, pulling at the ties and wrenching it over her shoulders. Her hands were still bound, but now her own clothing had pinned her arms to her sides. Jenne lifted the loose shift over her breasts and Ama stood exposed and helpless. Jenne pushed her again, slamming her back against the wall, eyes alight devouring the way her breasts flowed at the movement. She plunged forward, snaking her tongue around a nipple, not even attempting to be gentle. Jenne was feral and Ama was powerless against it. She didn't usually make sounds during sex, but this was something else. Jenne pulled deep moans from her throat through some strange power Ama couldn't imagine.

The feeling of being wanted so ferociously, so wantonly, caused a warm wetness to flood her centre. Ama had had plenty of partners. Plenty of experience, but had someone told her she could feel this way, want this much, *need* to be taken, she would not have believed them.

"Please" she uttered between ragged breaths.

She could feel Jenne's smile form wickedly against her breast. Jenne knelt, those indigo eyes meeting Ama's. Kisses peppered her skin, lower across her taut abdomen. She bit the small pocket of fat Ama wished she had more of below her navel. Her heartbeat pounded hotly between her legs. Jenne slipped her fingers beneath the band of Ama's trousers peeling them toward the floor, smiling crookedly at the parts between her legs where they stuck because they were soaked.

Jenne inhaled deeply, closing her eyes, revelling in Ama's warm honey scent. She placed her hands against Ama's hip bones, steadying herself like a drunkard. Ama felt the warmth of Jenne's tongue lap languidly against her lips. She quivered, almost falling apart. Jenne did it again, eliciting whimpers from her lover before she drew back and stared into Ama's eyes. Jenne drew her tongue across her lips, relishing the sin. "So that's what my smith tastes like."

Jenne smiled again, like some demon from a tale told in an alehouse before she returned to Ama's centre. Ama wailed with abandon as Jenne drew her tongue across her lips, parting them and settling on her clit. Her lithe fingers slithered and probed, stroking, coaxing the secrets from her innermost self. Ama fell apart and Jenne was there to catch her.

Ama had been so wrong, and now it was her turn to weep. Jenne stood quickly wrapping her arms around her smith, holding her tightly until it was over.

"I'm sorry," Ama hiccupped.

"I know." Jenne whispered.

The scene dawned on Ama and she laughed between her tears. Porridge's head was still through the window. She was awkwardly half undressed and still tied up. They were both covered in sweat and the smell of sex hung in the air.

"So," Ama sighed, trying, and failing, to catch her breath. "You killed them?"

"What?" Jenne asked. "That's what you wanted anyway, wasn't it? Tell me how that would have gone

– rushing at them in a blind range? Did you even notice the one with a sword? You would have been killed before you even grazed their skin."

"The one with the sword was the one I was going to kill first," Ama muttered.

"What? Why?" Jenne was taken aback.

Ama sighed. "Since you've already killed them, I guess you're in this as deep as I am now." Ama lifted up her hands sheepishly. "Could you maybe untie me first though?"

Jenne smirked. "You didn't seem to mind it a few minutes ago." Ama tilted her head and raised an eyebrow. "Fine," Jenne laughed as she untied Ama's hands. "Now talk."

Ama massaged her wrists. "A local lord found out that I was making steel in the orphanage. They liked what I had made, so they came to bring me to work in the fort. I refused to go and I ran." Tears began streaming down her face. "They took me anyway and after I escaped, I found that they had burned my home and everyone in it to the ground."

Jenne slipped an arm around her, drawing her in closer. "They're still looking for me. The one you killed was one of them. It's why I can't stay." Jenne worried her lip. She wanted to tell Ama that they were in this together now, that she would go where Ama went. That nothing bad would ever happen to her again, but she knew Ama would never believe her. Instead, she nuzzled into Ama's hair and held her while she wept.

Chapter Fifteen

Patentiae / Irae

The nascent fort stood, construction having barely started, on the foothills with the Pyrenes standing proudly in the background. There were no gates, only a couple of poorly outfitted boys standing around, pretending to be important. The men led her to a hastily erected squarish wooden building, housing a much better-quality oak table. It must have been brought here from elsewhere and it spoke to the ambition of what was to be built later. One of her captors spoke.

"Lord Idoya, the smith we told you about." Ama suppressed a smirk. His name meant *pond* in one of the local dialects and this area was nothing but silty swamps. Lord Idoya put down the parchment he was poring over. He appeared as though his title had only come recently, Ama thought. His brigandine was faded. It was worn and rivets were missing. When he stood, he seemed stockier than she expected of a noble. Either way, this man had clearly done physical labour.

"They say you're one of the Sisters at the orphanage." Lord Idoya looked her in the eye. It made Ama uncomfortable. "Tell me," he said, looking away, "how does a Sister forge iron, let alone iron like this?" He took the sword from one of her captors and waved it in her face.

"I read it in a book," Ama replied meekly. Laughter erupted around her until they realised Lord Idoya wasn't laughing, at which point, it stopped abruptly.

"How does a farmer learn to read?" Ama guessed at his previous profession.

"Perceptive." Lord Idoya smiled wryly, "but I suspect you know less about nobility than you think. Only the wealthiest of us can sit in the shade, eating fruit. I worked the fields alongside the serfs."

"Did they get to learn to read?"

Lord Idoya ignored this question. He couldn't decide if he should admire the provocation or pity her stupidity.

"These fools can't read either," Lord Idoya explained. The *fools* lowered their heads, shifting their eyes around the room as though it would cause Lord Idoya to avoid noticing them.

"Did you manage to bring the book?" he turned to one of her captors.

"Uh, no, milord," one of them stuttered. Lord Idoya swung at him, belting him across the face with the back of his hand. Ama flinched at the unexpected violence. Antòni flinched as well.

"Leave us and go about your patrols," he ordered. Antòni and two others she didn't know left hurriedly while the other one sat, cradling his nose.

Monségnor Rachid entered the building, huffing as though he had run here urgently. "My Lord," he breathed, "you cannot waste your resources on this metal, it's heathen nonsense."

"Like the witch that refused to move?" Lord Idoya spat.

"The *seer*" Monségnor Rachid emphasised, "is just a harmless old woman who no longer cares if she lives."

"Yes, well my men refuse to kill her when half of them vomited their day's rations after destroying her hut."

"Your men need spiritual guidance." Monségnor Rachid said patiently. "Which is *why* I was asked to come here."

Lord Idoya grumbled and shuffled his parchment. "Tell me, Rachid," he started, "has God made us a metal that will keep the Moors in their place?"

"My Lord, the Holy Father has sent me to minister to the souls of this fort. I am responsible for your salvation." Monségnor Rachid blustered. "And the salvation of all the souls within!" he added. "We need a smith for the building of a *church*."

"Think, Rachid," said Lord Idoya, tapping his skull with a thickly callused finger, "do you not believe God would have us victorious rather than virtuous? Why do you think the Romans never took the North?"

"That is heresy, my Lord."

"Is it? Who will be left to be virtuous when we are overrun?"

Monségnor Rachid turned a glorious shade of purple. "Have it your way then," Lord Idoya gestured broadly, "put her with the *seer*."

"But she is a Sister!" Monségnor Rachid protested. "She does not even understand what she has done!"

"Then perhaps our seer can rectify that."

Monségnor Rachid made the sign of the cross as Ama was led away to a hastily constructed wooden cage. Its sole occupant was a dishevelled old woman who actually looked like the witches in the stories.

Ponç stood guard outside, rocking uneasily on his feet.

"You're to tell her about the metal," one of her captors said brusquely.

"What metal?" the old woman croaked. She cleared her throat and spat viscously next to his feet. She grinned.

"Go fetch the sword" her captor yelled across the muddy courtyard to some lackey further away. Within minutes, the sword was presented to the woman. She didn't move.

"You know I can't see," she said. "I don't know what you're talking about."

Her captor thrust the sword through the bars of the cage. The woman didn't take it, so Ama tentatively reached out toward it. When no-one stopped her, she assumed she was to take it, and so she did. Ponç's eyes popped open.

"You're giving her a sword!?" he shouted.

"What the fuck is she going to do with a sword in a cage? Kill the witch? Ponç shifted uncomfortably, but didn't protest any further.

Ama stood, holding the sword, unsure of what to do. Her captor made a face and tilted his head toward the woman. Ama took the woman's hand and placed it on the sword.

"That is indeed a sword," the woman said. Anything else I can divine for you?

"How did she make it?" he said through gritted teeth, enunciating every word.

"How should I know? Ask her," the woman retorted. He turned and stared intently at Ama.

"With bones and clay," Ama said quietly.

"Oh, that's what this is!" the woman exclaimed. "I haven't seen ghost iron in years!"

"So, how do we make more?" the captor demanded.

"With bones and clay," the witch said. She was about to stop, but the captor's look grew tense. "And runes. And only a woman can make them."

"Runes?" Ama asked.

"The shapes you drew on the clay, dear," she said. The witch was now speaking to her as though she had been invited over to share some village gossip, oblivious to the cage and the two angry men staring at them.

"I didn't know what they meant." Ama said.

"No-one taught you?"

"No."

"How did you learn this then?"

"It was in a book."

At this, the witch burst into peals of laughter while Ama felt embarrassed and the two men grew angrier. When the old woman finally stopped laughing, she wiped the tears from her unseeing eyes and told the men, "I can explain this to her, but it will take some time." The captor huffed and walked away, no doubt to report all that had happened. Ponç remained and slumped against the cage. Discipline, Ama supposed, would have to come after the fort was completed.

The woman thrust out her arm. "Draw them," she ordered. Ama repeated the markings she had drawn on the clay while the old woman's smile grew.

"I haven't felt the names of our old gods for a long time," she said

"They cared for you?" Ama asked?

The old woman chuckled. "The old gods are not like that. They don't care for people. Mind you, yours doesn't either, you just pretend he does. You appease the old gods and they may grant you protection. There are very few people they actually like. Fewer that they actually care about."

Ama didn't know what to do with this information, so she just sat still and waited. The old woman continued.

"These markings bind the spirit to the metal. Spirits feed on blood to become flesh again, if only temporarily. Once vengeance is taken, they are freed."

"I was supposed to quench it in blood, but I didn't."

"Oh that. That just acts like oil. It makes the transition less painful.

"The what?" Ama nearly dropped the old woman's arm. She laughed.

"Come now, you didn't think that enchantments came without costs, did you? If they didn't, everyone would be pestering spirits and gods, day and night."

"I suppose," Ama muttered. How do you know all this? The old woman smiled, eyes shining, despite her inability to see.

"I loved a smith once." The woman took Ama's palm and traced a finger across it. "Someone loves you too." She grinned knowingly, but then her expression turned serious. A frown appeared. "I haven't seen this before," she muttered. "The line breaks. But there's a branch that connects them? This is…"

She was interrupted by Ponç pounding on the cage. "Are you about done with your sorcery, witch?"

"You say that like it's a bad thing, dear." The old woman smiled sweetly. Ponç's face turned sour.

"Give me the sword. I think you're done with it," he spat.

Several unfortunate things happened at once. Ama bent down to pick up the sword by its hilt. The old woman also bent down to pick it up, or at least, bent down to where she thought the sword would be. Ponç reached out his hand to take the sword, but as the old woman stood, she knocked Ama off balance. Instead of the hilt, Ponç wrapped his fingers around the blade. He drew his hand back to examine the thin red line that had appeared. Ama tried to drop the sword, but found that she couldn't. Her fingers only clenched the hilt tighter.

Blood dripped from the boy's hand, but instead of hitting the ground, some unseen force was drawing it to fall on the blade. The once superficial wound was now bleeding profusely. Ponç screamed in agony as the sword drank in every drop of blood that had previously been in his body. The boy's mouth grew dry and his scream turned to a crackling whisper and finally, dust. The desiccated husk that had been Ponç crumpled to the dirt. Once the sword had drunk its fill, the old woman watched blindly in horror as it now turned its attention to Ama. Thick drops of blood, terrifyingly red and viscous, swarmed the young girl like angry wasps. She screamed as it pelted against her, sticking, forming shapes, burning and burrowing into her flesh.

At once, the screams turned to an ear-shattering roar. Where Ama had once been, the dreadful figure of a bear made blood now stood. The cage had become splinters and the thoughts in Ama's brain could only focus on revenge and destruction. The bear careened toward the square building, its heavy footsteps squelching sickeningly through the dirt. Ama raised a bloody claw, tearing through the heavy birchwood posts as though they were made of parchment. Soldiers howled their throats raw. Limbs flew. Torsos thudded wetly against the ground. The dead eyes of men, slack and sightless stared back at her from the ground. The visions, the sounds and her own lust for vengeance became disconnected acts of violence and the euphoric rush of longsuffering justice sloshed against her skull, mixing like a well-stirred elixir of sleep.

Ama awoke somewhere in the woods, naked and cold. Every part of her hurt and she was covered in blood. Hers, the bear or someone else's, she didn't know. The answer to those questions, however, was of secondary importance. Right now, she needed to get back to the orphanage. To Sera.

She hurled herself forward, willing her burning legs to carry her toward safety. Her body careened into a tree, its rough bark tearing at her skin. She vomited hot blood and collapsed once again.

The second time she awoke, her thoughts were clearer. She remembered the horror of what she had done. This time, she followed the wet footsteps back toward the fort. She stared intently from the tree line and waited. She saw no movement, heard nothing. Ama took a few cautious steps forward, waiting to spy a guard from over the pointed logs, but she saw no-one. She saw no-one guarding the path into the fort either. A great splintered hole had been torn from the wall. That was probably her doing as well, she thought.

Ama continued to step cautiously, wincing as she trod carefully over the sharp gravel.

Bodies lay strewn about the ground. The witch was nowhere to be found, but she recognised Ponç's desiccated corpse and the captor who had brought her to her cage. She had never learned his name. Even now, she couldn't bring herself to feel anything but hatred toward them. She did not know the others. Lord Idoya either wasn't there or was so mutilated that she couldn't recognise him. She did not see Monségnor Rachid either. Now that she knew what this metal did, she understood why Lord Idoya had wanted it. And pitied Monségnor Rachid for his disbelief.

As she surveyed the rest of the damage, everything she knew told her she should feel an immense guilt at the scale of this destruction, but she could not. This was against what she had been taught since she was a baby. Retribution and vengeance would be doled out on Judgement Day, and not by her. She had taken what was God's alone to give. She had stolen from the divine, and it was the old gods who had made her Prometheus.

Ama looted some of the smaller bodies, taking boots and clothing that would at least preserve her flesh long enough to make it back to her Sisters. As she was about to leave, a glint caught her eye. It was the sword. Ama left it where it was. She quickly asked God never to let her experience that again. At once, she caught herself and whispered to the old gods whose names she had never been taught. A flurry of ravens settled near some corpses and cawed at her. Ama accepted it as an answer, though she did not know what it meant.

It took days on foot. Ama smelled the smoke before she saw it and when she did, she broke into a run, despite being near starving. Her orphanage had been put to flame, her Sisters slaughtered where they stood. Children lay lifeless in pools of blood-drenched earth. And Sera.

It is simply impossible to describe the madness that descends from the shock of sudden grief to one who has not experienced it. Humans, who pride themselves on being rational, even in their religious practices, do things that defy any semblance of logic or reason. When it strikes, there is a need by all beings with a modicum of intelligence to defy reality, though we are but motes of dust in a cold and desolate universe. From someplace deep within us, we feel a calling, a *need* to elevate and honour the dead in bizarre, and sometimes morbid ways. Some might even call these impromptu ceremonies of grief *inhuman*, but they are the most human of actions. These actions reveal our innermost selves, stripped of decorum, modesty or thought to how we may be perceived by others. These are but defences, costumes we wear that we pretend make us human, and in these costumes, we permit ourselves to commit the basest atrocities against the nature of our selves. We perform appropriate grieving ceremonies that do not disturb the sensibilities of others. Memorials are placed and speeches recited as though the ghosts care about stones and words said by the living. As though this will tie them to a time and place, as though they even feel the need to be remembered by the living.

But Ama was alone.

Ama had no-one to care about memorials and rituals There were no living eyes to gaze upon her in disapproval and her grieving, most human soul was free to honour the dead as she knew she should. And while the living may care about remembrance and memorials, Ama had firsthand experience. Ama knew the only thing that ghosts wanted. And after the weeping had passed and all the tears had been shed, Ama, dehydrated, starving and exhausted, lay beside them in the dust and ash. When she awoke, she got to work.

Chapter Sixteen

Concordia / Aavaritiae

He awoke with a start, gasping and clawing at the mud and dead leaves. He coughed, vomited and finally willed his body to sit up. As the blood started circulating through his veins, he slowly regained his vision. He could hear the owls, which meant that it was actually dark and it wasn't just his eyes. His fingers pressed into a soft rich fabric. The man he'd been hired to guard. He'd failed at that.

This was the problem with women, he thought. God had designed them to serve man, yet so often they rebelled. And you couldn't fight them – not unless one of them was foolhardy enough to challenge you directly. Beat, punish, discipline, certainly. You could cower most of them into submission well enough, but *fighting* them was simply impossible. Women were necessary to the survival of men, unless one wanted to live like those effete hermits, but even those small communes disappeared rather quickly. He *hated* that men needed women. That men *desired* women. And that women, in all of their weakness still somehow knew it. Other animals, he thought, either did not rebel or were easier to control. A cow did not threaten you. Sheep would obey their shepherds. Goats and mules were stubborn, yes, but they could still be rendered harmless. With women, you could never predict which bite may have poison or which plant they had stolen it from. The knowledge Eve had gained from that damned tree, he surmised, must have been witchcraft. And Adam's punishment was forever needing her.

But there was one he hated above all others. She had challenged him. He knew her face. He remembered her from when she had first toyed arrogantly with that sword. No, he wasn't there the day construction on the fort had stopped, but he had seen the aftermath. And she would learn her place. He rose to his feet and placed his hand against the bark of an alder tree, coughing for several minutes before limping off.

Hours later, Pèire arrived with a shovel and a lantern and began digging a hole beside the body, now stiff. Once he had finished, he did a quick search of the pockets and fingers for anything valuable. The robes were ruined and though impractical for life around here, they might have been traded to a merchant for something. Satisfied that nothing would go to waste, Pèire rolled the body with his foot into the hole and began filling it again. He looked around for the second body, assuming it had been dumped nearby, but didn't find it. Tired and annoyed at being ordered about by Hendrick, he decided the wolves would take care of it and went home to bed.

Jenne held herself tightly against Ama's back, wrapping her arm across her chest as Ama sobbed. And when the well of tears had run dry and Ama's cries became stuttering breaths, Jenne pressed her mouth against her hair, a soft, tangled mess that matched this beautiful woman who had endured so much and who, even now, only sought to shield her from those same horrors. Part of her regretted forcing her to reveal so much, to relive such pain. Another part of her wanted to know every secret she carried.

Naïve as she was, she wanted to know more about Sera. Perhaps out of jealousy, she thought, but even she understood that would bring more pain and she couldn't ask that of Ama. At least, not now. Her curiosity would have to wait. She decided to think of someone else to ask her about that might bring happier memories.

"Tell me about Sister Klara," she whispered against her ear.

Ama snuffled back the remaining tears and then rolled over to face Jenne. "She was," she paused, searching for the right words, "the strongest woman I've ever known. Her arms were bigger than my legs," Ama laughed wiping away more tears with the palms of her hands. "She told me once that she had had suitors and she had refused them. I can't imagine any man not being terrified of her."

Jenne smiled, glad she was able to summon some happy memories. She drew back some of the hair that had stuck to Ama's face. Ama continued.

"Imagine me, but bigger, wearing a dress, a kerchief and an apron." Jenne laughed at the thought. "I found out after she had died that her and Sister Hildegaarde were lovers. I think they had both come to the orphanage from the same place, but I never asked. Sera and I were always scared of Sister Hildegaarde. She was just an old woman, but everyone did whatever she said. She just had this air about her and I don't know how she did it. The only one it didn't work on was Sister Klara."

"I think we know why that is," Jenne grinned. She had no idea who these women were, but listening to Ama talk about them with such familiarity made her feel as though she were being invited into her world.

"What I wouldn't give to have heard some of their private conversations," Ama mused. "Well, not *all* of their private conversations." Ama made a face and Jenne giggled. "When I was little, I used to wish that Sister Klara had been my mother. I never knew her, whoever she was. I don't even know what she looked like. None of us did. Except for Sera, because her mother had been there when she was born. The Sisters told us that much at least."

"My mother," Jenne's look was faraway, "always seemed so sad. I think she was trying to protect me from my father." Jenne's face was stone, as though she had told this story so often that its reality had ceased to affect her. "He hit her often. And after he had left her, unburied with a stillborn twin in the forest, he hit me too."

"She had lost an eye, but she never told me how," Jenne continued, running fingers through Ama's ashy blonde hair. "I don't remember her face with both eyes, but if I ever see him again, I'll take one of his." Jenne rolled over onto her back, sniffing and blinking so the tears didn't show. Her revelation had affected her more than usual. It didn't always, but maybe, she thought, it was because she was sharing this with Ama. Everything felt different with her. She felt like if Ama asked her, she would throw everything she had built away. She would follow her from village to village.

Even she knew that was naïve and foolish. Ama was right. They had only just met.

"I found out later she had had another child," Jenne said, ignoring her feelings, believing that if she continued to reveal her past to Ama as though she were just another traveller, this pull to give up everything for her would subside. It did not.

"Before you?" Ama asked. Jenne nodded.

"Pèire told me she was left at an orphanage before I was born. Alfonso said that my father started hating her when he found out."

The colour drained from Ama's face as the realisation dawned on her. She was thankful that it was dark and Jenne couldn't see her reaction.

In the smouldering ruins of her orphanage, Ama set about rebuilding her forge. The thing about places that harness the power of fire, is that they are designed to withstand a great deal of it and so most of her tools were unharmed, despite being covered in soot. Some of her hammers would need new handles, but there was an entire forest nearby and that wouldn't be a problem. Besides, working kept her mind from thinking too hard about what she was doing.

Ama pulled the hot ingot, clay flaking off and placed it on the anvil. It had happened again, but she had been expecting it this time. She had been waiting. And when their eyes met, she nodded silently, accepting the horror of what she was about to do. Ama brought the hammer down onto the glowing bar, blow after blow, but no sound was made.

When she pulled the rondel from the quench, her gaze met a pair of dead eyes. "How did you?" Ama started but was cut off.

"You're not supposed to use human bone char for that," the witch stated.

"Did you..." but she was cut off again.

"Oh yes, the witch continued. I've seen it before, but I'd never been that close. You became a bear, correct? That's what it sounded like, at least. Those poor boys." She chuckled, seeming to have little sympathy for those *poor boys*.

"How did you get here?" Ama was at least able to finish her question this time.

"I'm a witch, dear. The old gods keep me around because I'm good at doing what they tell me to. You don't need to *see* to do that." She added "They're very interested in you, though. They're very interested in this *abomination* you're creating."

Ama stared pointedly at the witch and then returned to her work. Hammering silently. "She deserves revenge," Ama muttered.

"And how's that coming along?" Ama flicked her eyes upward to reach the witch's smirk. "What?" the witch cocked her head menacingly. "You remembered that a blind old woman showed up at your forge in a ruined fortress, but didn't think she could also show up when you were asleep and dreaming?" The witch sat on the edge of blackened stone and patted the spot beside her. Ama put down her hammer and sat beside her. "Now," the witch continued, "you remember that I asked you if you were sure that it was revenge she wanted? And I said that it seems like you had already gotten it? You never answered me. You said she nodded to you before she went into the iron. And I asked if you were sure that's what she had meant." Ama's eyes were locked on her soot-stained hands, a scowl on her face. The witch tucked a strand of hair behind her ear.

"What's done is done," the witch whispered. "But none of us were really expecting this to take quite so long."

"Who is us?" Ama asked.

The witch ignored the question and continued. "Ghosts and iron aren't really compatible. It burns them. And you've kept her there long enough." Ama's eyes went wide as the horror of what she had done, what she was doing, washed over her. She had locked the only woman she had ever loved in a burning iron prison. For years.

Ama grasped at the witch's filthy cloak, tears streaming. "How do I fix this?" She was frantic, pleading, "I didn't know!" she sobbed.

"No, of course you didn't," the witch huffed. "Does fire care if you don't know that it's hot? The gods don't care what you know. They care what you do. And even then, not so much." The witch pushed a sniffling Ama off of her and sat her upright, surprisingly strong for an old woman. "Listen," she placed a bony finger over Ama's lips, still quivering, "Now that you know, you have a decision to make. Give Sera her vengeance or protect her sister."

"So, it's true?" It was more of a statement than a question.

"Of course it is. You always knew it was." The witch stood and started brushing the soot off of her apron.

"What does she think of this?" Ama asked, her eyes searching for any signs of approval. She had done so much wrong unwittingly, caused so much harm. Jenne learning that her sister had been her lover's only love would crush her, wouldn't it?

"How should I know?" the witch turned to leave. "Do you think I just stroll into anyone's dreams? I don't have a blood connection with her, now do I?"

Chapter Seventeen

Fides / Incredulitas

Ama rose with the dawn again and left quickly. She found Porridge grazing nearby with a bustard standing on top of her. It flew off when she approached and Porridge didn't seem to notice it. In minutes, she found herself standing at the door of the bakers. Ama thumped on the door and was greeted by a short, angry looking man with a red upturned nose, covered in flour and reeking of alcohol.

"I'm here for Karlson," she said, hoping to be in his presence as briefly as possible. She noticed an older boy behind him, curious to see who was at the door this early. The man scowled at Ama and then swung violently at the boy. The boy had seen it coming and was able to step back out of the way. Ama wondered how long this man had left before his boys rose up against him.

"Get the orphan!" he bellowed, slurring his words. He turned back to Ama. "You're the smith."

"Did you need something?" Ama looked around for obstacles if she needed to run. She was close to his height, but knew she was no fighter. The man snorted derisively.

"Take the witch with you when you fuck off," he sputtered before slamming the door.

Moments later, Karlson appeared, bounding and full of energy. He danced circles around her and Porridge as they made their way over to the forge.

"Listen," she started, "you can't be jumping around the forge like that, so get it out now. You'll burn yourself like last time." Karlson sped off running and returned sweaty and panting. Ama made a face of disgust. "Once we're done today, you're going to bathe." Karlson rolled his eyes and they entered the shop.

Half the day had passed and Ama had shown Karlson how to operate the bellows and tell when the charcoal was ready for the iron. He had even managed to pull a piece out with the tongs without burning himself. After he had struck his first hammer blow, however, they had to stop as it went flying backward and hissed angrily in the dust. There was a long conversation about keeping the forge clean so that nothing would catch fire if he did that again. She had just set him to cleaning when Jenne appeared.

"I've brought you something," Jenne smiled, placing a loaf of bread and some hard cheese on the counter. She leaned in to kiss Ama, but Ama hesitated. Jenne noticed and gave a weak smile before stepping back.

Ama was still trying to process her dreams from last night and how Jenne would react. It turned out that her body had already betrayed that something was amiss. Now, when there was finally a glimmer of hope that she might be able to live a normal life, at least for her, she was about to fuck it up.

"Thank you," Ama said. "That was really sweet." She took Jenne's hand, trying to make up for her earlier hesitation, but the damage had been done. Karlson ran forward and tore a piece off of the loaf, cramming it into his mouth before running off again. "Don't run in the shop!" Ama yelled.

"Will I see you tonight?" Jenne asked. It hadn't been a question earlier, but given Ama's reaction, it was now. Ama ran her fingers through her hair, settling on the back of her neck.

"I said I'd look at the house Karlson's father left him. I'm not sure when I'll be finished." She said sheepishly.

"Ah, okay," Jenne said, trying not to let the hurt show. Something had happened and she didn't know what it was. Or more accurately, Jenne didn't know which one of the multiple things that had happened last night was causing Ama to act this way.

Maybe she shouldn't have been so forward when Ama was tied up. Ama was strong. *So* strong. Butterflies had settled in Jenne's stomach thinking about her arms around her. And Jenne had taken that away from her. And Ama liked to be in control. She liked to know what was happening and Jenne had barged in announcing that she had concocted an entire plan that didn't involve her. She had pushed Ama to the side and done things *to* her instead of *with* her. Maybe that's why she was upset.

Or maybe it was because she had seen Jenne with Alfonso. Maybe she was jealous? Of course, she would have gotten herself killed if she had attacked him, but maybe that didn't make her feelings go away? Did that mean she had feelings for Jenne? Real ones? Jenne felt her cheeks grow hot at the thought, but pushed it aside. She needed to fix whatever she had done.

Maybe talking about...Sera? Jenne had to force herself to continue down that path. She didn't like thinking of Ama loving someone else. She knew it was stupid and it was a long time ago, but she couldn't help the feelings of jealousy that started making her heart race. Maybe Ama knew she was jealous? Jenne's thoughts continued to spiral, growing more and more conspiratorial when she ran directly into Hendrick.

"You are definitely not okay," Hendrick stated. "What did you do?"

Jenne looked up at him pitifully and then burst into tears. The giant man wrapped his arms around her. "I ruined everything!" she sobbed into his chest.

Hendrick let her cry and when she had finished, told her to meet him by his wood shop. "Help me move some planks over to Karlson's house and tell me when you've cleaned yourself up." He didn't actually need help moving planks, but it would distract her enough so they could get to the bottom of whatever it was.

Within half an hour, Jenne was loading planks onto a cart, burbling about how she had wrecked whatever tenuous relationship she had had with Ama in one novel-sized run-on sentence. She sat on the edge of the cart, hyperventilating before Hendrick told her to stop and look at him.

"What did she say to you?" he asked

"What?" A confused look spread across her face. "What do you mean?"

"What. Did. She. Say?" Hendrick asked again.

Jenne shook her head, the confusion pressing her eyebrows together. "Nothing."

"Then why do you think you messed anything up?"

"Because she hesitated!" Jenne yelled. Hendrick was clearly not understanding.

Hendrick rubbed his chin and looked away in exasperation. "Look, I know this is your first relationship, but it's been a week. You need to use your words. If you think something is wrong, just ask her."

Jenne shook her head. "That's not how it works!"

"You've been with a girl for a week!" he yelled. "*You* don't know how it works! You don't know how *anything* works!"

"You talk to her then!" and then she muttered "since you seem to know how everything works."

"Absolutely not," he protested.

"Why not?" she pleaded

"I'm not your Santa Casamentero, not that you believe in saints."

"No, but you're my friend." Jenne reached out and took his hand.

"You have other friends," he cajoled.

"None that know about Ama," she whined.

Hendrick rolled his eyes. "The entire village knows about Ama. You two aren't as discreet as you think you are."

"Please?" she pressed.

Hendrik slid another plank onto the cart.

"Also, I'm afraid of her," he murmured.

"What?" Jenne exclaimed. "Why? What did you do?"

"The last time I saw her, I carried her off and tied her up. You didn't see the way she was about to launch herself into the inn and murder two men."

"Oh, yeah, I can see why she would be angry about that."

"And, now that I think about it, every time she sees me, I'm trying to make her do something she doesn't want to do," Hendrick complained. "She must think I'm a terrible person."

Jenne nodded, "I can see why she would think that."

Another plank was slid onto the cart.

"You're still going to ask her though, right?"

"Why do I let you talk me into this?" Hendrick whined.

"Because I'm the only one who keeps you company in the woods," Jenne grinned. "She's not that scary."

"To you. Has she made a single other friend in this village?"

"Karlson likes her."

"Karlson would befriend a toad."

"I thought you were bringing her planks today? You can't be that afraid of her."

"I am. I was just going to leave them outside Karlson's house and sneak away before she noticed."

"You don't think she's going to notice a giant man with a cart of planks unloading them in front of the house?" Jenne looked at him as though he were a fool.

"I was going to do it while she was busy at the forge, but now because of you making me late, I'll have to do it while she's there."

"Good, so now you have no excuse. Besides, she's not going to murder you if you're giving her something that she needs."

Jenne hopped off the edge of the cart and ran away before Hendrick could rebut her. She still felt uneasy about the situation, but she could always count on Hendrick. Hendrick always seemed to look out for her, even when she was smaller. He had always seemed to treat her well, like he was an uncle of sorts. Maybe it was because she was different, at least at first. Other Moors she had met passing through had told her that she should stay here. That things got harder when there were more of them in one place. Being here, by herself, she was *their* Moor. If there were more people like her, they had said, they would feel threatened; like they were trying to take over.

That didn't feel fair to Jenne. She had been completely cut off from that side of her family. She didn't really know her father's side either, it's just that most people they had met *looked* like him. She wouldn't even really know where to begin if she met a whole village full of Moors. Would they even accept her, being half Christian as she was? And she was different in other ways – ways that not many people were fond of, here or there.

Though at least *here* almost everyone liked her, except for Txomin and Markel. Even Nerea liked her, though, she thought, she couldn't imagine how she could be so friendly if she was married to Txomin. Something must have happened to him to make him so mean and bitter.

And then there was Ama, who was just *different*. Indescribably so. She didn't really seem to fit anywhere – at least, not anywhere Jenne knew of. She refused to be pinned down, always on the move. And Jenne wanted so badly to make her stay, but would that be fair to her? Would Ama even *be* Ama if she stayed? Jenne sighed deeply, reluctantly accepting that chasing Ama wouldn't get her what she wanted.

Ama would have to come to her.

Jenne sighed. Only last night she was willing to do anything to be with Ama and now that circumstances were changing, she was finding that it was waiting for Ama herself to change was frustrating. Maybe Ama was right. She was young and naïve and foolish and rash and everything else. Was she in love or was she just impulsive? What would it mean to wait for someone else she found attractive to come along?

The thought of *someone else* made her nauseous. Or would that feeling wear off too? Jenne decided she would go for a walk in the woods and then find Ama and talk with her herself.

Chapter Eighteen
Stabilitas / Instabilitatis

The house was in better condition than Ama had expected. There were areas where the pebble walls would have to be chipped out and remade but most of the slate on the roof was still in decent condition. Only a few tiles were missing or would have to be replaced. Unfortunately, those spots had allowed moisture in and the wooden floors would have to be pulled up and redone. It was a good thing that Hendrick was coming by with planks today. Tomorrow, she would teach Karlson to make nails. A lot of nails.

She heard the planks being unloaded in front of the house, but no-one knocked on the door. Porridge was just outside, so they must have known she was here. She fished a few coins out of her pocket and handed them to Karlson.

"Go take Porridge and buy her some apples," she said, pressing the small copper pieces into his hand.

Karlson bounded off. She heard him yell "Hi Hendrick" as he ran out the door. She might be able to ignore him if she started pulling up planks inside but then heard the sound of his boots clomping up behind her. She folded her arms across her chest and turned to stare at him. Cowed, he looked at the floor.

"I shouldn't have tied you up, but to be fair, our plan was better," he said.

"Was it?" she asked. Then she remembered the rondel. She had no idea what such a scene would have looked like inside the inn if it had tasted blood. Their plan *was* better, but only because she didn't *have* a plan. She wasn't going to let him know that though.

"Also, Jenne wants to know what's wrong."

"Who said anything is wrong?" Ama started reefing on the planks in the corner.

"The way you're pulling on those planks, for one." Ama ignored him and continued to pull planks. "Look," he continued, "I might not know a lot about women…"

Ama snorted. "That's for sure." Hendrick stopped, shocked and confused.

"Did Jenne say something to you?" he whispered.

"What? No. I know Surgoi. Merchants may travel, but we do talk." Ama stopped and stared at Hendrick.

"Okay then," Hendrick breathed a sigh of relief.

"I know about your hatseller too," Ama teased. "So does Surgoi, by the way."

"Right," Hendrick wasn't amused. "Well, then I suppose half the folk in this area know about you and Jenne then."

Ama shrugged. "And that's why I need to leave." Ama wasn't entirely sure on that point anymore, but she wasn't about to elaborate on the new developments that had happened last night. The developments that had caused her to regret getting involved altogether.

"Don't pretend to be cool about this. I know she's more than just another bed for you. I was at the inn." Hendrick narrowed his eyes.

"Yeah, you were there," Ama admitted. "But why are you here?"

"To deliver planks, like I told you I would."

Ama deserved that, after she had played dumb earlier. "Why do you care so much about Jenne's business?"

"For the same reason you keep getting involved in Karlson's."

"I'm not..." but she couldn't really rebut his accusation. She could have refused to take him as an apprentice. She could have left his house to rot. But here she was, trying her best to rescue him from an abusive baker and then do what? Leave him here? At eleven? In a house she had helped repair? Her actions made no sense if she was planning to leave. She just kept trying to do what was *right* in the moment and that had led her to *this* moment.

Ama slumped against the wall. The witch had told her she had a choice. Jenne, who was very much alive, or Sera, who she had unwittingly trapped in a burning iron prison for years. If she left, Jenne would be safe. If she stayed, she would be found. She would fight. Sera would have her vengeance. And how would Jenne feel if she learned that Sera was likely her half-sister?

Hendrick sat down beside her. He waited for a few moments for her to talk, but Ama didn't. There was a maelstrom in her head and just sorting through them was taking its toll.

"When Jenne and her father got here," Hendrick started, "we all thought he was a pompous ass. But it's a small place. Bigger than some, sure, but still small. And in small places, you become needed, you get along, or you leave. No-one needed a ropemaker. Sure, ropes are handy, but he probably would have had better luck in a city closer to a lake instead of a river. He knew it and so he left. But Jenne; everyone *liked* Jenne. She arrived shy and quiet and we could all see what her father was doing to her, but he also wasn't the attentive sort. He didn't care if she didn't come home. Jenne would disappear first thing in the morning, pester us all day and not return until late at night. Eventually she stopped returning altogether. And so, she *thrived*. She made friends. She became like a daughter to the herbalist who had lost her own years ago. *We* became friends. I was out felling trees while she would gather herbs beside me. And I loved it."

Hendrick paused and his face grew morose. "When I was younger, I was part of a logging team. We would hire ourselves out to whoever needed some trees felled. In those days, we feared only the fae. Occasionally we would run into a witch's hut, but they were usually abandoned. We used to fear them too, but when the church came, they convinced most that the fae didn't exist and the witches had no real power, only tricks. We grew bolder, cutting without regard to the ways our fathers had taught us and nothing evil happened. The church taught us not to fear our superstitions."

"But," he continued, "they taught us to fear other things. They had a parcel of forest. A big one in the mountains of Thuès-les-Bains. It was good money, near the river Têt. We would have had work for years. But my kind wasn't welcome. They told me I would corrupt the rest of the men and that if we wanted the job, I would have to leave." Hendrick sighed. "Those boys and I, we had worked together for years."

"So, I left. I couldn't make them give up a job that big for me. And they let me" he said with an undertone of bitterness. "I tried to join some other teams, but it was becoming the same story everywhere. Everyone who had treed land seemed to have ties to the church and no sooner would I be hired than I would be told to leave again. Here, though, I'm just a woodcutter who supplies a settlement that might even become a town one day. We're too far off the main roads for them to build a church. I suspect if that happens, I'll have to move on, but until then, I'll stay. It's lonelier working out in the woods by yourself. Some days, it was so bad that I would wind up at Pèire's until dawn. Until Jenne came."

A smile beamed across Hendrick's face. "The herbalist would send her out, only during the day when there were no dangers, mind you. And she would find me and talk until it grew dark. I think she'd been storing up all her words the entire time she had been alive just to unload them on me! I never needed to visit the inn for gossip because she knew *everything* that was going on in the village. The things she would tell me!" he laughed. "I knew she liked girls before she did." He paused. "And I taught her to be discreet."

"You absolutely failed at that," said Ama.

"Yes, well, I told her how and why. It doesn't mean she listened to me."

"I guess not," Ama shrugged.

"I suppose I was too good of a teacher because she didn't learn about me until a few days ago," Hendrick shrugged back. "But then again, no-one can really prepare you for your first love."

Ama worried at the inside of her cheek and nodded slowly, staring straight at the wall opposite. There was that word again.

"And when her father left for good, there was no question of her staying here. I don't even think he asked her if she was coming with him."

"What about your first love?" Ama teased.

"That's a story better told over an ale," he said.

"Does it involve a silk merchant?" she asked.

"No," he sighed. "Anyway, like I said, in small places, if you're needed, you're a bit more protected. Cities don't *need* people."

"Right," Ama nodded. "What happens when small places no longer need you?"

"Then you'd better hope you've made some friends."

Friends Ama thought. Even at the orphanage, she had only really had Sera. Sister Klara and Sister Hildegaarde were more like parents than friends. Ama wasn't good at friends. She was too ugly. Too stubborn. Too *masculine*. But here she was, knowing these people for only a short while and she had made two friends. Well, one friend and one woman who was absolutely besotted with her for some reason she couldn't fathom. And an eleven-year-old. Not friends *per se* but, she was sure he was only around because she was teaching him to forge. But he did insist on going with her to pick up her tools. She couldn't understand why people wanted to be around her.

"Why do you want to be my friend?" she asked quietly into the fading sunlight.

"You're joking right?"

Ama frowned.

"I can see you're not good at talking. Neither is Jenne, by the way, which is why she made me come here. You have that in common." Hendrick looked amused.

Ama was not. "I thought you said she would talk your ear off in the woods."

"Ah," he smirked, "she is excellent at telling you things about other people. Not so good at talking about herself."

"Look," he continued, "within days, you've shown up, taken a boy under your wing and forged a bunch of things we've been needing for months. It only took a little bit of harassing because you're a good person. Also, my best friend is clearly in love with you."

"Well, she won't be for long," Ama muttered.

"Still planning on leaving?"

Ama took a deep breath. "How many witches have you met?"

Hendrick laughed. "No real ones. The superstitious fools killed one any time they had a bad harvest and the Romans killed the rest. Now no-one even believes in them anymore. You're going to have to explain where this is going."

"You remember the rondel I showed you?"

"Of course. It was too beautiful to be a bar brawling weapon. I'm still not sure what this has to do with Jenne." Hendricks eyes went wide. "Unless you stole it from her! Did you steal it from her?"

Ama pinched the bridge of her nose. "Please stop talking." Hendrick sat, subdued and staring intently. "I swear to god, I will murder you if you *breathe* a word of this to anyone." Hendrick nodded, mouth shut, unblinking. "The knife contains a ghost."

"That's rid...." he started, silencing himself immediately once Ama shot him a look.

"The ghost of my best friend. And first love."

Hendrick narrowed his eyes in confusion. "So, you think she'll be jealous of your dead lover?"

"Are you always this crass? Also, it's her sister."

Hendrick sputtered several "What's" and "How's" with no real intelligible sentence forming. Finally, once he regained his composure, he stumbled upon "You're full of shit!"

Ama shook her head. "Why would I make this up?"

"Yeah, you are kind of dour," Hendrick half-teased, attempting, and failing, to lighten the mood. "Seriously though, how do you know it's her sister?"

"I didn't, at first," Ama said, "until Jenne told me her mother was a Moor with one eye. And that she had left her first child at an orphanage. And a witch confirmed it in a dream," she added. "But I need to let her out. I didn't know the rondel was a prison. She's been burning in there for all these years. If I stay, they'll find me and I can finish the job, but it would bring disaster to your village. And Jenne. If I go after winter, you'll be safe, but she'll be trapped in here forever."

"There's a third option."

Ama knew the voice. Jenne was standing at the threshold with Karlson in tow. Her eyes dark, moonlight reflecting off the tears streaming down her face. She was vibrating with restrained fury.

"You can leave now."

Chapter Nineteen

Patefacio / Pervicacia

Ama drew her sleeve across her face, wiping the tears from her eyes. She stood up and hurried past Jenne and Karlson, ignoring Hendrick's pleas to stay. Porridge protested being led away, but Ama decided it was because she hadn't received enough pets and not because she didn't want to leave. Within minutes, Ama had loaded up her tools from the forge and was on her way. The darkness had already fallen, but it didn't matter. She needed to get away as quickly as possible.

Ama only had one home – the forge at the orphanage. She only belonged one place and to one person. And that person was gone. By the time she reached the woods, it was too dark to go much farther. Even the moonlight couldn't penetrate the thick branches and she was forced to rest for the night. She stepped off the trail and tied Porridge to a tree and then found a spot to curl up with a blanket. It wouldn't be warm this late in the fall, but she wouldn't attract attention. Ama took the rondel out of her boot and cradled it like a doll, crying herself quietly to sleep.

When morning broke, Ama noticed that she had slept under a copse of alders. *Fool* she scolded herself and then thanked God that she was still alive. Looking around, she noticed that Porridge was missing. She must have come unhitched during the night. Ama followed the trail of hoofprints and broken branches to a brook, where she found Porridge happily being petted by the witch.

"You again," Ama snarked.

"You're rather sour before breakfast," the witch retorted. Ama huffed.

"What are you here to tell me this time?" she asked. "Out with it, no more beating around the bush." Ama crumpled into the forest floor, legs crossed, waiting for the witch to respond.

"Dear, I'm an old crone. My entire purpose is to tell younger people things. Younger people who don't listen."

"I did listen" Ama protested. "You said I had a choice. Either I had to leave and protect Jenne or go and free Sera!"

"Is that what I said?" the witch smirked. "I don't recall saying anything about staying or going."

"It was *implied.*" Ama said through gritted teeth.

"Was it now?" The witch said sweetly. "For a girl who reads so much, you're not as bright as I thought you were."

"Then spell it out for me. I have no patience left and I'm in no mood for your games." Ama slumped, defeated.

"That's very obvious," the witch laughed. "Let's look at what you've done so far. You trapped the ghost of your first love in a blade and then you've been running ever since. Is that what she would have wanted for you?"

"No," Ama muttered pitifully.

"And would she also have wanted you to break her sister's heart?" the witch mocked.

"Jenne told me to leave." Ama hissed.

"Of course she did. You had just told her that you were responsible for trapping the ghost of the older sister she had always wanted. You do have to admit, that's a lot to take in."

"So, what do I do?"

The witch rolled her blind eyes. "Stop wallowing and listen. What do you need to do to release Sera?"

"Feed the knife blood. Preferably the blood of anyone who survived the bear," Ama said bitterly.

"And what do you need to do to protect Jenne?" the witch continued.

"Keep those men away from her and the village."

"Exactly," the witch said, satisfied that her point had been made.

"So, you want me to get captured away from Jenne?"

"I suppose that's one way to do it."

"You can't seriously think I could just march up to the fort and fight them?" Ama blurted loudly.

"Gods no!" the witch laughed. "You're no fighter! You're no assassin either, clomping around like you do." Ama sulked, unamused. "But there's a reason you made a rondel. It's small. Easily hidden. It doesn't require a sheath because the only way it will draw blood is if you stab someone with it. You knew you would be captured and that no-one would even notice it."

"So, I should turn myself in." It was more of a statement rather than a question.

"That would probably be quickest," admitted the witch.

Ama sat quiet with her decision for a few moments. It would solve things quite neatly. She could go, surprise an attack when the moment was right and then return to Jenne. But would Jenne even want her back? Even in the fading twilight, Jenne's eyes had been so full of hurt. Full of venom. For her. It would be best to simply disappear. The village would find another smith. Karlson would grow up without her, especially if he had Jenne and Hendrick to look after him. She hoped.

It didn't sit right with her though. How would she have survived if Sister Klara hadn't taken her in? Or Sera? Would they simply have been abandoned? Left to die in the woods? Or would they have been carried along by parents incapable of caring for them? Suffering each step of the way? Why was this falling on her? She was barely capable of caring for her own needs. She was only good at hurting people. Hurting the people she loved and running away. But she still couldn't help but feel responsible.

Ama's resolve hardened. She knew what she had to do. At least, the first part. She would go to the fort and turn herself in. She would decide whether to stay or leave once she had finished that. Finished freeing Sera. She raised her head to look at the witch. She hadn't moved.

"Why are you still here?" Ama asked.

"Why are you?" the witch retorted. Ama frowned. "You still want to ask me something, so I'm still here."

Ama thought. "When I was making this rondel, you said I shouldn't use human bone char for it. You said it was an *abomination*. Why?"

"That wasn't the question I thought you were going to ask," the witch laughed grimly. "But it's the same reason you don't eat people. We are made of the same meat as pigs, but you eat one and not the other. Why?"

"Because humans have souls?" Ama ventured a guess.

"Exactly," the witch responded.

The witch still did not leave.

"What will happen when I use the rondel?" Ama said quietly. She noticed that she had said *when* and not *if*. Her mind was made up.

"What happened when you used the sword?" the witch asked.

Ama was not in the mood for the witch's questions, but knew she wasn't going to get a straight answer anyway, so she might as well play along. "I was pelted with blood and I became a bear. All I could think about was violence. Rage. I was so angry."

"And then?" the witch prodded.

"And then, it left. I passed out. Vomited," she said quietly.

"That's because bears do not have souls," the witch lectured. "Humans do. And souls are like water."

"So, Sera's soul will make me wet?" Ama furrowed her brows.

"Well, she did when she was alive," the witch grinned. Ama frowned, disgusted. "Alright, I apologise. I'm an old woman, let me have my fun where I can." The witch waved her hand in dismissal. "Listen. What happens when you pour one cup of water into another? Can you tell what water came from which cup?"

Realisation spread across Ama's face. "So, I will become Sera? Forever?"

The witch shrugged. "Or Sera might take you when she leaves. No-one has been foolish enough to do this before."

Chapter Twenty

Spes / Desperatio

Jenne sat alone on the floor, shutters drawn, poking aimlessly at the fire. It was the third such day and she had run out of food, aside from the onions hanging from the rafters. She could probably eat the fermenting cabbage from the crocks, or open the dried fruit stores, but she would still need those for the winter and her solitary mood didn't appear to be going anywhere for the foreseeable future.

There was a small knock on the door. It couldn't be Hendrick, he tended to pound loudly, and she didn't want to see him anyway. It was his fault Ama had even stayed – his insistence that the village *needed* a smith when they had been doing just fine without one since last winter. She also knew that wasn't entirely true. Hinges had rusted off. Latches had fallen apart and ploughs had chipped and broke. They could rely on travelling iron merchants for tools, knives and smaller items, but a plough was much too large and required trips to a larger settlement or a city. If they remained broken by spring, they would lose days of travelling, not to mention the expense.

Part of her knew that Hendrick wasn't at fault, but she needed to be angry with someone right now. Someone who was *here* to be angry *at*. The other problem is that she wasn't sure what exactly she was angry at Ama *for*. More precisely, Jenne wasn't sure which of the things she had overheard she should be the most furious about. Ama knew her sister. Ama had been *in love* with her sister! And then she had trapped her somehow in a knife! What kind of person could even do such a thing? Witchcraft was something old superstitious people believed in; it wasn't real! So, was Ama lying? Why would she make up such an insane story? Was any of it even real? None of it made sense!

Jenne's eyes glazed over as her mind continued to spiral, trying to piece together what she had heard into some sort of rational story when the knock on her door interrupted her thoughts. She didn't want visitors, but it might be an emergency so she forced her unwilling legs to stand and carry her to the door. It was Karlson, holding a basket of apples.

Jenne motioned for him to step inside. Without speaking, she picked up one of the apples, cut it in two and passed half to Karlson.

"You look awful," he blurted out. Jenne frowned. Karlson lowered his eyes, cowed.

"Yes, well, people look awful when they get their hearts broken."

"Yeah, but you're the one who told Ama to leave," he said.

"She made up a story about trapping my sister in a knife. What kind of person does that?" Jenne couldn't believe she was explaining this to an eleven-year-old who could only see the world on the surface and unclouded by the desires of the heart. He couldn't possibly understand but it had been three days and she still hadn't made sense of any of it. It felt cathartic to at least articulate what she was angry about.

"She didn't make that up," Karlson said.

Jenne narrowed her eyes. "What? Why would you believe that?"

"I've seen it!" he burbled excitedly.

"Seen what?

"The ghosts," he said.

"Which ghosts? In the knife? What are you talking about?"

Karlson rolled his eyes like he was explaining things to a child. "Not the ghost in the knife. The ghosts in the place where she makes things."

"And you *saw* ghosts?"

"Yeah. I waved at them. They waved back. They're not as scary as I thought. Well, they were scary at first, but then they weren't so scary. Also, Hendrick wants to talk with you, but he thought you wouldn't let him in, so he gave me the apples and sent me instead."

Jenne blinked in confusion. It felt like everyone was on a different plane of reality. "Where is he?" she asked finally.

"He's in the woods where you usually meet."

An hour later, Jenne found the spot where she and Hendrick would have their lunch. It was covered with brown and yellow leaves, the rot of late fall setting in. A crisp breeze from the Northwest would bring snows in the mountains soon. Here as well, but rather than cover everything with a blanket of pristine white, it just made the ground muddy and impassable for anyone other than solo pilgrims, who tended to only travel during the warmer months, and traders without carts. And since those traders rarely had anything worth selling to small villages such as hers, they were never seen out this way.

Jenne thought back to when she had first been here. Alasne had sent her out to find feverfew while it was still plentiful. After listening attentively to the skinny herbalist's lectures on the differences between it and chamomile, Jenne was mostly sure she would find some. It had been summer then. Finches and sparrows were fluttering about, chirping obscenities at each other while the sun splashed brilliantly against the bright green leaves of the oak and chestnut trees.

Alasne had explained that they kept the land from soaking up too much water and turning into a silty swamp - a lesson the Romans had learned the hard way. When the Goths came, they mostly ignored the sandy swamps and foothills, preferring the other side of the mountains and the farmland to the east. Here was just a stretch of road to pass from one to the other. Some of the forest had regrown in the centuries in between. Even now, ragtag groups of soldiers, ambitiously calling themselves *armies* mostly left them alone, sticking closer to the southern passages or travelling by boat. Various rulers kept claiming this land as theirs, but for all intents and purposes, it was just ink on someone's map. The people here had been living and minding their own business for generations. The land wasn't worth fighting over, nor was it on the way to anything worth fighting over and the people were unimportant enough to be left alone. Mostly.

When she had first laid eyes on it, this had been a clearing. Its trees had been felled a long time ago, though one was still on its side, huddled close to a circle of blackened rocks. Green shoots of a rowan sprouted from its rotting trunk. Jenne had scanned the brush looking for her feverfew when she heard the rustle of boots in the soft earth and Hendrick had appeared.

She had seen him before and recognised him from the village, but she had never spoken to him. When they had first arrived, her father had purchased some planks from him, intending to build a small house. After the death of her mother, Jenne had proven unskilled at making rope, at least for now. Her father decided that he couldn't both sell and make rope and so he would need to settle down for a time until he could find a new wife or his daughter's fingers grew long and sturdy enough to twist the braids properly. Jenne was not used to living in a village; she was used to cities, with their noisy squares and crumbling buildings, torn apart and repurposed for whatever makeshift structure was needed at the time. The powers that had built them had long since disappeared and humans had taken over, flourishing like weeds and destroying whatever grand design had once existed.

Though she hated him, she could admit that her father was a charming man. He made friends easily among the other merchants and had a knack for selling. Often, she would peek from knotholes in their cart to watch him flash his bright blue eyes and straight teeth, ensorcelling whomever happened to approach. They almost always walked away with a coil of rope – rope he never made.

The rope was made by her mother. She would sit quietly in the shade of the cart, twisting and braiding strands of hemp or jute, humming softly. Jenne would occasionally try to coax her out to meet other merchants or introduce her to the friends she had made that day, but she preferred to remain secreted away. It was only much later that she learned why.

When times are good, even in a strange land, your differences tend to be accepted. People are willing to trade knowledge and embrace cultures. The worldly man with many experiences is esteemed. But when times are bad, those same people look for anyone to blame. It was other Moorish merchants who had told her this. They had warned her not to be around too many other Moors, lest the city's population feel threatened. Jenne's protests that she was only half Moor or that it wasn't fair was met with only sympathetic smiles. They understood that she would learn the hard way.

And she did. That summer, her and the other merchant children – at least the ones who could get away for the afternoon without being put to work, had run around the market. Discarded bits of straw, a stray stick and loose cobblestones became soldiers, swords and castles. They played joyfully and carefree all afternoon until one of the boys grew hungry. He left and returned with two handfuls of berries, which they all accepted greedily. The sweetness of summertime spilled over their faces and no sooner had they finished than they turned back to their games.

That is until the shadow of a large man darkened their make-believe battlefield. Soldiers, sticks and stones transformed back into the detritus of the streets as the angry merchant began thrashing Asim for stealing his fruit. Asim, of course, had not stolen anything; he was simply darker than the other children, who had scattered before the merchant's wrath turned on them. Jenne ran as quickly as her small legs could carry her to Asim's parents.

Jenne had assumed that they would rise up in righteous fury, that they would hurry to the site of this grave injustice and set things right. Instead, they shook their heads sadly and waited for Asim to return. *This is why your mother remains in her cart* was the only explanation they gave when Asim arrived, limping and with his right eye swollen shut.

Later that evening, nestled together in their cart, Jenne told her mother the events of the day. As usual, her father was away at the local alehouse with the other merchants, trying to secure a steady contract for this area.

"Why did Asim's father not help him?" she asked.

Her mother combed her fingers gently through her hair. This close to the sea, she was able to trade another mother a coil of rope for olive oil. Carefully, she separated the deep brown strands and then began new twists. She hummed softly as her nimble fingers, deft from years of twisting rope, worked away at her daughter's hair. Jenne grew impatient for an answer and looked up at her mother. She sighed.

"Oh Ghnima, she sighed.

Her mother's accent was thick, but Jenne only knew a few words of Kabyle. She was born into two cultures, but one slipped further away with each passing day. And yet, she knew her daughter would always be seen as an outsider. She hoped only to keep her safe as long as she could.

Her thoughts travelled back to the other; the one she had left with the godly women. That one was fully of her people. She suspected that as long as she stayed there, she would not suffer the same hardships. It had been a mistake to tell her husband about her. He had grown cold and distant – more angry when things did not go his way. More violent as well.

"I told you I like *Jenne* better!" she protested.

"That's the name of a stinky bush. You are not a stinky child!"

Jenne huffed. *Ghnima* was too hard for the others to say. Also, she liked the juniper bushes. She loved the feeling of picking apart the tiny, multilayered berries and the resinous smell they left on her fingers, even if her mother didn't appreciate it. But she would not win this argument, so she dropped it.

"What do you think would happen if Asim's father had helped him?" her mother asked.

"He would learn not to hit other people!" Jenne said, interrupting her reverie.

She nodded slowly, spreading more oil through her curls. "Lessons only work for children and those willing to learn. If Asim's father had risen up, they might have decided we had overstayed our welcome." She added "Or turn their violence on us."

"But that's not fair!" Jenne protested.

"Listen," she turned her daughter's face to hers. "You must never return violence. Or you will bring death to us all."

And so, she had. Jenne had perfected the art of bearing taunts and insults. When others sought to trade barbs, she returned kindness. It had served her well in this village. Soon that difference was forgotten. She ceased to be a Moor and instead became *their* Moor. And while she wasn't happy about being *the village Moor* at all, she much preferred her current treatment to the latter.

Hendrick raised his hand in greeting lest he startle her with his voice. Jenne raised her hand silently in return. He sat on the log and opened his wineskin, taking a deep draught. He fished around in his sack for a few plums and held one out to Jenne. She had no real reason to be afraid and it would be rude to refuse, so she approached and took it.

"What does Alasne have you doing today?" he asked, mouth full.

Jenne carefully chewed and swallowed the bite of plum, trying, and failing, to keep the juice from falling down her chin. "Feverfew."

Hendrick nodded. "I spied some over there, behind that ash tree." He gestured broadly with his fingers, now sticky with plum. Jenne looked toward the ash and then back at him. Hendrick smiled.

"Thank you," she said, trying to keep her voice as neutral, yet cordial as possible.

"Your father is heading off again?" Hendrick asked before Jenne could leave.

"Yes," she replied.

"You're staying in that house by yourself then?"

Jenne nodded.

Hendrick nodded back knowingly, as though she had given him the answer to a riddle. "Alasne doesn't mind you spending so much time making rope, then?"

"I guess not," Jenne shrugged. "She hasn't said anything."

"No, she hasn't." Hendrick muttered, though he didn't offer to elaborate. "I'll be here tomorrow at the same time if you want to take a break from your gathering." Jenne nodded, grinning and then headed off to find her herbs.

*

The Hendrick that emerged from the woods this time was significantly older, more grey hairs and a thicker waistline, but he still cut an imposing figure. Jenne supposed she had aged too – probably more dramatically. Whatever age Hendrick might be, he couldn't compete with Jenne's tear-streaked face and her kerchief unable to hide the mess of her braids. Soot stained her fingers and she was certain she reeked of smoke. Yet Hendrick was undeterred and he pulled her deep into his giant arms.

Jenne wept anew and Hendrick absorbed it all. His massive palm rested against the back of her head and she allowed herself to fall apart against her best friend. Hendrick held her by her shoulders and stared into her red rimmed indigo eyes with the sympathy of a man who somehow understood everything. "You're a mess," he said, finally.

Jenne was unable to suppress her laugh. She wasn't sure what she had expected him to say, but it wasn't that. Hendrick spoke before the renewed emotion could spark another fit of sobs. "I say this as your friend – you're an absolute fool."

"But," Jenne protested but Hendrick cut her off.

"Whatever you were about to say, it doesn't matter. Look at you."

Jenne's head sunk to her chest, cowed.

"Remember all those years ago when I told you to stop staring at the butcher's daughter?"

Jenne nodded. "Eneko," she offered.

"Yeah, that one. I had forgotten her name," he waved it away. "It doesn't matter because you were about to catch every fly in the village the way your mouth hung open every time you were around her."

Jenne nodded again, but kept her mouth shut this time.

"I told you to meet me here and you did and then I told you something. Do you remember what it was?"

Jenne cleared her throat. "You told me that Eneko wasn't for me. I thought that you were going to tell me that I could only feel that way about boys, but then you told me that if I was patient, I would get my chance with a girl who was even better."

"I also told you that you would need to be discreet about it, and you completely fucked that up because the entire village knows." Hendrick said tersely. "But this is your chance," he continued. "Don't fuck up that part because Ama is in some shit."

"But how could she," Jenne started.

"Has she ever lied to you?" Hendrick cut her off.

"No," Jenne muttered.

"Has she led you on?"

Jenne shook her head.

"Taken advantage of you?"

Jenne sighed and her shoulders fell, defeated.

"Ama is a good person. Too good. That's why she's in the position she's in."

At this, Jenne's face melted into an ugly visage of pained sorrow. Great heaving sobs erupted from her chest and her arms wrapped tightly around her quaking body. She was the picture of grief that sculptors would fail to capture centuries later. "She left!" she choked between gasps of air. Hendrick wrapped his arms around her once again.

"So, you can wait for her to return, or we can go and find her."

Jenne nodded against his shift. Hendrick turned and walked her back to her house. She would need to stock up on food, but it was growing late. That was a task for tomorrow. As they exited the woods and her house came into view, Jenne spied a grey Konik with its head stuck through her window. Without a word, Jenne bolted away from Hendrick. She threw her weight against the door and burst into the room, but Ama wasn't there.

Chapter Twenty-One

Fides / Cynicismus

Antòni picked at the small piece of boiled chicken on his oat bread. There was crab-apple verjus to season it, but he was in no mood for eating today. He had approached the fort, now significantly larger, and offered Lord Idoya information on the whereabouts of the smith he had been hunting for years. The fool had merely smiled maliciously and waved him away. One of his captains had offered him a position if he wished to remain and then ordered a servant to bring food. He decided that if this was the quality of food being offered, he would rather stay working as hired muscle. Yet, the roads were growing wetter and the trails would be impassible soon. He may do well to stay the winter at least.

The door opened and a draft blew across the floor. Antòni looked up, expecting to see the captain returning for his answer. Instead, it was Monségnor Rachid. His previous tonsure was non-existent as his pate was now completely bald. Deep wrinkles carved through his skin like canyons, but he wore a wry smile. He was in no mood to bear the admonishments of an over-religious, sackcloth-wearing martyr.

"Out with it," he growled.

"She's already here," Monségnor Rachid said. "She surrendered herself this morning."

Antòni frowned. "Why would she do that?"

Monségnor Rachid shrugged. "The Lord has come to test me, I suppose. Do you know what happened the last time she was here?"

"I saw the aftermath. To be honest, I didn't know you'd survived."

Monségnor Rachid pulled at the corner of his cloak, revealing a network of gashes ending in a stump. Antòni nodded. "I don't want that heathen witchery here," Monségnor Rachid hissed.

Antòni laughed. "I recall that you believed it was superstitious nonsense."

"And yet, here we are," Monségnor Rachid said, unamused. "It appears there are devils yet to vanquish."

"And your plan?"

Monségnor Rachid eyed him suspiciously. "Searching for a morsel of information to sell?"

Antòni scoffed and picked again at his chicken, now cold. "I have information that you'd appreciate."

Monségnor Rachid cocked a greyed eyebrow. "Your price?"

"I want to be nowhere near this place when whatever you're planning happens."

"You're free to leave right now. Nothing is stopping you."

"Then consider it revenge."

"I'm listening." Monségnor Rachid sat next to him.

"There's a village. It's not on the maps, but I can point to where it is. I brought a man there looking for a wife. There were rumours of witchcraft."

"And you expect me to do what about cunning women in small villages?" Monségnor Rachid frowned.

"Ah, this village," Antòni continued, "is just about large enough that it should no longer escape the church's notice."

"Go on." Monségnor Rachid tapped the fingers of his one hand on the table.

"And this cunning woman engages in...shall we say, *unnatural* relations."

Monségnor Rachid's other eyebrow raised. "You have proof of this?"

Antòni smirked and rose from the table. "If you find the village, the Baker will confirm it. Or you could just ask your smith."

Monségnor Rachid strode across the courtyard. Though his robes were a dirt brown, a colour chosen to represent his humility and vow of poverty, the elegant manner in which they swished in the rhythm of his gait belied their expense. The church, and his order, was growing wealthier, and as a result, the vestments he was expected to wear had changed.

When he had joined his order, Monségnor Rachid had believed that he would be spending his days hearing confessions, tending to the sick or sitting in contemplation and prayer. And it was, at first. It was only as he grew older and was sent abroad that he learned that most of what the church did was political. Helping the poor required buildings. Buildings required land, materials and people. Those were granted by kings and in exchange, the church provided an overarching framework from which to govern. Rather than spending their efforts appeasing disparate gods, devils and fae, the people would look to the church and their one God, who had chosen in his infinite wisdom their lot in life, as well as their rulers. To be fair, Monségnor Rachid felt a sense of unease about it.

The problem with wealth and power, however, is that once gained, it is exceedingly difficult to relinquish. Further justifications are always needed and principles are often bent, if not broken altogether. Monségnor Rachid did have principles, though it was only recently that they had become clear. Being the third son of a minor noble, whose family had only been granted a small parcel of land for their support in replacing the Merovingians, had merely walked by faith into the priesthood without probing too much into the details.

In reality, he had thought so little of his future and simply blundered forward with little intellectual curiosity and found himself where he was. Years in beautiful solitude, however, tends to lead to introspection, and upon it, Monségnor Rachid had to admit that his current position was achieved less due to *walking by faith* and more due to the *faithlessness* that carried his feet to where he was. He hadn't really *believed* anything, at least not with the sort of fervour that might have been expected of a man of his stature. His journey was the result of simply refusing to engage with his own life out of fear of making a misstep and so he had been carried here by the currents, not against his will, but not because of it either.

His newfound principles had been borne out of this sense of unease through introspection. Humility. Grace. Forgiveness. Even love. But those all still required funding, and so Monségnor Rachid wore the robes he was expected to wear.

He followed the sound of hammer and anvil to the forge. The previous smith had been relieved of his duty, much to his delight as he had been trained to stab people and the forge was hot, tiring work. A pile of twisted and broken iron lay in a pile – a backlog of items needing repair or replacement. Ama did not look up as he approached.

"You built the forge in a stupid place," she said.

He scoffed. "I can assure you; I did not build it." When Ama offered no retort, he asked "Why is that?"

Ama pointed her chin at the stables nearby and then returned to her work.

"Do the horses not need shoeing?" he asked.

Ama rolled her eyes exasperated. Monségnor Rachid had clearly never been in charge of anything more than reading scriptures in a language most did not understand and feeling self-important. "Oh, they do. But horses can move. Fairly easily too."

Monségnor Rachid looked at her with a look of utter befuddlement. It was obvious he had no idea where this was going.

Ama sighed. "Fire also moves. You fools have straw scattered everywhere. Next to the stables."

Monségnor Rachid nodded, at last catching her meaning. He looked toward the ground. "You should not be here."

"No," she said. "But neither should you. And neither should this forge," she added.

"You know you can't make more of that metal."

Ama laughed. "I thought you didn't believe in those superstitions."

"I didn't believe in a lot of things."

"And now?" she asked, placing her work back under the coals.

"Sister Aurea…" he started.

"You would dare!" Ama shouted. She dropped her hammer, staring him down with fury. "After what you let them do." Tears welled up, but she choked them back down and steeled her jaw. Monségnor Rachid lowered his head.

"I have paid for it," he said quietly. Carefully he pulled back his robe, revealing his arm. He flashed the flesh-coloured gashes and rough-healed stump where his hand used to be. Forearm muscles rippled in the pattern of his fingers wiggling, a garish mockery, given they were absent.

Ama could not find the sympathy. "I assure you, you have not," she hissed. "*I* returned to them *You* never did. You haven't even seen the destruction you allowed."

"And how do you know I haven't seen it? Haven't mourned it?" Monségnor Rachid refastened his cloak.

Ama narrowed her eyes. "Because you wouldn't be standing here if you had. You may preach forgiveness, Monségnor, but the Sisters no longer believe in it."

Monségnor Rachid was about to call it superstitious nonsense, but thought better of it. Ama caught his expression though.

"Are you sure you want to test that, Monségnor?"

"I do not," he said quietly.

Ama pulled her piece from the forge and continued hammering. She worked the iron for several minutes before he spoke again.

"If you do not intend to make more of that metal, then why are you here?"

Ama glanced up at him and continued hammering. Monségnor Rachid nodded. "I cannot expect your forgiveness, or that of your Sisters," he continued. "But I might be able to help you. It will never make amends, but I beg of you to let me."

Ama grunted and turned away.

"Then let me put it another way. They already suspect you are here to cause some harm. Without assistance, you'll never get the chance."

"I don't need your help," Ama growled. "The fools didn't search me when I arrived," she added.

"I have also received orders to travel to a village a few days from here." Ama ignored him and kept hammering. Monségnor Rachid continued. "This village has no name. Appears on no maps." Ama put down her hammer and braced herself against the anvil. "This village is in need of a priest to provide guidance. It seems that at least one of the women requires quite a bit of it."

"Why do you provoke me?" Ama said through gritted teeth.

"Because if you refuse to allow me to help, you will both fail in your aims *here*, and a church will be built *there*."

"So, you would use me to assuage your conscience." Ama spat.

Monségnor Rachid sucked his teeth before nodding slowly. "I am not a good man. I thought I was. I believed I was helping others. Providing light in the darkness. Giving counsel." He paused and inhaled deeply before continuing. "But I would have to be blind to not see that the only help I am providing is to the powerful."

Ama worried at the inside of her cheek. She too, had tried to do good, and had so often failed. That's what had led her here, where she would make things right. Or at least, she hoped she would. She hated this man with every part of her. It was he who had scorned Sera. He who had brought those men to the orphanage. He who had done nothing as they burned her home and murdered everyone she had ever known.

But she could not bear the thought of attempting to do right and only making things worse yet again. And so, she grit her teeth and decided to try to find guidance from someone outside of herself. And Monségnor Rachid was the only person here who was even remotely on her side.

"Did you know?" she said, barely audible above the gentle hiss of the coals.

"You'll have to be more specific," he said with a touch of haughtiness. Ama frowned. "Sorry," he muttered.

"About Sera," she said, refusing to look at him.

Monségnor Rachid nodded. "I knew about Sister Klara and Sister Hildegaarde as well."

Ama looked up at him in disbelief.

"There were some merchants who had relayed the information, hoping for some reward, I suppose."

"And you didn't do anything?" she sniffed. Her face turned contemptuous. "I suppose you want me to thank you for ignoring us?"

Monségnor Rachid huffed. "We didn't care. At least not then. You know how the world works."

"I was raised in near total isolation. You'll have to humour me."

"Very well then," he started. "No-one cares what peasants do. You believe that you're at the bottom. You're downtrodden, abused, mistreated. It is your lot in life to suffer while the nobility rule."

"That sounds fairly accurate to me."

"It is," he continued. "But in that, you have an unbelievable amount of freedom. Having a child out of wedlock or multiple lovers? No-one cares. You have nothing and so nothing is at stake."

Ama laughed. "I've seen peasant's care a great deal if their wife takes another lover."

"No-one important cares," he reprimanded. Ama hid her smirk. "If you have nothing, no land or title, your children are insignificant. Your dalliances are insignificant. But when you do, daughters suddenly become useful to fathers. You cement alliances – between businesses and noble families alike. Surely, you've had other men propose marriage to gain control of your trade?"

"No, I haven't. It's my sunny disposition, Monségnor. Also, I'm ugly," she mocked.

"Your Jenne doesn't think so."

"You learned her name?" Ama said, angrily.

"I'm told a peasant in your village was very informative. At any rate, none of that matters. The only thing that does is your womb. Any suitor determined enough would have simply beat your attitude out of you."

Ama shrugged. "What does this have to do with the Sisters then?"

Monségnor Rachid sighed. "When I was a boy and it became clear that my older brothers would survive and there was no need for me to carry on the family title, I was told I could learn to fight or join the priesthood. I had no talent with a sword and so the choice was made for me. I was *gifted* to them. Back then, it carried little weight. Now, we have wealth and power." He tugged at his robes, showing off the cloth.

"But you wouldn't be using women in the church to make alliances anyway," Ama said, confused.

"No, we wouldn't. But with wealth comes comfort. The cloth becomes a much more attractive option for young women who would refuse a husband. And if they learned that they would still be able to have certain...*needs*...met?"

Ama made a disgusted face. "Why would anyone care? No children are being made."

"No alliances either. Imagine the chaos that would befall us should a greater number of noble daughters refuse their duties to live happy and fulfilled lives as Sisters? We like to pretend that we are above this mortal plane, guiding the affairs of the nobility from on high with our wise counsel. But they would turn on us like a pack of ravenous wolves if too many of their daughters came to us. We would lose everything."

"And so, you accept their gold and their land so you can provide divine legitimacy to their rule over us." Ama said through clenched teeth. "And barter God's children like cattle."

"Women have a purpose."

"Do they?" she spat. "Are the Sisters part of that purpose? Living isolated and never bearing children?"

"They continue to be helpmeets to men. All mankind, not just a single man."

"But they must be miserable while they help. Or else it all falls apart, does it?"

Monségnor Rachid stood silent. The church had the answers to these questions. These accusations, but in the moment, they felt hollow. More than that, they felt *wrong*. It was this *wrongness* that had carried Monségnor Rachid here. The injustices that his Brothers allowed and perpetuated that did not seem to bother them made it easy to simply go along with them. Made it easy for him to believe that it was simply the devil placing doubts in his mind. Made it easy to believe that he simply wasn't wise enough to understand. Made it easy to believe that he was doing the right thing. And when those beliefs had crumbled, they were replaced by despair. Who was he if not part of his order? What would he do if he left? Even if he did leave, how would that change anything? And then the perfect opportunity had presented itself in a fool of a woman; a low-born orphan witch who could have simply given herself over to be guided through life by the hand of God, but instead, had only ever done what she thought was right.

"I have no right to ask for forgiveness, for myself or my Brothers, but I beg of you to let me help you."

"How could you possibly help me?" Ama bit her words. "You know why I'm here and now you've told me you're going after the village." She paused, blinking tears back. "And Jenne," she choked.

"My entire life has been spent providing counsel and comfort. Allow me to do that much for you at least and when I am finished, you can choose whether you want my aid or not," he said quietly.

Ama wiped her eyes with her arm, smearing a streak of iron dust across her face. She nodded.

"I have known you since you were a child. I was visiting the night a man brought you to us. He didn't speak any language I could understand and I don't know if he was your father, but that's irrelevant, I suppose. Every time I visited, you were in trouble. You were fighting back against your tormentors. You were stealing from the kitchen because Sister Klara had said she was hungry. You gave a girl a black eye because she made fun of Sera. You always did what you thought was right."

"And it always got me in trouble," she retorted. "Just like it does now. Whenever I do something that I think is right, it always makes things worse. I guess I should have learned that as a child."

"No, you learned the right lesson," he smiled weakly. "When you do what is right, the world will fight back. You're just a bad fighter. You always wound up with more bruises than they did."

Ama couldn't help but laugh through the tears that wouldn't stop falling.

"But it doesn't make what is wrong right." Monségnor Rachid sighed. "It's a lesson I should have learned a long time ago. So will you let me help you?"

"How?" she murmured.

"You've given me an idea, but I cannot tell you what it is yet. I will cause a distraction in the night and make sure you are not locked away. You can do what you came here to do."

Ama nodded, thinking.

"I've seen what happens. I likely will not survive this time."

Ama met his eyes. She could see the sincerity in his remorse. It wasn't just his arm that was marred. The years of unease and worry had carved deep lines across his face. Dark circles under his eyes sagged with the weight of it.

"And the village?" she asked.

"If I leave now, I may arrive before my Brothers. Those who need to flee will have the choice to flee. But I will not be able to help you here and I don't believe you will have the opportunity you seek."

Ama cursed the witch silently in her head. The choice she thought she had made was to simply leave Jenne and grant Sera her rest. Now, she learned it would doom her to whatever punishment the church thought fitting to make an example of her. Nothing she had done since that day had turned out to be the right decision. Or rather, she hadn't been able to outwit the world yet. This was her problem – she preferred action over inaction. Movement, rather than stillness. It wasn't that she wasn't *right*. It's that she lacked the patience or the intelligence to figure out how best to *be* right.

"You must do both," she said finally.

"I cannot. The time simply does not allow it."

"Listen," she said, staring Monségnor Rachid in the eye. "There is no good in doing what's right if nothing good comes of it. I'm tired of always doing what's right only to cause evil. I refuse to. Because the evil that I cause always hurts the people I care about the most."

"But it isn't *you* causing the evil, Ama," he said.

"Dammit, stop trying to console me!" she yelled. "If your whole life has been spent sitting and thinking and offering advice to others, use it for good for once, and help me figure this out!"

Monségnor Rachid nodded in contemplation. He thought of the day he was moved to managing the abbey's resources. The first thing you did was take stock of what you had. It may be hopeless, but he asked anyway. "What do we have available?"

Ama looked around. "I have the clothes on my back and the rest of my tools in Porridge's saddlebags."

Monségnor Rachid quickly put together an idea and erupted into a flurry of activity. "Grind some soot with water and make yourself a pen from some straw!" he ordered, cloak whirling as he spun away. "I'll gather some parchment." Ama plucked a lump of charcoal and began crumbling it with her hammer.

"How smart is your horse?" he yelled as he walked away.

"She'll do anything you want, as long as you pet her enough first!"

Chapter Twenty-Two

Parsimonia / Avaritia

W e need to go, now," she yelled across the field. Hendrick looked visibly confused and he strode faster over the dying grasses. The *swish swish swish* of the brown stalks marking his pace. "Why?" his voice boomed when he got close enough.

"Go and get Karlson. *Now!*" There was no further explanation, only the sounds of glass clinking and metal banging together as Jenne hurried about the house. Hendrick wondered briefly if she was having another breakdown, but those tended to come with tears and isolation rather than a fit of ordering him about. Jenne was impulsive at times, occasionally manipulative, but never *bossy*. Whatever it was, now was not the time for questions. Hendrick changed course and headed back to the village.

Karlson spied Hendrick running down the hill that led to Jenne's house. He was lumbering awkwardly, the way that men of a certain size tend to do when the angle of the terrain seems to launch you forward further than you expect. Combined with being, on average, more top-heavy and heavier in general, Karlson was sure he heard Hendrick yelling multiple profanities, though it was difficult to understand *which* profanities in particular since the ground jolted his mouth shut with every step

Karlson couldn't fathom why Hendrick was running so fervently in his direction. Sure, he was dressed inappropriately for the fall winds that were starting to pick up, but it mattered little. The energy he burnt fencing with Mikal and Inigo had sweat dripping down his face. All three of them were covered in splotches of dried mud and dust as fencing had turned into wrestling. Hendrick had never cared about any of that before.

"Karlson!" Hendrick yelled. Karlson was already standing, watching the great, heaving man bellow, out of breath. Mikal and Inigo were also watching him as he was quite the sight.

"What happened?" he asked.

"Uh," Hendrick's brain stalled. He actually had no idea what had happened or what needed to be done, nor whether this was something that the entire village needed to know. He settled on "Jenne needs you."

Surely, Jenne needing something could easily be handled by Hendrick, especially something as urgent as to require him hurtling himself down a hill, but Karlson's childish sense of self-importance got the better of him. "Is Ama back?" he asked. "I saw Porridge."

"That's why she needs you," he guessed.

"Okay." Karlson waved at his friends. "I'll come play tomorrow," and followed Hendrick back up the hill.

When they arrived at Jenne's house, they found Porridge's saddlebags overloaded and Jenne administering pets and apples to coax her along.

"Are you ready to explain what's going on?" Hendrick asked, exasperated.

"Can you read?" she asked.

"A little," Hendrick said. Karlson just shook his head.

"We need to go north through the woods and then around the village. Give it a wide berth. Then get to the swamps and from there, Ama said Karlson will be able to show us the rest of the way?"

"Ama told you that?" he asked.

Jenne flashed a piece of parchment in his face. "It was tied to Porridge."

"Ama is coming back?" Karlson said hopefully.

Jenne shrugged. "All I know is that she said there is a group of men coming here to set up a church and that we aren't safe. And that you would know where to go."

"Where are we going, Karlson?" Hendrick asked.

Karlson shrugged. "The only place I've been is her orphanage, but it burned down."

"I guess that's where we're going then," Jenne shrugged back.

Pèire was wiping mugs in preparation for the evening influx of patrons. The days had been growing shorter and thankfully, a honey seller had stopped by last week with extra wax that he could use to make candles and ward away some of the darkness. The oak door creaked, announcing the first visitors, a draft making the hopeful flames flicker. Four figures, three with tonsured hair and cloaked in brown sackcloth with rough jute belts. Smaller ropes of many knots hung from them with a wooden cross, rubbed smooth. The fourth appeared to be a hired guard – an inexpensive one, given the state of his gambeson. It appeared to be mottled grey and moth-eaten and hung loosely from his slender frame. Though, *slender* was being polite. *Emaciated* would be more accurate. *Even Ama's fit her better*, Pèire thought. *And hers was second-hand and made for a man.* Even he could probably best him if needed, sword or not.

One of the tonsured men stepped forward to present themselves while the others kicked the mud from their shoes at the door. "Greetings in the name of the Lord. May I know the name of this village?"

"None that I know of," Pèire replied. He continued to wipe his mugs.

"Then is this the village with a mill and a smith?" he asked.

"It might be." Pèire squinted in the dim light into the bottom of one of his mugs.

The man gave him a confused stare. "Why might it not be?" he attempted.

"Depends if the smith stays."

The man nodded. "I am Monségnor Xavier. These are my confrères, Monségnor Basajaun and Monségnor Anders." The other two men bowed their heads in greeting. The hired guard found a seat. "Has Monségnor Rachid arrived?"

"Don't know no Monségnor Rachid," Pèire replied.

Monségnor Xavier thought about this. The innkeeper seemed rather brusque, but he had no reason to suspect that he was being obstinate on purpose. They hadn't been given the funds to bribe the man either. All they had been directed to do was determine whether this settlement required their attention and if so, to begin the process of setting up a church.

"Might we await him here?" Monségnor Xavier attempted.

"Suit yourself," Pèire grunted.

The three tonsured men found a table nearby and rested their legs. Their escort, such as he was, was already seated. Half an hour passed, by which time their guard had fallen asleep, head motionless against the hardwood table as though it were the finest silk pillow. Several more drifted away, the evening patrons had come and gone and the candles Pèire had lit flickered and disappeared in whimsical curls of white smoke. They were used to sitting in silent contemplation and their ability to simply exist with minimal reaction to the world around them was, Pèire thought, unnerving.

"I'll be going to bed then, boys" Pèire said as the last few candles gave up their ghosts and the only light left came from the hearth. They turned to face him, expectant for something he didn't know. "If you'd like to stay, you'll have to pay now," he muttered. Their expressions were unchanged. Clearly, that wasn't it. In unison, they stood, save the guard who may or may not be dead, given his stillness.

"Perhaps you know another, then," Monségnor Xavier said, finally breaking the tension. "Is Txomin in this place?"

By his expression, Monségnor Xavier knew he was.

"What do you lot need with a baker?" Pèire asked. The only answer he received was a beatific smile that was more unnerving than the hours of stillness. They left as silently as they had sat, appearing to float out the door. Pèire quickly barred it, ignoring the guard. He would ask for payment tomorrow.

When Txomin opened the door and saw the three tonsured men, his lips pursed in an ugly smile. He yelled for Nerena to fetch sagardoa and bread as he invited them in to sit. Danel was crouched by the fire, poking at the cinders when Txomin shooed him away. "Go and fetch Markel," he said as Danel left.

"I understand that you're the one who requested we build a church here," Monségnor Xavier started.

"That's right," Txomin sniffed, eyes narrowing. "You'll understand in a moment." Markel shuffled in, dark eyes bleary and even darker dishevelled hair. "This is my eldest." Txomin gestured at the boy, though he was more of a man at twenty-three. "Tell him what that witch did to you."

Monségnor Xavier rolled his eyes. "Witches do not exist, sir," he stated matter-of-factly. "I hope you'll appreciate that we visit villages and small towns several times a year and each one of them would swear on his mother's grave that it was a witch that caused some malady or crop failure."

"But she poisoned me!" Markel blurted out suddenly.

"That may be, but it is not witchcraft, boy," Monségnor Xavier reprimanded. Markel clamped his mouth shut and hung his head, looking toward his father.

Txomin clenched his jaw. "There are other things."

"Such as?" Monségnor Xavier asked.

"The woman has unnatural passions."

Monségnor Asajun and Monségnor Anders exchanged glances while Monségnor Xavier ran his tongue over his teeth in thought. "Also, not witchcraft," he proclaimed at last. Txomin's mouth flew open, about to protest, but Monségnor Xavier raised his hand to silence him. "But," he continued, "clearly this settlement is in need of guidance." A smirk formed over Txomin's face and he nodded at Markel, who went back to bed. "The question now, is whether that guidance would be best delivered in the form of a church." Txomin frowned, but Monségnor Xavier continued. "You have built a mill, true, and I also saw a forge. Does this mean you have a smith?"

"She's part of the problem," Txomin growled.

Monségnor Xavier's eyebrows shot up and the other two exchanged a second set of glances. "You mean to be rid of her?" he asked.

"She was meant to be on her way. She seduced our herbalist through some witchery..." Monségnor Xavier glared at him. "Sorry," Txomin corrected himself, "turned our herbalist unnatural somehow, and was convinced to stay since our smith passed last winter."

"You haven't had a single smith who wanted to stay, save this woman?" Monségnor Xavier asked.

Txomin shook his head. "I don't know about smithing. I took in his boy, but he's too young for the forge. They tell me the forge is a good one, but no smith wants to live all the way out here, so far from cities. And they all want pay in gold, rather than in kind."

Monségnor Xavier nodded. It had been this way since the last wave of the sickness that had started with Justinian. Any peasant with a modicum of skill believed their worth to be higher than it was, and with no competition, they could usually get what they demanded. "Is she still here?" he asked.

Txomin shook his head. "Left last week."

Monségnor Xavier inhaled deeply. "Here is my dilemma, sir. Should I instruct my Brothers to build a church and no smith arrives, your settlement will disappear. As important as we believe we are to the welfare of mankind, very few flock to us without other amenities. Such as a smith. This would waste precious funds and simply be a poor use of the Lord's resources with which he has entrusted into our care."

"If I can find her?" Txomin asked.

Monségnor Xavier thought a moment. "That may change things somewhat. It depends on what it takes to fix her."

Chapter Twenty-Three

Amor interior spiritualis / Amor exterior materialis

Monségnor Rachid was not a brave man. In fact, he would be the first to admit to it. He was not a captain, like his brother, or even like one of the men under his command – or so he thought. What no-one tells men about bravery, is that almost no-one is *brave*, at least in the way we believe bravery is defined. The ones we say are *brave* are either fools with no regard to personal safety or the safety of others, or they are propelled to hurtle themselves into danger by some greater fear.

Sometimes, we will say that *bravery* is being afraid and doing it anyway, and certainly, that may be an adequate definition of bravery in the absence of other circumstances, such as learning to ride a horse, or learning to fence. A man may seek glory against a savage beast, or chase down some rogue, but only if his fellow mates are there to witness the event and provide backup should something go awry. The stories of lone knights on quests to right some great injustice are just that and any man who dreams of being such a hero will quickly abandon his quest and instead retire to the local alehouse to spin tales instead.

The greater fear of the men under his brother's command is simply that they will meet their end should they flee as well as be forever branded cowards and bring shame to their families. They face death either way and if the least they can do is avoid pissing themselves while they do it, they are *brave*. It's just that no-one mentions that part. It also makes for terrible stories as well as making it much more difficult to convince young men to agree to join some campaign against whatever problem the wealthy have decided requires violence to solve.

Monségnor Rachid's motivation was that he was much more afraid of Ama than he had let on. It wasn't Ama herself that he found terrifying, although he would still wake up screaming in the dark, feeling claws formed of coagulated blood ripping through his flesh. It was what she represented. Women were the weaker sex, or so he had been taught to believe his entire life. They existed to help *men*. Failure to do so, which was not unexpected, usually resulted in discipline. But if a woman was more *powerful* than a man, that meant that some sort of devilry was involved. It was more than simple practical magic – love potions, divination or location spells that even priests were known to practice, as long as they consulted the saints or angels. It was consorting with darker forces that worried him.

In the old days, Ama would have been accused of conspiring with the fae, and if word spread, it would bring back accusations of *witchcraft*. Monségnor Rachid had not ever heard of witches, at least not *real* ones. Even the cunning woman they had caged a decade ago had only been a seer that lived too close to the spot they wanted to erect their fort. What Monségnor Rachid feared wasn't Ama herself, it was that if she was not removed from this place, more women *like* Ama might appear. More women might *reveal* themselves to be witches. More women might decide that they had had enough of being subservient to men and they might take back power for themselves.

And so, while he was disillusioned with the creeping corruption of his order, he could not imagine that a world ruled by women who could turn into bears made of blood would be *less* violent. Nor did he know how he would fit in such a world. What he feared most of all, however, is that women would exact their revenge on *all* men for being kept in subservience from Eve until now.

That was not all.

Monségnor Rachid also feared for his soul. His life had not been the same since that night. Out of respect, or possibly in awe that God had spared his life when most of the rest of the garrison had been killed, he had been promoted within his order to prior. As prior, however, he had made the unfortunate mistake of voicing some of his concerns about the growing symbiosis between the church and kings, and had since been passed over for the position of abbot multiple times. His life was to be wasted away, managing his small monastery's books while the pain in his arm throbbed, each beat marking another second until his inevitable death. Monségnor Rachid feared giving an account for those seconds to his Maker. If he could die preventing the creation of more of that metal, and by extension, Ama's discovery by the rest of the world and subsequent uprising of women, he might spend a lesser amount of time in Purgatory.

Of course, Ama had none of these grand designs. Monségnor Rachid knew this, but he also knew that intention matters little once one becomes a symbol. Killing her would also solve this problem, but that would both lead to his death in vain at the hands of Lord Idoya, who had also managed to survive, barely. He also doubted he would actually succeed, given his missing arm and that no-one had removed Ama's weapon.

And so, he went to the stables.

Porridge was easy enough to find. She was, by several hands, the smallest horse there. Monségnor Rachid placed his hand on her muzzle only to have her press into him, expecting pets and apples. He produced both and Porridge accepted happily.

Soon, he heard bootfalls against the pine floorboards. The stable boy was here to water the horses and clean out the stalls. He looked to be about fourteen, brown hair, lanky and with a smattering of wispy hairs on his lip. His shift was filthy and he smelled almost as much of horses as he did of adolescence. This was due to the fact that there were no launderesses here and therefore men were sent with carts of fetid clothes to the nearest known settlement with a wife willing to do it. However, as winter was rapidly approaching, carts would be unable to pass. Someone had proposed that bridges be built over some of the swampiest areas, but that was rapidly discarded as they had neither the time, materials, nor the manpower. Roads, they had decided, would be built once the fort was complete and more permanently manned.

"Hello Monségnor," the boy croaked. His voice had deepened considerably, but his confidence was still rather shaky. "Uh, are you here for something?"

"No, son. Just admiring God's creatures." Monségnor Rachid continued to stroke Porridge's mane lovingly.

"Uh," he chuckled nervously. "That one wouldn't be my first choice."

Monségnor Rachid shot him a contemptuous glance. "You would judge the perfection of His creation?"

"U-uh, no! Um, sorry, uh." The boy quickly bowed his head and made the sign of the cross, backing away.

"Perhaps you should seek penance at the chapel." Monségnor Rachid suggested.

"I need to finish watering the horses," he protested. "Uh, but then I'll go, right away," he stammered.

Monségnor Rachid approached the boy, placing his good hand on his shoulder and causing him to look into his eyes with terror. "I shall relieve you of this burden for tonight." The boy nodded and made to move away, but Monségnor Rachid held fast. "I'll need your keys if I'm to complete your tasks." The boy thrust the keys forward and ran away as quickly as he could manage.

Once alone, Monségnor Rachid pocketed the keys and took Porridge's saddlebags. He wrapped Ama's note around one of the straps of her harness and secured it with some twine. A quick prayer was said and then he began unlatching all of the stalls. Part one was complete without a single lie told.

In the darkness, Ama heard the soft *click* of her door being unlocked. When she had arrived, surrendering herself willingly, she had been assured that she would not be kept in a dungeon. Lord Idoya had said that she would have her own accommodations. He did not say that she would be left to her own devices.

Lord Idoya had somehow, through some unseen act of Providence, escaped the attack eight years ago unharmed. At least, it appeared that way. She did not ask how, though she assumed he had either fled the instant he had heard a commotion or been covered by rubble, bodies, or both.

He paused writing when she was brought to his hall, setting aside his pen. This time, though, he stood.

"They told me you came here of your own free will," he said, waving off his guards. They bowed their heads and left. "Why?"

Ama flexed her calf, feeling the rondel tucked inside. She had half expected them to search her for weapons, given the chaos she had caused last time. Though she was obviously not a threat and rondels don't require holsters. The rondel, as far as weapons go, requires almost no skill to wield. As long as you can tell the hilt from the blade, you can use a rondel. It has three distinct sides and a point, which is the only sharp part of the weapon and so as long as you don't sit on the point, you can wear it anywhere on your body. Each side is hollow ground, which allows blood to flow freely, and so they are colloquially named *blood grooves*. This also allows easy retraction of the blade so that you can stab your victim multiple times in the span of seconds, though since the base is about 2cm wide, one well-placed stab, is usually all it takes to ensure death in minutes. It is a crude and inelegant weapon, but extremely effective, making it the choice of alehouse brawlers everywhere. The key difference between them and Ama is that their rondels are often hung from their belts on full display, whereas Ama's was tucked into the calf of her boots.

She did, in fact, have a plan for what to do if they did begin to search her and it was simply to stab the person nearest to her. Yes, this would use up the weapon, but she decided that whatever happened, she would be close enough to the culprits that Sera would probably still have her revenge and at the very least, she would be free. Ama would live or die with the consequences of their souls merging and Jenne would be safe. At least, that's what she had believed until her conversation with Monségnor Rachid.

"I was tired of running," she said at last. Lord Idoya raised a sceptical eyebrow. "Your fucking lackeys are like the plague. They kept turning up. It was impossible for me to make a living." Ama hoped the profanity would convey the appropriate level of distain.

"They did their job then," he said, one corner of his thin lips curling upward.

"It's been eight years," she said, quieter now. "Why not find someone else?"

"Oh, we did," he gestured for Ama to come closer. She hesitated, but then cautiously stepped forward. Lord Idoya cleared his table and then unfurled a map. "I don't think you appreciate how rare you are. At least around here. Have you ever seen a map?"

"A few small ones on folios," she admitted. "But they were mostly text with arrows pointing in various directions."

Lord Idoya nodded knowingly. "We are here." He pointed to a drawing of a ridge of mountains separating a peninsula from the rest of the land. He then traced his finger northward along the coast, across the sea until it came to rest on some islands. "Your people are from here. Or thereabouts."

"Then how do you even know about them?" she asked.

"Because they've been trying to settle here." He traced his finger southward along the coast again until it rested along a spot of land across the sea. "A few tales have reached us. Most of them were not believed until we came across you."

"I don't even know if they're my people."

Lord Idoya shrugged. "It doesn't really matter if they are or not. We sent some envoys to inquire whether we could buy the metal, but they would only sell it to us once it had been spent. We then tried to capture some of their smiths, but the ones we needed are hidden away even further north. We still require you if we are to survive."

Ama scoffed. "You think I'm going to make enough metal to drive them off? When I barely know what I'm doing? One novice against how many master smiths?"

Lord Idoya laughed. "We don't care about them. That's for the northern kings to deal with. Our concern is across the mountains. The Moors," he said darkly.

"The Moors are only this far north because they were promised rewards for participating in your squabbles. The ones who are on this side of the mountains are only merchants and refugees."

"They are now," he admitted. Lord Idoya rolled up his map and placed it back onto the shelf. "You are not a ruler and so you don't think like one. But," he paused and sighed. "I don't believe there is anything special about noble blood. You are aware that my nobility is scant. I worked the fields alongside my father's labourers."

Ama stopped herself from rolling her eyes. She wasn't in the mood to hear this man's populist act, but understood the position she was in. Lord Idoya continued.

"Therefore, I don't believe you are *incapable* of understanding, so I will do you the courtesy of attempting to convince you instead of simply locking you away like your mount and forcing you to work when required."

"Because you need me to believe in your cause. You're afraid that if I don't, I may still decide to flee or subvert you somehow?"

A sly smile crept across Lord Idoya's face. "As I said, I don't believe you're incapable of understanding."

Ama huffed. "Go on, then. Convince me."

"Let us say that your people are unsatisfied with the land they have. Let us say they decide to come further south. Nothing is stopping them, save the number of men we can produce to defend us. We still have the numbers, after all."

"Alright. Where do I become necessary to your plans?"

Lord Idoya held up a finger. "And let us say that the Turks decide to make further advances westward. Or perhaps the Arians decide they have the numbers to overthrow the one true faith."

Ama shrugged and shook her head, still not understanding where he was going with this.

"Now bring in the Moors. We are here, not because they are a threat *now*. We are here because we may not have the numbers when they *become* a threat. That's where your metal becomes necessary."

Ama worried at the inside of her cheek and nodded slowly. "It seems to me the job of a ruler is to jump at shadows of his own imagination and convince the rest of us to be afraid."

Lord Idoya frowned. "They told me you had a soft spot for them. Just because you knew one, doesn't mean you know them all."

Ama realised this meant he hadn't yet learned about Jenne, which gave her some hope that she was doing the right thing for once in her life. "How many do you know?" she retorted.

Lord Idoya scoffed and waved his hand in dismissal. "You'll be given a cell. You were a Sister, so you should be used to the accommodations. You will not leave it when you are not at the forge."

Ama smiled, remembering the conversation. It felt good getting under his skin, though it had felt good goading that boy with her sword all those years ago and look at where that had gotten her. Ama unfastened the top buckle of her rondel and withdrew it. She brought the odd shaped blade to her lips and kissed it. A tear welled up and ran down her cheek as she thought of all the years she had trapped her lover in this weapon. Now it was time to make things right. She tucked the rondel into the waist of her trousers for easy access, steeled herself and opened the door.

Chapter Twenty-Four

Reverentia /Scurrilitas

It was evening the next day when Porridge, Karlson, Hendrick and Jenne made it to the orphanage. The first tendrils of winter had started to creep through the trees and whispers of white frost clung starkly contrasting against the blackened stones. Jenne dug a wool blanket out of Porridge's saddlebag and passed it to Karlson. Her and Hendrick had travelling cloaks, but Karlson did not.

Grazing was sparse in the woods and Jenne was kicking herself for not bringing anything but apples for Porridge. The long winter shadows also kept the weak rays of sunlight from reaching too deeply into the ruins, making everything colder than it should be. This should have been an ideal resting place for any traveller, but something felt very wrong. It wasn't just Jenne and Hendrick who felt it either. There was no evidence of a fire pit or any encampments nearby. Other travellers must have avoided this place as well.

Except for Karlson. His snub-nosed face with blonde wisps of hair poking through the dull grey blanket wrapped around him was grinning ear to ear. And he was waving frantically at absolutely nothing. Jenne frowned at him.

"What are you doing?" Hendrick finally asked when he had had enough of his unusual behaviour.

"Waving?" Karlson replied, believing it a silly question.

"I see that. Waving at who?"

"The ghosts," he said. Ama can see them. Can't you?

Hendrick and Jenne exchanged uncomfortable looks.

"Is this where Ama lives?" Jenne asked.

"Uh huh. Over here." Karlson led them to the forge. Its stones were blackened as well, but the walls were intact and the roof had been tiled with slate. There wasn't a speck of timber, which, Jenne decided, was probably wise when working with fire. Even the anvil, though it was smaller than the one Karl had used, rested on a pillar of packed earth, framed with mortared brick. Jenne traced her cold fingers over it, taking in the colder stone. Trying to summon the essence of her smith.

Ama was right. She hardly knew her. She had no comprehension of the desolation in which she lived. The coldness of it. The loneliness. What does such isolation do to a person? How much had she suffered to believe that living here was the best choice she had available to her? Toward the back of the forge, she spied a doorway with no door. Behind it was a simple straw mattress and a leather apron - about the only things flammable in here. In the corner she found a sack of oats, mostly empty, but enough for Porridge for tonight. She shook it, looking for signs of mice, but found none. Either extremely lucky or mice didn't ever come here, which was highly unlikely. Come to think of it, she didn't see anything growing between the stones either. There was simply no life here at all. Maybe that's why she felt odd about the place?

"Do you know where the fire starter is?" she called to Karlson.

Karlson scrambled up behind the forge, covering himself in soot in the process and brought down a piece of flint.

"Did she teach you to light it?" Hendrick asked.

Karlson nodded vigorously. He ran outside and gathered some twigs, placed them carefully and started the process of making a fire. Within minutes, the coals had come back to life and Karlson was hard at work pumping the bellows, heating the small space almost beyond what was comfortable.

"He might be able to run the forge by himself yet," Hendrick muttered.

The two adults shed their travelling cloaks. Karlson had long since abandoned his blanket and they brushed iron dust off of some surfaces to sit while they pondered their next move, though something else had to be taken care of first.

"Can you tell us about the ghosts, Karlson?" Jenne asked quietly, unsure if speaking of them too loudly would summon something awful.

"They're the Sisters," he shrugged. "Some of them are the orphans," he added.

"And they're the ones killed by the men who are after Ama?" Jenne choked on the word *killed*. True, she had also killed, but she couldn't fathom taking lives after she had already gotten what she had wanted. It made no sense.

Karlson nodded.

"And Ama lives here with them?"

"Not all the time. Only in the winter." He poked at the lumps of glowing charcoal. "This is where she makes the things she sells all year, though," he added.

"And what do the ghosts do?"

"Ama says they protect this place. They make sure no-one comes here but her."

"But we're here."

Karlson shrugged again. "Maybe it's because they know me?"

Hendrick interjected. "Are we safe here?" He scanned the horizon, but all he could see were the stones illuminated by the forgelight.

"I can ask them." Karlson hopped off of the stone he was sitting on.

"That's like asking a bear if it won't rip your head off!" Hendrick yelled.

Karlson didn't listen and ran out of the building. Jenne and Hendrick watched as he had a conversation with the air several metres away.

"So, ignoring whatever is going on here," Hendrick gestured toward Karlson, "what are our options?"

"Ama's note said that they were coming to build a church in our village and that we needed to flee. I haven't really been anywhere as an adult, have you?" Jenne asked.

Hendrick nodded. "I could probably build us a cart and we could sell herbs. We could find a smith in a city and see if they'll take on Karlson as an apprentice."

"I doubt Karlson would like that very much," Jenne said.

"We could always send him back to the village."

"To do what?" Jenne hissed. "Be beaten and inherit nothing?"

Hendrick threw up his hands. "Right. That won't do. Travelling it is then. At least for a while. People will assume we're a family."

Jenne shook her head laughing. "You've got twenty years on me. They'll assume you're my father and keep pestering me for marriage."

"Except you don't look anything like me. They're more likely to believe Karlson's mine than you are."

Jenne winced. "Your niece maybe?"

Hendrick shrugged. "Maybe. What about Ama?"

Jenne sighed. "She told us not to come looking for her; that it would be dangerous and impossible."

Hendrick chuckled low. "And is that what you're going to do?"

"Of course not."

Hendrick threw a pebble at her. "You're a fool."

"You're the one who scolded me for letting her go."

"That doesn't make you not a fool. What can we do to help?"

Jenne's shoulders slumped forward. "I don't know. I don't even know where she is."

"I do."

Karlson suddenly appeared. They weren't sure how long he had been standing there.

"You do?" they said in unison. "How?" Jenne demanded.

Karlson pointed to a patch of empty space. "Sister Hildegaarde told me."

Jenne narrowed her eyes. "What else did she tell you?"

Karlson shrugged. "She said that Ama was always getting in trouble and that Sera always helped her hide it and that she was Sister Klara's favourite, so she kept getting away with things and that she wishes she had said what she had really wanted to at Sister Klara's funeral, even though she told her to say what was written on the parchment because she knew Sister Klara so well and it would have been a lot funnier if she had and Sister Klara would have thought it was funny as well."

"What?" was all Jenne could manage.

"I dunno," he shrugged again. "Ghosts are weird, I guess."

"Did she say what Ama was doing?"

"I can go ask." Karlson was about to turn and run away again, but Hendrick stopped him.

"Maybe go ask in the morning. Did she say if we were safe here?"

Karlson nodded. "She said we're safer here than anywhere else."

The sun rather rudely struck Hendrick in the eyes. Ever the gentleman, He had allowed Jenne and Karlson to share the mattress which was also mercifully rat-free. His back, though, had paid the price. A packed earth floor under a woollen blanket was not appropriate for a man his age. Hendrick forced himself to sit up, cursing under his breath and looked around the room. He really couldn't believe that Ama lived like this all winter. There wasn't a hint of anything warm within these walls. No mementos or treasures from her journeys. It was almost like a dungeon cell. Hendrick couldn't decide whether it was because she was used to living like a Sister or because she was punishing herself.

Hendrick's eyes moved over toward the mattress. Jenne was still sleeping, but Karlson was nowhere to be found. He decided to get some water and then set about gathering timber. Their food wouldn't last long and the trails would turn to mud soon, so they had better get on with their plan.

As he stepped outside, he heard shrieking. His head snapped in the direction of the noise, exhaustion immediately disappearing, but it was only Karlson leaping from stone to stone, dashing here, hiding there. He briefly begrudged him the boundless energy of children, but then realised that there was no-one to play with.

"Karlson!" he shouted. Karlson turned and ran to him.

"Yeah?" he huffed.

"What were you doing?"

"Playing." Karlson said this as though it were the most obvious thing in the world.

"With who," Hendrick asked.

"Them." He pointed to some stones.

"Aren't the Sisters a little old to be playing with you?" Hendrick still hadn't gotten used to the idea of a child seeing ghosts.

Karlson shrugged. "Maybe. But the orphans aren't."

Ah yes, the orphans. Hendrick had forgotten. As the cruelty of what had happened here all those years ago washed over him, Hendrick began to feel a deep melancholy. He couldn't imagine the banality of being forever a child, trapped with no-one among nothing but blackened stones to play with. It's little wonder

Ama was the way she was; guarded and overprotective of her privacy. Overprotective of those she cared about. What must it feel like to constantly leave the ones you love? Or refuse to love for fear of bringing this sort of hell down on them?

Jenne emerged from the forge yawning and with a wool blanket wrapped around her. *It's not because she thought Jenne was naïve,* he thought. *That was just an excuse. She actually cares about her.* Hendrick strode over to Jenne and clapped both his hands around her shoulders, jolting her awake.

"What was that for?" she protested.

"Think," he demanded. "Where would Ama go if she wasn't planning on coming back?"

Jenne blinked the blurriness from her eyes. "It is far too early for this."

"What danger is she trying to keep us away from?"

"The church," Jenne muttered. "At least, that's what her note said."

"That guard," Hendrick said. "The one who showed up with your husband."

"Please stop calling him that," Jenne mumbled angrily.

"She threatened to kill him. Why?"

Jenne stretched and furrowed her brows, resigned to having this conversation too damn early in the morning. "I don't know if you noticed, but Ama doesn't like a lot of people. Men in particular."

"Yes, but she doesn't threaten to kill them. Where was he from?"

"Alfonso said he hired him coming up from the south, so somewhere in the mountains, I guess. But there are half a dozen cities between here and Barshiluna."

Hendrick frowned and slumped against what used to be a wall.

"They're in the fort," yelled Karlson.

"What? What fort?" Hendrick sputtered.

"The one on the trail that goes that way and then there's a road to the mountains." Karlson gestured vaguely.

"How do you know that?"

Karlson pointed at the air. Hendrick sighed, resigned. "Right."

"Who's *they*?" Jenne asked.

"Ama and Sera."

"I thought Sera died?" Jenne was incredulous. She tried to avoid feeling a spark of hope that her half-sister she had never known was alive, but it was impossible. Instead, she pushed it down, knowing that it was just likely the cruelly innocent babblings of a child.

"Who's Sera?" Hendrick asked.

Karlson shrugged. "Ama's... friend. From the orphanage," Jenne said, awkwardly. A flood of conflicting emotions raced through her. Hope. Jealousy. Fear. What would it even mean if Sera was still alive? Who would she be to Ama? Would Sera even want to be around her? Her thoughts were interrupted by Karlson walking away.

"Where are you going?" she yelled.

"To get Porridge," he yelled back.

"You can't go off by yourself," Jenne huffed, running after him. Hendrick followed. Chasing after a horse was a poor start to the morning if they wanted to build themselves a new life.

They spotted the grey Konik by the creek, being doted upon by an old woman. Even from where they were standing, they could see that her eyes had gone milky white.

"Excuse me!" Hendrick called. The woman didn't budge.

Karlson got to Porridge first and began petting her. The old woman smiled at him and Karlson smiled back. Jenne walked faster.

"I swear, that child has no sense of self-preservation," Hendrick muttered. That, the old woman heard.

"He'd probably be taken by the fae in the old days, but they're long gone," she said. Hendrick caught up to them. She continued to happily pet Porridge, unfazed by the new people.

"Can we help you?" Hendrick asked. "This really is no place for an old woman."

She huffed. "I live here."

Jenne exchanged glances with Hendrick. "I thought no-one lived here."

"*Live* is such a strange term," the old woman mused. "Anyway, your horse is ready. I know she needs a little attention before she'll move." She smiled sweetly. "You'll need to bring them here and it's a fair way off, so you should get going."

Jenne's eyes widened. She ignored the strangeness of the affair and hoisted Karlson onto Porridge's back, leading her away. There was only one thing she needed to do now and that was to find Ama. Hendrick grumbled and ran after.

Chapter Twenty-Five

Iustitia / Inustitia

Fire. That was all it was. All everything was. The world as far as Ama could see had transformed to flame. Every building was alight as though hundreds upon hundreds of dragon's tongues had materialised, savagely caressing, savouring structures. Wood, stone, metal, it did not matter. It was everywhere.

Ama did not even feel the heat at first. The sheer luminescence of the flames assaulted her eyes after being locked away in her windowless sleeping quarters. She blinked once. Twice. But the intensity seared any moisture away. Ama crouched, keeping her head lower where it was marginally cooler and then catalogued her surroundings.

The forge was gone. It was already ash. The fools had built it mostly out of timber and the sacks of charcoal left in the corner had increased the temperature at which it burned. As instructed by Monségnor Rachid, she had *neglected* to douse the coals that night. She assumed the rest was his doing. The stump used to ground the anvil was gone and, in its place, lay a glowing lump of metal peeking from beneath the falling ash. The grindstone was nearly dust and the treadle that held it had disappeared. Her pile of incomplete work was still there, but was now black and radiating yet more heat.

Next to the forge were the stables. They would be blamed for this conflagration when all the dust had settled. She did not know who was responsible for planning the layout of the fort, but it was likely the stable boy who would be punished for failing to keep the straw away. Someone always has to take the blame and it is rarely those actually responsible. One wall of the stables had completely collapsed. Charred spikes of wood rose from the earth like some demon's teeth. The doors were open and flames vomited through them along the ceiling. She did not hear any whinnying, and so she hoped that Monségnor Rachid had kept his word and allowed the horses to escape. Porridge making it to the village was her only shot at warning Jenne of what was coming their way.

The keep was next to the stables. It was largely made of stone, but the timber beams holding the higher floors were not. They had not caught fire yet, but they had blackened and jets of steam could be heard hissing from rapidly desiccating wood. It would not be long until the entire building collapsed and it would occur without much warning when it did.

In contrast, the chapel next to it and facing the stables from across the courtyard, was nearly gone. The wooden cross was ablaze in a mockery of an omnipotent deity. His followers would later justify it as in accordance with his will and punishment for failure to suppress the wickedness of the peasants in the area. It would only spur further violence on the innocent as humans will almost universally punish the defenceless rather than the powerful, no matter how at odds this may be with their stated beliefs.

At last, she came to the barracks. Almost everyone in the fort who was not a craftsman or a labourer slept there. From the distance and the distortion in the air caused by smoke and heat, Ama could not make out *who* was fleeing, only *that* they were fleeing. This distressed her as she wanted revenge on exactly three people still living; Lord Idoya, Antòni and Monségnor Rachid, though given that Monségnor Rachid had somewhat redeemed himself, she would settle for the other two.

In truth, she had no idea who was ultimately responsible for the massacre of her home. She did not know whose hands held the knives, whose hands held the torches. She did know whose fear compelled them to act. She did know whose self-righteousness justified the murder. She did know who had caused the church to take an interest in Jenne's village.

But revenge had now become the secondary motivation. Her primary task was to free her friend, her love, from the torment that her own hand had caused in grief. In that, she was just as guilty as the rest of them and should Sera spare her, it would be grace. If not, it would still be justice.

Ama walked, crouched toward the heavy wooden gates through which everyone who could flee was doing so. Here, it was easier to identify individuals. Soldiers, boys really, hair slick with grease and sleep, eyes squinted from the smoke, streamed through. A few she recognised. This one escorted her to her sleeping quarters. That one brought her meals. Over there was the previous smith, who had done such a piss-poor job that she had to redo almost all of his work. Monségnor Rachid was not among them, nor were Antòni or Lord Idoya.

"My lord!" she heard above the roar of flames. It came from behind her and she recognised the voice. Ama turned and saw Monségnor Rachid standing outside the chapel, the remnants of the burning cross glowing in angry cinders. His face was stained with soot and the hem of his expensive robe partially burned. His eyes met hers across the courtyard and then he opened his mouth.

"My lord, this way!" he cried, not breaking eye contact. Ama stood and sprinted toward him. Moments later, Lord Idoya appeared, covering his face with his sleeve. He was stumbling, and missing one boot. His bare foot was red and angry. Blisters had started to form. Lord Idoya picked his way across the courtyard from the keep to the chapel, hopping on hot blackened stones. "Over here, my lord, follow my voice!" she heard Monségnor Rachid say.

Ama wasn't sure he was going to make it, and yet he did. He collapsed into Monségnor Rachid's arms. Lord Idoya was led forward, his eyes screwed shut and his head lowered to avoid the ash. Monségnor Rachid stared directly ahead, eyes watering, red-rimmed and grey with smoke, locked on to Ama. "Hurry, my lord," she heard him say. "Follow my voice! The Lord will guide us!"

Ama reached them. They stood, pathetic in the face of something as simple as fire. Mortals. Frail old men who played at being gods, who unquestionably believed their duty was to guide the fate of common men who were just as blind and weak as they. Ama withdrew her rondel from the drawstring of her trousers.

"You aren't forgiven, but I don't hate you," she said, her eyes piercing into Monségnor Rachid, which was about as much grace as Ama was willing to give the man.

The tip of her rondel slipped free. She spun the rowan wood handle between her fingers; a move she had practiced over and over until the wood had worn grooves. When she closed her eyes, she had imagined her fingers tracing Sera's beautiful face - her cheekbones that framed her deep brown eyes and how sparks danced in them when she smiled. It made her cry every time. Except this time. Ama did not shed tears, or if she did, they evaporated instantly in the heat.

The weapon felt lighter this time, like a second pair of hands was guiding it toward its singular purpose. Lord Idoya's eyes flew wide in shock as the blade slammed into his lung, black, smoke-saturated fluid streaming through the blood grooves. This is what a rondel is designed to do – bring a final resolution to a problem. But Ama knew better. She knew what was about to happen. So did Lord Idoya, though he would likely be dead from the wound before the true horror had even begun.

Blood and black ichor flowed freely, but did not touch the ground. Instead, it wound in a three-stranded black twist across Ama's arm. Ama grew nauseous with anticipation. She had done this before and she feared having it happen again. Yet, she knew she deserved every shred of pain coming to her and she embraced her punishment.

But it did not come. Instead of the pelting droplets of blood, bulleting into her like the previous time, it simply soaked into her skin, as though she were a cleaning rag. Ama turned her hand this way and that, marvelling at what had happened when a sonic shock from the sudden temperature change knocked her from her stupor. Every flame had disappeared and a blast of icy air rushed in to fill the void. Monségnor Rachid ran in fear. Lord Idoya collapsed into the greasy soot. The remaining guards who had been trapped behind fallen timbers clambered out from the rapidly collapsing keep. Antòni was among them. Ama narrowed her eyes hatefully at him, which is when it happened.

Ama's body exploded into flame, but she did not burn. *My love,* she felt echo in her mind. *You have returned for me!* Ama felt her fingers flex into a fist, but she could not recall commanding it to do so. Her body dashed forward, tendrils of flame flickering in her wake. She remembered what had happened. Men had come. They had come to collect Ama. No reason was given, only that she had to come with them. Ama had fled into the woods and she had tried to stop them from following. There was a kitchen knife in her hand. The knife Ama had made her. Sister Hildegaarde had tried negotiating with them. She had pleaded with Monségnor Rachid to explain himself. She had said that without Ama, the orphanage would not be able to continue. They would need to rely on travelling ironmongers who rarely came this way. This would drain their already meagre funds. She had said that Ama's goods were sold to merchants and that she kept the tables balanced.

He had said that God would provide. Sera had lunged forward, her face contorted in silent rage. Sister Hildegaarde had tried to stop her, but she was too nimble and she slipped through her arms like water. Her blade had landed against a boy's shoulder. Antòni had drawn his sword. There was a gash from her neck to her arm. She had fallen. She had heard Sister Hildegaarde scream. Monségnor Rachid had called him a fool. She had watched, unable to move, growing colder as the blood pooled around her. As her vision grew darker. As Ama was marched to their wagons. But Ama did not see her. Ama would never know what had happened.

Ama had not known that Monségnor Rachid had ordered the orphanage burned to hide the crime, but Sera did.

Ama withdrew her fingers from Monségnor Rachid's chest. In her burning hands, was his heart, slowly turning to ash. Monségnor Rachid's face contorted, hands grasping at the cauterised hole as he collapsed. *If there is a hell, you will burn in it* she felt herself saying. She felt only relief as the light in his eyes disappeared.

Ama's hands flew to her neck. She felt where the gash had been, but it was gone. There was only the unmolested skin of her neck. It felt rougher than she had remembered, as if it had aged. There were small callouses, as if a garment the wrong size had repeatedly rubbed against it. She traced her fingers upward to her jaw. This, she remembered. The way her face angled. Ama had always hated how sharp her features were, but she had loved it. Her skin was all one colour, one shade, but Ama's was spotted. Like someone had splashed her with ochre.

She had joked once that Ama was like one of the leopards she had found in a bestiary. Ama had frowned, both because of the way she hated her freckles and also because of the way the leopard's mouth looked. This delighted Sera to no end and for half a year, she called Ama *my leopard*. Several months after she had stopped teasing her, Ama had appeared in the kitchen with a new tool. It was a pair of tongs, but Ama had filed the teeth to resemble a leopard's head. Sera could not thank her the way she had wanted to in front of all the Sisters, but she had made it up to her later.

The way her fingers traced her bones in the dark. The way they gripped her stick-straight hair. Ama made the sounds that she could not. Not then. Now her voice was her own. Their voice.

A scrabbling sound against stones broke her from her reverie. She turned and saw him. Antòni. The smarmy prick that had started it all. The one who had been humiliated because she had twirled a sword and he had been scared in front of Ponç and Sergei. They had run as well, but Antòni couldn't let it go. He couldn't be *beneath* women in any sense. Men were warriors. Doers. Active. They commanded, women obeyed. They planted the seeds, women bore them.

When his body had reacted in fear that day, he hated himself. He had confessed to Monségnor Rachid as though running away were a sin. When he was brushed off, he had gone off to gather sticks with which to beat himself. She could still see the marks on his back as he attempted to hoist himself over the burning stones, most of his shift nothing but charred rags.

He had seethed about it in silence since that day, but his mood had changed. He was meaner. Bitterer. He lashed out at every slight. Ponç and Sergei, whose good-natured teasing had once been a staple of their friendship, stopped. They began to distance themselves from him. He stopped being fun to be around. And then he simply became unpleasant. Antòni had become trapped in a prison of his own making, hating everyone and everything. It was almost amusing for her to watch. She pondered allowing him to continue festering away in his cell. It would be delightful to simply follow him around and watch as he destroyed his life, pushing everyone away as he desperately sought validation of his manliness.

Alas, that was impossible.

She sauntered over to him, hopping over the blistering rubble. He turned and saw her before turning back, jumping, grasping even more furiously. Even more uselessly. Even as his shame grew from doing so, the panic he felt overcame every other emotion. She stood, hip cocked slightly, revelling in the sight. Feeding off of it. The reek of fear pouring off of him, along with a few other bodily functions that had let themselves go. She wrinkled her nose in disgust.

Had she been herself, Ama might have even felt pity watching every shred of imagined self-importance fall away from this wretch. But a ghost does not exist for pity. A ghost exists to finish what could not be completed. A ghost exists for vengeance.

Antòni stopped attempting to flee and turned to face her. There was only one thing left that he could do, and that was fight. He surged forward raising his fist, only to beat against the air. He was exhausted and Ama had easily stepped out of the way. It had thrown him off balance and he stumbled, falling against the earth. Ama stepped closer. He reached out to grab her leg and pull her down, but his fingers came away as though he had grasped hot iron and death itself. He screamed, holding his blackened and desiccated hand, like some ancient relic held in a wooden box in a stone chapel that may or may not have been cut from some saint and venerated by simpletons.

She did not know if *hell* existed – she had not been there. And the only heaven she had tasted had been Ama beneath her lips. *Here* was all she had known. Monségnor Rachid and the Sisters had taught them about *justice*. About how all things here on earth would be balanced in the end. There would be a final accounting by God himself, but so far, she had not seen it.

The triptychs and tapestries portrayed hell as this place where you would be overcome by your sins. Your own folly would torture you forever. And since God had yet to show his face, she would have to oblige in his stead.

Antòni knelt, weeping in the foetal position, utterly defeated. That would not do. *Surrender* was not this man's sin. His folly was *wrath*. She took a step backward, waving her hand, beckoning. Taunting. She could feel his cortisol rising. His heartbeat racing. His temperature climbing. He lunged again, missing. Again, this time tripping on a loose stone, tumbling forward against the soot. She smiled as the hot blood bloomed from his knees and hands.

He wanted to give up, but she wouldn't let him. She snarled, forcing adrenaline through his veins. He screamed, his eyes bulging. Again, he dashed toward her. She could see the steam pouring off of him as his temperature spiked. He had spent his years loathing the fragility of women and more so, how they would refuse to accept it. But what he truly feared was his own. His *weakness*. Being *less than* what he hated. And she drank it in. Revelled in it. The ambrosia of his wrath as it consumed him, brought him low and sputtering to the ground. Coughing foamy blood as his brain baked in his anger.

His fingers twitched for a few more minutes after he had collapsed.

Chapter Twenty-Six

Cosmicam viniculum / Disorientatio

Ghosts are not a well-studied phenomenon. We might feel a tug or a warmth at the thought of a deceased loved one, but those are not ghosts. A seer may communicate with the dead, but those, too, are not ghosts. Ghosts, we think, are those who have not *passed on*, whatever that might mean as *passing on*, is also not a well-studied phenomenon, despite those who would claim otherwise. There may be a place where they go. They may merge with other ghosts or some deity. Or they may simply cease to be.

The second thing we think we know about ghosts is that they are linked to a place or an object. They usually cannot move beyond it. Because in order to do so, they need to complete something that they cannot, at least not without the help of the living. Which is why we hear of *hauntings*. Ghosts are simply trying to ask us for help in the best way that they know how – by being annoying. That is the third thing we think we know about ghosts.

Sera's ghost did not possess Ama's body. *Possession* implies that the body was taken by force and that the person who currently inhabits the body is elsewhere – either tucked away in some corner of the mind, unable to control themselves or is perhaps absent the body altogether. And while Aristophanes was correct in that humans search for their missing halves, it was the body itself that was divided in two. A single divided human body cannot contain a whole person, especially when each half is destined for different fates. And like a cart pulled by two horses that try to take different paths, the cart goes nowhere.

Sera's path had ended. Her vengeance was taken and now she had no more purpose. Had her path continued, she would have kept loving Ama, but that requires more body than they currently had at the moment. And so, their thoughts continued to swirl in a danse macabre, trying desperately to love the other who was not there. Their body's fingers reached out to twist hair that was not there. To kiss lips that were their own. Speak with sounds they had never produced.

Like the cart with two horses, Ama's body went nowhere. It slumped against a soot-stained wall, eyes, half open and unseeing as the winds drifted in from the north west. Snow and ash fell together, but their body felt neither. They fell into a catatonic madness, reliving their memories. Together.

The spring air had been fresh that day. Sera's brown face peaked from behind the cool stones, staring at Ama. Her arms flexed as she lifted the hammer, flesh rippling each time she brought it down against the glowing metal. It was obscene, Sera thought, and it was hers.

Ama was normally quiet – possibly a consequence of being so close with a mute girl. But she was very much a troublemaker. She would break any rule for the people she loved, even Sister Hildegaarde. And she loved Sera most of all. Those arms would do anything for her. She imagined them around her waist. She would scold her for staining her apron with soot, but not tell her to stop. Ama would lift her off the ground and Sera would feel weightless. Already a burning heat pooled inside her.

She noticed Ama smirk as she worked. She must have been caught.

"I can feel you watching me," Ama said, refusing to look at her.

Sera hopped up, white teeth beaming. That earned her a look, and a proper smile. Ama set her work aside and rested her hammer on top of the anvil before crossing her arms. The way it made her forearms stand out nearly sent Sera over the edge. She bit her lip and controlled herself, holding out a bottle of oil. Ama's smirk grew deeper.

"It's that time again, is it?" she asked, though it wasn't really a question. Sera nodded and Ama poured water over the coals. "Alright, let's go." They headed to the creek to gather water, but as they were being *discreet*, Sera didn't take Ama's hand until they had left the courtyard.

After Sister Klara had died and Ama had taken over the forge, her fingers had become much larger. Sera's hand felt tiny in comparison. She loved her quiet confidence. Ama simply *did* things and because she was useful, she tended to get away with them. Sister Klara had been the same, which is probably why Ama had liked her the best. Sera allowed herself to lean against Ama's shoulder as they made their way to the creek, the feeble rays of the spring sun splashing themselves across her face. She closed her eyes and allowed herself to enjoy the scent of earth, the new greenery, and of iron. Ama would make sure she didn't stumble or trip. She would bottle these moments if she could. There were *other* moments she would bottle if she could, but she would have to hide those bottles.

Sera handed Ama her bucket, looking up at her through her dark eyelashes. Ama rolled her eyes and took it, picking gingerly through the mud and river rocks while Sera sat on a stump, watching. Ama crouched and leaned forward, dipping the bucket in the icy creek. Her shift hung a bit more loosely than was appropriate and Sera had to cover her face to prevent herself from fainting.

All of the Sisters wore aprons, which kept their shifts in place and also spared them from even more laundering than they already did. Ama's was made of leather to avoid catching fire, but it currently hung in the forge, just the way Sister Klara's had. However, Ama had made other adjustments to the smith's habit. She wore her shift larger, on the grounds that it would keep her cooler. She had also traded some iron goods for a pair of trousers, arguing that it would be less likely to catch sparks if one made it past the leather apron. In truth, Ama believed she was ugly and tried desperately to hide herself behind bigger clothing.

Ama's belief about what her clothing choices looked like and how they actually appeared were quite different. Her shift would billow and cling in places she thought she was hiding. The trousers accentuated, rather than downplayed her curves from behind where Ama couldn't see. The effect was that she stood out even more and presented as a lazy, but wealthy rake, well-versed in women's pleasure and come to steal the hearts of unsuspecting wives and daughters. Sera knew she had hers already.

Which is why she always made Ama fetch the water. From here, she could appreciate all of Ama's body without making her embarrassed. Ama couldn't see the effect she had on her and rush away to cover up. She was too busy trying to avoid falling in the creek. Alas, it was too brief, just as always and she would have to wait another month.

They made their way back drifting apart so as to avoid another lecture from Sister Hildegaarde. She had threatened to take this monthly chore away from them if they didn't behave, but they all knew that would be impossible. Ama was the only one left who could do it.

When Sera was four, a group of merchants had passed by, one of which was a Moorish woman. The Sisters had approached her and begged her to teach them how to do her hair. They did not want to keep cutting it short, it seemed *wrong* to them, but their brushes and combs were not made for her. The woman laughed and asked that Sera be brought to her. Sera was terrified of the woman, having never seen another person with the same skin or hair as her before and she refused to go. She only relented when the Sisters said Ama could go with her. That afternoon, Sister Estelle, being eighty and unable to do much else, was given the task of learning to care for Sera's hair. Ama held her hand and stared, wide eyed, as the woman taught Sister Estelle what to do. They traded for some combs just for Sera and, though it was not strictly necessary, every month, Ama would be by her side when Sister Estelle did Sera's hair.

And so, when Sister Estelle passed, the task had fallen to Ama even though Sera could do it by herself by now. That bit of information never seemed to have made it beyond themselves and so the task stayed with Ama.

Ama arranged the oils, soaps and combs on the table of the bathing house waiting for Sera. She rolled up her sleeves and tied them fast around her elbows. Sera entered, carrying the bucket of now-scalding creek water and poured it into the basin. She unfastened her kerchief and shook her braids, sitting so Ama could undo them. Despite growing more muscled, her fingers were still deft. Once undone, Sera stood and lowered her head to the basin of soapy water. She could probably do this part more easily herself, but she liked the feeling of Ama's fingers against her scalp. Her pads of her strong fingers pressed against her head as Sera practically melted into the water. Ama gently teased the last of the twists of her hair and let Sera wring the water from it herself. Ama returned with a linen towel and then they sat, waiting for it to dry enough to braid.

Maybe one day a merchant will show us how to do your hair, Sera signed. Ama frowned. Her hair was fine and hung limply. She had tried once to twist it like she did with Sera's but it only tangled more. Using a kerchief was more to hide it than for modesty. She decided not to take the bait. "Which oil do you want today?" Sera pointed to the bottle with chamomile stalks floating in it.

Ama went to take the towel, but Sera leaned back against her, resting her head against her hard stomach muscles. "You're going to get us in trouble with Sister

Hildegaarde again," Ama muttered, but Sera could hear the smile through her voice.

She reached back to pull Ama's arms around her, tugging her down until she could reach her lips. Ama teased, skimming just above her reach. Her breath fell across her face like wisps of morning fog above the foothills to the south. Sera narrowed her eyes and lanced upward, catching Ama's lower lip. Ama gave in and the sand in the hourglass started falling. They had only stolen minutes.

Ama's fingers pulled hastily at Sera's shift string, slipping her hands roughly to her breasts. Nipples pebbled stiffly against her palms and she dug in her fingertips. If they had had more time, Ama would have been gentler. She would have taken every second to savour the softness of her, awestruck over her beauty, but she did not. Sera's fists burrowed into Ama's shift, pulling her closer, tongue piercing, searching for something deeper. She sighed into Ama's mouth, feeling the pinch on her nipples. Sera too, wanted desperately for more. More time to run her fingers across her hard muscles. Explore how they transitioned into soft breasts. Worship her reluctant goddess. But she did not have it and she needed Ama. Now.

She pushed Ama away and spun around on her stool to face her. Sera pulled her hand to her lips, kissing the pad of each finger. She shifted forward, hitching up her skirt, dragging Ama's hand with her. She had done this to herself before, as had Ama. In the quiet hours of the night when even the cicadas stopped making noise and dreaming of each other, but never *with* each other. They thought they knew what to expect. How it would feel. The press of flesh against flesh. The rush of endorphins. The slickness of desire.

They were very, very wrong. Ama's touch felt like the sparks flying off of a bar of hot iron. Sera's core burned against her fingers. She stiffened and pressed against her palm, blood hot and racing, pulsing away the seconds they had left. Sera shifted her hips, bucking against Ama's fingers, taking them inside her, one hand grasping her forearm, feeling the muscles flex against her, the other wrapped around her neck. Ama felt her own arousal pool against the gusset of her trousers. Perhaps it had been a poor choice of clothing after all. Sera could not sign like this and so brown eyes stared into brown eyes, fingers flexing against taut muscles telling Ama everything she needed to know. Ama thrust the way she remembered she liked, hoping that Sera would also like it. Sera's hips matched her rhythm. Nails bit into skin and Sera's pupils exploded as something in her body shifted. Suddenly, nothing could be deep enough. Nothing could be too much. Nothing could satiate. Her need of Ama became all-consuming.

Sera tipped and fell and came undone. This was new. It was wonderful and would have to be repeated and explored again and again. She manoeuvred herself off of Ama and sank into her arms, tracing her fingertips over the marks she had left. Ama kissed her forehead and pulled back to look at her. *Mine* Sera mouthed. Ama smiled and turned to get the oil. The sound of gravel crunching outside told them they had only just made it.

Chapter Twenty-Seven

Beatudo / Miseriae

When they arrived, most of the fort was gone. The keep had toppled over and most of the spiked logs that were serving as a temporary wall were heavily charred. The stable was ash, as was most of the barracks. Only a single charred beam remained of the cross in front of the chapel. The arms had long since disintegrated. Small grey snow drifts now covered almost every surface. It was eerily quiet.

"Look for her!" Jenne screamed, as though Hendrick and Karlson weren't already on their way.

They found Antòni first. His body was stiff and nearly naked, with only ribbons of charred cloth clinging to him. A pool of blood surrounded him, frozen and pockmarked with snowflakes, gruesomely glueing pebbles and ash to the ground. Monségnor Rachid was next. He was crumpled, hands gripped around a sizeable hole in his chest. Without examining too closely, it appeared his heart was missing. Jenne tried to cover Karlson's eyes, but he refused and promised he wouldn't have nightmares. Next to him was a man they did not know, but he appeared to be burned and desiccated. It seemed strange that two completely different fates could have befallen two men so close together.

"I don't see her," Hendrick said morosely. "Are you sure she's here?"

Karlson shrugged. It was becoming an annoying habit, Jenne thought. "That's what they said!" he protested when she gave him a cross look. They stood around for several seconds, scanning the ruined fort for any sign of movement. The only motion was the occasional fat flake of snow drifting down from grey skies.

"Do you hear that?" said Karlson suddenly.

"No?" Jenne replied.

Hendrick shushed them. "He's right, I hear something too."

There was a low murmur coming from where the keep had stood. The three of them picked their way over to where the almost inaudible sound was coming from, only to find Porridge.

"This is hopeless!" wailed Jenne.

Karlson scrambled over the stone to fetch Porridge. "No, it's not!" he yelled. There, slumped in the corner of a fallen wall in front of Porridge, was Ama.

Jenne ran over to her, brushing the snow and ash from her head. Her eyes unseeing and unblinking. Those lips that had once tasted her body were now blue, pressing and unpressing together in some sort of trance. The fingers of her left hand were locked, clawing into her right forearm. Jenne shook her, trying to get her to wake up, but she just kept opening and closing her mouth. She concluded that Ama must be trying to tell her something important. Jenne lowered her head to her lips, straining to hear. A puff of air escaped her frozen lungs, repeating over and over. *Mine.*

"Hendrick!" she screamed. He hoisted himself over the rubble. "Get her on the horse. We need to get her back!"

"What about your sister?" he asked.

"I don't know where she is, but Ama will die if we don't get her back now."

Hendrick lifted Ama onto his shoulder, remembering the last time he did that, she had tried to beat him. This time, she was about as cooperative as a sack of oats. Hendrick draped her across Porridge's saddle.

"Sorry Karlson," he said. "She gets the saddle on the way back. Your job is to make sure she doesn't fall off."

Karlson nodded and they made their way back to the orphanage.

The door opened, but it wasn't Sister Hildegaarde. Or more accurately, it wasn't *just* Sister Hildegaarde. All of them were there. Even the children. "We need you to come with us," they echoed in unison. Sera and Ama looked at each other, confused. "I haven't finished her hair," Ama protested.

She frowned. "To where?" she asked.

"Outside," they replied. Sister Hildegaarde beckoned, extending her hand.

She took a few steps, but Sister Hildegaarde motioned for her to stop. "Not you."

She looked around. Condensation had gathered against the cool stone. Oils and soaps sat on the shelf. Everything appeared to be normal, but there was an eeriness about it. As though the room itself was an uncanny valley. She took the towel from her hair and shook it free so she could turn her head more easily.

Her fine, limp hair caught. She became aware of the oil on her hands. She wiped them on her apron and looked around again. There was no-one here but her.

"That's unfortunate," Sister Hildegaarde hummed. She turned to the throng of others behind her. They simply stared, resolute. Why was the whole of the orphanage here?

"I did say you needed discretion."

It was true. She had said it. She had heard it. She had remembered it.

"I remember," she said. Her hands touched her lips, as though she weren't sure she could speak.

"But this didn't happen," Sister Hildegaarde continued. Her brows knitted together in confusion. "You were dreaming you had two bodies again," the chorus of voices behind her said.

"But this body is *mine*."

The chorus nodded. "It is," said Sister Hildegaarde. "She gave it to you, or she would have. Long before you lost yours. She was always yours."

"Who is *she*? What are you talking about" she screamed.

"I'm sorry," Sister Hildegaarde said. "I felt the same when my Elke left. I wouldn't wish that feeling on anyone."

"Who is Elke?" she said, feeling herself reeling into madness.

Sister Hildegaarde tilted her head. "Sister Klara. I forget sometimes." She sighed. "I felt like I wanted to lay down beside her in her grave, but I knew." She sniffled and wiped at her face. "I knew that Elke wasn't there anymore. It was just her body. There was no way I could be with *her* anymore."

She looked down at her hands. Brown skin and thick fingers, covered in calluses.

"But you," Sister Hildegaarde continued, "you have the opposite problem. She is yours. Her body is yours. But if you stay, Ama's body will die. It is already dying. And when it does, you will have achieved nothing."

"But this body is *mine*," she said weakly.

Sister Hildegaarde nodded slowly. "It is. But it can't be anymore."

She slumped forward onto her knees and began to wail. Her cries echoed off of the stone walls, reverberating so that the entirety of her being felt her sorrow. The ghastly chorus began as well, the resounding destruction of a whole human heart carried over the hills. The aspens shook. The oaks groaned. Chestnuts dropped their fruit like tears. Greasy soot climbed the walls of the bathing house and the orphanage burst anew, flames licking at the timbers.

Sera tore herself from Ama, a gaping wound across her chest and blood splattering against the rocks in sticky gobs, falling into Sister Hildegaarde's arms. Ama toppled forward, grasping at her heart, fingers trying in vain to keep the blood in. She had never felt so cold in her life. Her breath stuck, unable to inhale. She careened, arms outstretched to where Sera had been, but there was no-one there. Sister Hildegaarde had gone. The orphans had gone.

Sera had gone.

Ama awoke with a start, eyes wide. Her hands flew to her chest. It was undamaged, but she had never felt such emptiness before. It was as though her entire body was hollow. She heard Jenne yell for Hendrick, but her eyes only saw vague shapes. A large figure stepped inside the room. *Her* room. This was her mattress. These were her stone walls. Someone had lit her forge.

"What did you do?" she tried to yell, but no sound appeared. Her arms flailed, but Jenne did not know how to sign. She leapt off of her mattress and grabbed a piece of charcoal, scrawling on the wall. She hoped Jenne could read.

"All we did was bring you here!" Jenne protested. "Why? What happened?"

Where is she? Ama scratched, frantic.

"Who?"

Sera

Jenne stood still, her face blanching. "We didn't find her," she whispered. "Do you know where she was?" A small amount of hope was in her voice, but Ama only fell to her knees. Jenne looked to Hendrick who only shook his head. A small mouse scurried past his feet and disappeared through some forgotten hole. It was glaringly obvious to Ama what had happened. The threat was gone, but she could no longer stay here.

Ama wanted to lash out at Jenne. At Hendrick. Instead, she stood, clothes twisted and in disarray, crouched as though she were about to pounce. Her fingers flexed and unflexed, trying to grasp something that wasn't there. Or some*one*. "I need..." she managed to whisper out.

Jenne took a step backward, eyes locked on Ama.

"I need... to leave."

"And go where? Hendrick asked cautiously

"I can't…" she panted.

"We're all leaving," Hendrick said. The village isn't safe for us anymore.

Ama shook her head. "It is. He's dead," she whispered. Her breathing began to slow to a more regular pace. She braced herself against the wall. Hendrick and Jenne exchanged glances. "I can't…be around you. I can't forgive."

Ama briefly thought about trying to explain what they had done, but they wouldn't be able to understand. It was more than just Sera's death. She had already mourned that eight years ago. She felt like she had been torn apart and the remaining shreds dumped gracelessly back into her body. And even though Jenne had not done it, she had brought her here. She knew it was not her intention, but she couldn't help but feel furious toward her.

She kicked herself off of the wall and hobbled slowly outside. Porridge and Karlson stood, watching. Ama managed to get to her Konik, leaning heavily against her. Burying her face against her grey brown mane. It was a small comfort, but it was a comfort nonetheless. Ama sniffed away the last of her tears and steeled herself. She would have plenty of time to grieve later, but now she needed to do what she did best.

Run.

She mounted Porridge and started off, picking her way through the rubble. Karlson followed. Ama paused and looked at him quizzically. He turned to look at Hendrick and Jenne, a mixture of confusion and worry on their faces.

"You haven't finished teaching me," he said

Ama couldn't think of a good reason why Karlson shouldn't come with her. She wasn't angry with him and she didn't really feel good about sending him back to live with Txomin. She turned and spurred Porridge onward, but she didn't stop Karlson from following either.

"Should we...?" Hendrick started.

Jenne shrugged. "I don't... neither of us have room."

"Unless we finish fixing up his house?" Hendrick offered. "Though he's probably better off with her anyway. I don't think he wanted to be a baker."

"Txomin's a terrible baker anyway. He also has enough kids to run both the mill and the oven."

Hendrick nodded.

"Do you actually think it's safe back at the village?" Jenne wondered aloud.

"Well, you read a note from Ama attached to a horse and got us all to leave before we found out what was really happening, so, maybe we should see for ourselves?" There was an edge of annoyance to Hendrick's voice.

"We haven't made much progress on actually leaving, so maybe we can come up with a better plan if we need. We've also exhausted our supplies. And Ama has Porridge, so a cart wouldn't do us much good."

Hendrick sighed. He understood what happened when a place gathered enough people that decided being different was a problem. He also understood that it was likely they would be able to scrape together a few days before the real problems started, especially if they were about to leave anyway. In retrospect, leaving so suddenly had been rash, but then again,

Jenne *did* tend to act rashly. If the church had indeed come, they wouldn't have had the numbers to put them in any real danger right away. It would have taken weeks, if not years to convince all of the people they had helped through the years that they were a threat to their salvation.

Well, maybe not Txomin. Txomin had always been bitter and angry toward anyone different. Even after everyone had gotten over the novelty of Jenne's half-moorishness, Txomin kept making remarks. At first, it would earn him a round of laughter. But over time, as Jenne proved herself more and more useful to the well-being of the settlement, the laughter had turned to weak chuckles and eventually, people just ignored him.

That was probably what chewed at Txomin more than anything else, even more than Jenne poisoning Markel. His ability to gain approval by shitting on Jenne had grown stale – even more so than his bread. Milling and baking were never Txomin's dream. Txomin had always wanted to be a soldier. Whenever he would travel to the cities for supplies, Txomin would point them out to his sons. "Look at how those filthy beggars run," he would say, wishing he was the one inciting such actions.

As a result, Txomin spent more time drinking and simply being angry than he did being a baker. His loaves were undercooked or burnt. Edible, but barely. But since no-one else had built a mill or an oven, Txomin was who they went to for bread. This annoyed everyone, including Txomin, who knew enough about building things to make his equipment, but no desire to actually use it well. Txomin had his faults, but he didn't enjoy people coming to him begrudgingly. Txomin wanted their respect and admiration.

As a boy Txomin had fenced with wooden swords and spears, dreams of keeping the undeserving in their place. His father had been the one to dash those hopes. While most third or fourth sons would be pushed to learn to fight or join the clergy, Txomin's father insisted he learn to bake, even if he would never inherit the ovens.

He did get his chance though.

After several days of waiting for Monségnor Rachid to appear and no smith, Monségnor Xavier and his tonsured brethren had decided that they would send a priest to perform rites as needed once a year. To build a church, however, would be a poor use of the Lord's resources. For now, they would take their leave before the snows set in. This would have been much more irritating for him if not for the fact that the herbalist who had poisoned his son seemed to have disappeared along with the woodcutter and the smith's brat.

And while their disappearance did not make him any more popular, it was when two soldiers burst through the inn door, covered in ash and soot while Txomin was in his cups that his fortunes changed dramatically. A dragon had attacked the fort on the main road toward the mountains, according to these men. Lord Idoya had perished and since he had no heirs, whoever slew the dragon would be set to become the new lord, they had explained. Other men who had escaped were currently scouring the country to recruit bands of men, who would be handsomely compensated should they succeed, mind you, to aid in their quest.

Never mind that the snows were setting in and it would be impossible to drag carts through the mud. The bravery of whomever joined their quest would sustain them, as well as God's favour in slaying this Moorish beast. They knew it was Moorish because although Lou Carcolh lived in a cave nearby, he did not breathe fire as this monster did. In fact, it was likely the Moors who had *trained* this beast to attack the fort. They were certain of it.

Several rounds of ale were ordered for the men and the story grew in direct proportion to the amount of ale consumed. There were at least two dragons, bright flaming eyes, but one of red and the other of gold. They had black and green scales and Moors rode on their backs. By the time evening had fallen, Pèire had to practically shovel the lot of them out the door. When morning arrived, the first of the bleary-eyed adventurers set about rousing his comrades and gathering whatever meagre arms the village could spare.

It turned out that there wasn't much in the way of weaponry, but there were fools in abundance. Several young men who had grown bored of waiting until spring to leave and seek their fortunes. Txomin, despite being on the older end, also grasped the opportunity. The mill was passed to Markel and the ovens to Danel until his return, which, he promised, would be accompanied by treasure enough to turn this village into a *real* town. He could invest in building a proper road, setting up a night watch and become something akin to a *mayor*.

The snows came and the bread improved somewhat, which wasn't normally the case during the winter. Danel turned out to be a decent baker. Markel sold the mill to the maltsters and then promptly disappeared one evening with the maltster's daughter and a purse full of coin. Though the words were never uttered, no-one was particularly upset about Txomin being gone.

The problem still persisted, however, that the village had failed to attract a smith and when the winds calmed and the heat of spring began in earnest, the forge lay just as quiet as it had last spring. Jenne's first action in the morning was always to look toward it in the hopes that smoke might be rising, but it never did. She wondered when she would stop.

Chapter Twenty-Eight

Pax / Contentio

The sights and sounds of late spring were thick in the city. Though the days had lengthened since midwinter, as they did every year, today was the first truly nice day in a while. The cold wet winds had been nice enough to slow to a gentle breeze and warmth, rather than the chill they had become accustomed to, radiated from the stones. Things were a bit different on the north coast than they were even a day's ride to the south.

By afternoon, every un-shadowed surface had dried. Cats sprawled lazily in sunbeams, unbothered by the crowds bustling around them. One in particular, an old grey tabby with a chunk missing out of her right ear, lay on the worn, heavy oak slab that served as a counter of sorts. She sat there for two, possibly three reasons. The first was that it was extremely warm, being just opposite of the forge. The second was that she was likely deaf and therefore, didn't mind the constant ringing of the anvil. The possible third had something to do with ley lines, though Ama knew better than to dabble in that sort of nonsense again.

To be fair, Ama didn't go near the counter either. She left that to Karlson, who turned out to be surprisingly good at interacting with customers. In between taking orders, Ama would make him practice on the more basic projects. He had more or less mastered horseshoes and nails and was working on roughing out swords in fewer than three heat cycles. Ama still refused to let him create the billets out of fear of accidentally trapping a soul, even though he had never even seen, let alone learned the runes.

All things considered, Ama was as contented as she could be, which is to say, positively miserable, but she had arranged her life in such a way as to make her misery as acceptable as possible given the circumstances. She would wake every morning, light the forge and pound red glowing metal saying as few words as possible. The forge she had built out of recovered stones from some crumbled Roman structure mostly kept out the light and so the only way anyone would know she was there was by the sound of the hammer and anvil or the occasional glow of the forge splashed across her angular face.

Her face had changed. Since they had moved further north, she had had the opportunity to meet northern traders. The first few had eyed her sceptically, a strange woman who did not know their language, but working metal in a way they recognised. They brought some of their smiths who laughed and said she was using *old ways.* Ama simply nodded and continued hammering.

It was Karlson who won them over. His constant chatter and questions amused them and they agreed to show them some more *modern* techniques. When they were satisfied that she would forge iron the way they needed, they retrieved armloads of work for her to repair.

In the process of doing so, Ama caught the eye of one of the women. She was taller, with lighter, hair, styled in rows of miniature braids, but she had the same angular features and wiry build as Ama. She carried her own bearded axe at her hip and had a gambeson that fit, as though it were made for her. Ama also noticed that she wore trousers. That was not something she had ever seen another woman do. The woman stole glances as the men bartered with Karlson. She heard great peals of laughter when the men realised they had underestimated the boy's skill at negotiation. All the while, she kept flicking her soot-stained eyes toward the woman. She had not taken her eyes off of her.

She was the one who had spurred the men to invite Ama and Karlson to dine with them. Ama was hesitant, wary of being kidnapped, but Karlson's instincts for self-preservation were significantly less developed than his customer service skills. Ama relented, convincing herself that she would fetch a poor price as a woman anyway. They already had one like her and she didn't appear to be a slave. Ama's instincts were correct. Her admirer had obviously wanted something else. Ama already knew what, and she couldn't honestly say she was opposed.

After sharing a bowl of what appeared to be lamb stew, the woman approached her and introduced herself as Astrid. Ama allowed herself to be led away to talk while Karlson joked with his new, much older, friends.

"How is it that you come to live here? Were you taken?" Astrid asked, touching her leg a bit more than was strictly necessary. Ama allowed it. It had been months and she had been too busy looking after Karlson and setting up her new forge to even think that way.

"How do you know I'm not from here?" she attempted. This only earned her a sceptical look from

Astrid. Ama's features were not rounded. Her hair was sandy-brown and fine instead of the thick flowing reds and blacks that she envied the women here. It tangled constantly. She was taller than even some men, though Astrid was taller still.

"I'm not even sure where I'm from. I was raised south of here," Ama said quietly. "In an orphanage," she added.

Astrid's face betrayed its shock. "How do you know metal, then?" Ama related the story. She debated leaving out the parts about the bear. About Sera. But she decided that there was no longer any harm. Her pursuers were dead and Astrid would leave. Astrid might even provide some insight as Ama felt entirely disconnected from her people.

Astrid, it turned out, was a good listener. She sat calmly as Ama told her story, firelight dancing across her features. When she had finished, she took her hand, interlacing their fingers. They were nearly as thick as her own. "So, you are malmr-kona." Ama stared at her blankly.

"A metal witch. They do not usually use the things they make." Astrid laughed in disbelief. "The people who do usually do not survive either, but you have done it twice!"

Ama shrugged. "I don't know much about where I came from. I don't know anything, really." she admitted. It felt strangely freeing to be this vulnerable. Though, she thought, was it really vulnerability if she'd never see Astrid again? That was not something she was going to dissect right now.

"And with a human soul!" Astrid continued in amazement. Ama winced. Sera was not just a *human soul* to her. Astrid must have noticed, because her expression turned into one of worry. "I apologise," she said meekly. "It is only that there must have been someone who held you very tightly to keep you here. *Very* tightly," she emphasised.

It wasn't something Ama had thought of before. She remembered the feeling of being whole, but part of her had suddenly left. Had *chosen* to leave. Somehow, something had spoken to only that part of her. Someone else entirely had *kept* her from leaving. And she knew exactly who it was, even if she didn't want to admit it right now.

Ama pushed those thoughts away. She could not bring herself to think of her. She was the reason Sera was gone. She was the reason Ama was still here. Or what was left of her. Often, she would wake up and feel as though her skin was the wrong colour. Her hair the wrong texture. Like her body itself was *wrong*. On bad days, it was only when she saw the glowing yellow metal on her anvil that she could focus, lose herself in her work in order to remember who she was.

"I'm not sure all of me is actually here. Or that all of Sera left," she said. "Is that normal?" For some reason, Ama desperately wanted it to be, despite not being normal all her life. For some reason, Ama wanted to be normal *somewhere*.

Astrid only shrugged. "I've never heard of it before, so I don't know." Astrid squeezed Ama's hand tighter. Ama fell quiet, unsure what else to add. "I do know one thing though," she smirked coyly. Astrid lay back on the grass, pulling Ama with her. Ama let her. It would feel good to be loved.

Astrid's fingers were quick on the ties of Ama's gambeson. "I think you need a new one" she laughed as she worked. "This one doesn't seem to fit right."

"They don't make gambesons for women here," Ama protested.

Astrid laughed. "Then maybe you are in the wrong place?"

What would that feel like, Ama wondered. *To be somewhere you were accepted, even if you weren't useful to them?* Ama slid her hands to Astrid's hips. Though they were wide, they were toned and pointed, like hers. Ama could feel Astrid's muscles flex beneath her touch. Ama had always loved women's hips. The soft and sometimes dramatic curves that called to her. That made heat pool between her legs. And she found that Astrid's hips, though different, still called the same way.

It was then that Ama realised what Sera had seen in her. What Jenne had seen in her. What other women had seen in her. She wasn't *ugly*. She just wasn't attractive *to men*. It should have been obvious from the start. She had been so wrapped up in trying to prove herself to everyone she cared about because she couldn't fathom that anyone would like the way she looked. She was more than just a tool for others and maybe they wouldn't discard her the instant she stopped working.

Ama wasn't sure what to do with the idea of being *attractive*. It was clear Astrid wanted her, but was that because she was *available* or because she was *attractive*? She decided this new idea would take some time to get used to and she wasn't ready to fully accept it yet. Ama pushed those thoughts away for now and willed herself to relax. Astrid's fingers slid across her collarbone, finding the laces of her shift. Ama closed her eyes in an attempt to shut out the intrusive thoughts. She wanted this. She did.

Her shift came undone and she could feel the pressure release from around her throat. Her shift hung open, billowing in the darkness, freckled breasts on display.

Ama pushed down her anxiety. *She was attractive* she told herself. *Women liked the way she looked.* She felt Astrid's hands carry the heft of her breasts through the warm linen. She sighed into her touch, nipples pebbling.

But Astrid could see.

"You don't like women?" she asked, releasing Ama and propping herself up on her elbows.

Ama shook her head. "No." She huffed a mirthless laugh. "I *very* much like women. It's just… my head is full." She spun her hands around her head as if to demonstrate how full it was. "And I can't get rid of my thoughts."

"Of the person who kept you here."

"You're unnervingly perceptive," Ama teased, and then lowered her head. "I'm sorry. It's really not you. You're beautiful."

Astrid blushed. *Did she blush when women complimented her?* she wondered. This was becoming a whole evening of revelations.

"I just feel like I've suddenly become aware of all of these new parts of myself that didn't exist before. And are they even *me*?" Ama blurted. Astrid simply listened. Ama became suddenly conscious of how much this sounded like an excuse. "Really though, if you were staying for longer, I could get to know you, and..." Astrid cut her off by rolling her eyes.

"Please. I would fuck you and leave," she laughed. "Though you look like you would have been fun," she teased.

Ama felt a pang of regret, but knew there was no going back now. "This is going to sound strange after I just turned you down," she said, "but... would you show me how to do my hair like yours?" Ama dragged her fingers through the tangled mess on her head. Astrid's eyebrows knit together in confusion. "These southern women all have beautiful hair," Ama whined. "No-one knew what to do with mine."

Astrid's look turned sisterly. "These southern women have *boring* hair. Wait here," she ordered and marched off to find a brush.

When morning came, Ama's hair was in a series of braids and neater than it had ever been. Her hair wasn't meant to be in flowing black or red locks. It required a bit more discipline and effort, both of which Ama had in abundance.

And even though Ama still hadn't been able to bring herself to have sex with anyone since Jenne, she awoke in Astrid's arms. She didn't recall falling asleep. She had provided no service to these people and yet they had cared for her. They had decided she was *theirs* and had acted accordingly. True, Astrid had been *attracted* to her, but even after it had become clear nothing would come of it, she had allowed her to stay.

Ama slipped out from under Astrid's arms and rose to hunt for Karlson. She found him, sleeping next to the dying embers of last night's fire. Three large men with markings on their hands and arms sat around him on guard. As Ama approached, one of them rose his head to meet her disapproving eyes.

"He drank more than he should have," he stated.

Ama's expression softened and she shook her head, "He's twelve. I doubt he's drunk anything before."

The three of them bowed their heads with a modicum of shame and so Ama decided to take advantage of it.

"Those markings on your arms. How did you get them?" The three men looked at each other and smiled.

By the afternoon, the group was mostly packed up and ready to move on. Astrid found Ama and Karlson with their three new friends poking soot into her arms. Porridge stood by dutifully observing and receiving the occasional pet. Ama smiled up at her while Karlson tried to avoid becoming nauseous at the sight of Ama's blood. "What's this?" Astrid asked, as though she were scolding children. The three men grinned up at her impishly.

"She asked us to," Jorge protested.

"Yes, but malmr-kona don't get markings," she said.

"This one does," Ama responded plainly. Perhaps she would never be *normal* anywhere.

Astrid couldn't help but smile.

"Listen," Ama started, "I don't know runes."

"Yes, I know. I believe you told me that's how you got into this," Astrid said.

Ama ignored her remark. "If I sound out a word for you, could you tell me the runes for it?"

Astrid rolled her eyes, but she still asked. "Tell me what you want."

Chapter Twenty-Nine

Timor Dei / Inais Gloria

Jenne was not happy. She was not happy a lot these days. Yes, they had gotten through winter and the merchants were beginning to wander through along with the warmer weather, but Ama was never among them. She had tried to put Ama out of her mind by distracting herself with the ones who came through. She had even tried flirting with a glass maker, but her husband had quickly put a stop to that. Her heart hadn't really been in it anyway.

She slumped forward, resting her head on the table during one of the quieter moments at the inn. It had been quieter than usual more often. Without a smith or a miller, this place wouldn't last another winter. More families were leaving than joining. It would become a downward spiral in no time.

She heard the door open, but didn't raise her head. It was too light out for the merchants to visit, so it could only be one person. Hendrick shuffled noisily into the seat across from her.

"You're a depressing sight." It was true, but there was no malice behind the statement.

Jenne raised her head to stare daggers at her friend. "You're here early."

Hendrick shrugged. "Fewer people mean less wood needs to be cut." He slapped his hands down on the table as if to make a point. "We should probably start making plans so we can leave by the fall. I can still add a roof to that cart," he said, quieter this time.

Jenne dragged her body off the table and sat up properly. Respectably. She nodded, even though she didn't want to leave. What she wanted was for Ama to come back and tell her everything was forgiven. She wanted to bury her face into Ama's neck, to inhale her scent of linen and chamomile. To be held and know that she would stay forever. "What if she comes back and we aren't here?" she mewled pitifully. Her friend gave her a sympathetic look.

"You really are a mess." Hendrick moved to the other side of the table and scooped her up into his giant bear arms. Jenne sniffled away the tears as they came, soiling his shirt. Thankfully, Hendrick never minded, or if he did, he never said anything.

At once, the room erupted into chaos. Three men burst through the door, cheering and smelling worse than Pèire's mutton stew he had once forgotten about in the middle of summer. Several others followed, waiting with baited breath. After ordering a round of ale, one of the men began telling the tale.

"Only a days' ride south, and the hounds picked up the scent of the dragon!" he said, in hushed tones to enhance the dramatic effect.

"How'd he know what a dragon smells like, eh?" someone in the back yelled.

"They smell like brimstone, gobshite! Everyone knows that!" yelled back one of the man's comrades. This earned him a stiff slap against his chest and he cowered, keeping quiet as the man telling his tale continued.

"The hounds led us through bog and swamp. Every night we would set up camp, we could feel the eyes of winter hags upon us. We could hear them cursing our fire, so it only gave off weak flames, no matter how much dry tinder we fed it." Now the children gathered round, pushed to the front by their parents so they could hear.

"In the night," he continued, "one of them got close enough to *touch* Txomin!" Audible gasps were heard through the crowd. "First his toes turned black, then his entire leg. We could see his maggoty flesh falling off his bone!" A child shrieked and cried, but was quickly shushed by their sibling wrapping her arms around him in comfort.

"We had no choice but to leave him, but Sorne, here had a better idea." Sorne stood up and waved like a celebrity. "Sorne said we should tie him up as bait for the dragon and hide ourselves." Though no-one was especially fond of Txomin, no-one had wished that fate upon him either. Nonetheless, the crowd restrained themselves to only low murmurs of disapproval.

Reading the crowd, the storyteller tried to assuage their guilt. "Now, now," he said, hands waving in a calming motion. "Poor Txomin was too delirious to understand what was happening. He was actually the bravest among us, offering to sleep near the outside of the circle, which is what got him touched in the first place!" This earned him somewhat more approving noises from the crowd.

"Txomin *the brave* would have died anyway and so he *offered* to be used as a sacrifice to lure out the dragon." This earned him a few cheers, and even chants of *Txomin! Txomin! Txomin!* ignoring that the storyteller had just said he was delirious.

"So Sorne and the lads tied him up, hung him from a great ash tree and we watched and waited." He quieted his voice, re-enacting the scene. "There were no fires for us that night. Me and the boys, we shivered in the cold for hours, watching *brave* Txomin wriggle and squirm trying to attract the attention of the beast!"

"And then," he paused for effect, "we saw it! Great beady red eyes and smoke billowing from its hungry maw! Skin, black and greasy as soot and flecks of gold! Hideous wings as dark as night and twice its length! I recognised it immediately from my grans tales! A coulobre!"

"But don't those live to the east of here?"

"Of course they do!" the storyteller yelled. But they must have come west when the cities fell and they had less to eat." This made a certain amount of sense to the crowd who murmured and nodded as though this man had bestowed enlightened truths upon them instead of spinning entertaining nonsense.

"Me and the boys ran after it, chasing the sound of its wingbeats in the night! We caught up to him once and he turned to spit fire at us! Koldor got caught and was torn apart by the beast! But Sorne," (Sorne stood up and waved again) managed to snag its paw with his pitchfork! We followed the trail of black blood through the swamps until we found a fort, burned and ruined, but it looked to have done it a long time ago."

Hendrick exchanged glances with Jenne. They must have found the orphanage, now that the ghosts had gone.

"We thought it might have been its lair, but we found no sign of him," the storyteller continued. "We had to wait until the hounds caught his scent again. We spent many nights, huddled in those cold, black stones, always alert, always on guard for the coulobre to attack at any moment!"

He quieted his tone again, shaking his head mournfully. "We'd used the last of our arrows and we saw few rabbits. We lost Alesander and Mattin to starvation and Lander wandered off in the night." The crowd fell still and silent in anticipation. "And then, one morning, Tuste spotted him against the rising sun!"

"Where's Tuste?" someone yelled.

"We'll get to that," the storyteller waved him away. "Off we went, running after Tuste and the hounds. We spent all day chasing them, but Tuste refused to stop, lest he get away. But then," he paused again, "Tuste fell down, exhausted."

Cries of *no!* could be heard from the crowd. They were very invested now.

The storyteller nodded sadly. "Tuste had given up his life so that we might not lose the beast!" Cheers went up and chants of *Tuste! Tuste! Tuste!* rang throughout the inn.

"As we were mourning Tuste, we could see the mountains in the distance and it was there, I spied the coulobre, black as midnight against the snowy peaks!" Another cheer rang out. "We chased that beast, never letting my eyes off it, though it be a horrible sight! We climbed through the snow, and rocks until we were face to face!" More cheers.

"He spat fire!" *Cheers*

"He clawed at us with his great wings!" *Cheers*

"He tried to blow us off the cliffs!" *Cheers*

"But we SLEW THE BEAST!" he shouted, hoisting up a sack, presumably containing its head. The room erupted in a raucous joy. Sorne waved and shook hands. Rounds and more rounds of ale were bought and drunk and the sack paraded around the inn.

When the noise finally died down, a man Jenne recognised sidled up to their table. It was the silk merchant. "May I sit," he asked, an unnervingly wry smile on his face.

"You're the bastard who told me about a husband," Jenne said acerbically.

"True, though I'm told you handled the matter yourself." The smile didn't leave his face.

Hendrick blushed. Hendrick never blushed. Jenne furrowed her brows. "Should I leave?" she asked.

"No, no," the silk merchant waved. "I have more news for you."

"Is it about the dragon?" Hendrick asked.

The silk merchant laughed. "I've seen it. It's merely an unfortunate looking goat." Hendrick joined in his laughter.

"Sit, please!" Hendrick pointed across the table. The silk merchant sat daintily. "Jenne, this is Surgoi." Surgoi nodded his head as an introduction. "He's, uh..."

"I know who he is," Jenne teased. "What I don't know is why I'm still here. Clearly you have some catching up to do."

Hendrick inhaled as though he was about to speak, but promptly thought better of it and clapped his mouth shut.

Surgoi took the opportunity for him. "As you know, I visit many places."

"Including this one for some *mysterious* reason," Jenne joked.

Surgoi cleared his throat. "Yes, well. Most of the places I visit are not so small." Jenne waited for him to continue, unsure of where he was going with this. "And merchants, well, we talk."

"Have I done something worthy of merchant gossip? Defiled a merchant's daughter, perhaps?" Jenne knew full well she had done no such thing, but it made her feel like she was on more of an even footing in this conversation.

Surgoi gave a small shrug. "Not that I have heard."

"What did you hear then?" Jenne grew more serious.

"I heard you were looking for a woman smith. I happen to have heard where one might be."

"Where is she?" Jenne whispered. Her eyes widened as though she might miss it if he spoke her whereabouts and she had blinked.

"North of the forests. Burdigila."

Jenne's heart raced. The din of the room had disappeared and only the sound of her blood rushing in her ears remained. Finding it difficult to breathe with how quickly she was hyperventilating, she nonetheless managed to demand "How do you know it's her?" even though she was ready to fly out the door on the merest rumour.

"I do not. They say she is spotted. Muscled. Her hair is the colour of wet sand, in braids, with markings on her arms."

"Some of that fits," Jenne nodded. "She could have braided her hair and gotten markings." Her breathing slowed as she tried to calm herself and think rationally. Ama always did tease her about being young and rash. The memory of it brought new waves of heat to her core that she tried to brush away. Now was not the time to get distracted.

"They also say she has a boy with her."

Jenne's heartbeat sped up again, even as she willed it to slow. Her eyes flew fervently to Hendrick.

"Lots of women have children and no husbands," he said. Hendrick did not want to go chasing a rumour. Not when they had planning to do. Burdigila was five days ride away and they needed to use the summer to prepare to be merchants themselves.

"They say he's the one who takes the orders. The woman does the work."

"Is there any more information?" Jenne said frantically. "Out with it! All of it!"

Surgoi sighed and finished the last of his drink. "Stop interrupting and I will."

Jenne sat, cowed and nodded for him to continue.

Surgoi placed his tankard on the table. "I did not get her name. The boy, however, is called Karlson."

Chapter Thirty

Salus Animae / Varietas

A ma shook her braids, enjoying the sensation of them bouncing against the back of her neck. It was good to have her hair out of the way, but still feel it's presence. Like a friend that never left. The thought of Sera came, unbidden. Ama was still getting used to having part of herself removed, but, like her hair, things had changed. She allowed the memory of Sera to enter her. She felt grateful to have had such an amazing person in her life.

And then she let go.

Ama sighed and led Porridge to the forge. She had no real need for her anymore, but she refused to sell her. There was plenty of space outside the town where she could graze and it felt like Porridge was the only thing that tied her to her old life on the road. A life where she ran from everything, where she felt like she was a danger to everyone. There was no real love in that life. Porridge had been there through all of it.

Yes, there was the occasional release whenever she had been fortunate enough to find a settlement with another woman like her, but they were always just as nervous about being found out as she was. Not Jenne though. Jenne had rushed naïve and headlong into an absurd infatuation with Ama. She had damn near brought ruin on her village because of it, too. But Sera had also been young when she had known Ama. Younger even. Would Sera's feelings have changed over time if they had been allowed? Or would she continue to be that same mischievous imp Ama had adored? Why had it been so hard for Ama to let Jenne in?

Ama finished brushing Porridge and went to light the forge. Karlson was already there, ready to take orders. He had grown at least a handspan since they had arrived here.

"Where are your sleeves?" he asked, noticing that Ama had torn them off her linen shift.

"It's too hot in the summer," she said. "Besides, the women like my arms." As if on cue, the brewster's daughter passed by, eyeing her scandalously. Ama smirked. She had leaned into her newfound appreciation of her body with a confidence she was unaware she possessed. It felt surprisingly good to allow herself to be admired. To not shy away from stolen glances. To not immediately believe the looks you got were because you were ugly.

It was far from perfect and a lifetime of self-doubt does not erase itself overnight, but Ama had felt more and more like herself every day. She liked who she was becoming.

"You're going to get us in trouble," Karlson teased.

"I have no intention of doing anything untoward as far as that woman is concerned," Ama promised. Karlson gave her a side-eye. "Or any woman."

"What about Jenne?" Karlson asked.

"You weren't really supposed to know about that."

"The whole village knew about it." Karlson rolled his eyes.

"Yes, well, it doesn't matter now." Ama sulked and placed a billet into the coals.

Karlson watched her for a few moments. She became weirdly uncomfortable under his eyes.

"What?" she asked tersely, once she could stand it no longer.

"Just," Karlson shrugged. "Thanks for taking me with you." Ama blinked, unsure what to say. She wasn't good at receiving praise or thanks. She knew that it was something about her that irritated other people, but then again, she didn't like most people. She would like a *person*. Singular. And she would latch onto them and be the best person, the best *everything*, they had ever known. She would burn for them like the heat at the very centre of the forge. To everyone else, she would be *useful*. It felt like a strange betrayal to be more than that to anyone else.

She knew that other people were not like that. Other people could love more than one other person. She didn't understand it. Her mind could not conceptualise how *love* – this all-encompassing, all-consuming feeling could be directed at more than one person without it becoming less-than for someone else. But she had accepted that other people somehow, inexplicably, could.

Karlson interrupted her thoughts. "I know that you were promised my father's forge in exchange for teaching me and you didn't get it." Ama had forgotten that part of the deal, but now it made sense why Karlson was thanking her. "I know that the settlement is probably gone by now, but if you want, we can go back with a cart and bring some of it here. I don't know why anyone would take any of it with them when they left."

Ama turned to face Karlson directly, leaning against the anvil. The square was beginning to stir and the tabby sauntered over to its spot on the edge of the counter, but nothing pressing was about to happen. "Is it because you miss your father?" she asked.

"I guess," he said. Karlson would not admit it because Karlson was twelve, but he felt ambivalent toward his father. His world had already ended when his mother died. It was when Ama took him in that his life had started again. Ama interpreted his reluctance to talk about his father as a reluctance to be emotional. She did not understand that Karlson felt the same way about her as Ama felt about Sister Klara.

"Yeah," she said. "I'm sure someone around here has a cart we can rent. It'll take us about two weeks though, so we'll have to leave by fall." Karlson rushed forward and hugged her. Ama did not know how to process this, so she let him. And when it became clear she was standing awkwardly at the anvil with a child wrapped around her waist, she put her arms around him too.

Porridge nuzzled the grey tabby, who protested with a grumpy meow. Karlson let go of Ama and Ama took out the billet that was now a glowing yellow. They had a lot of work to get through today. She settled into the rhythmic clanging of metal on metal. It was soothing, like a meditation. Without realising it, most of the afternoon had passed. She was only jolted out of it by Karlson yelling "Hendrick!"

Karlson and Hendrick chatted animatedly for at least half an hour while Ama pointedly ignored them. He related the story of the dragon and the news of how the settlement was shrinking and the church would not be establishing any sort of presence. Eventually, though, he got sick of Ama's behaviour and roped her into the conversation.

"You look different," he teased.

Ama allowed her guard to drop. She smirked. Hendrick was always good at that. "You like?"

Hendrick winced. "Not really my thing." Ama laughed. "I do know who's thing it *is* though."

Ama frowned. She felt herself getting agitated. Hendrick saw it immediately. "Stop it," he ordered. Ama was taken aback. "You have no idea," he continued. "She has been absolutely intolerable for six months!"

"Wait," she said. "You want me to… because you're annoyed with her?"

"Yes!" Hendrick's arms flew above his head. "But also, because she really, really misses you."

"But," Ama's look was one of pure confusion. "Why? Why me? I always pushed her away." Ama knew why she was attracted to Jenne, despite her desperate attempts to avoid it. Jenne's infectious energy. Her inability to accept *no* as an answer. Even her rashness and refusal to stop and think before doing something she was passionate about. Also, Ama was completely mesmerised by her whenever she was around. Which is why she should be as far away from her as possible.

Hendrick pinched his forehead. "You're an idiot." Ama frowned again. "First of all, you are the most loyal, selfless person I have ever met." Ama blinked in confusion. "Which is why you have such a singular focus and you refuse to let anyone in and it's annoying as hell."

"That doesn't sound…" she started

"It does," he interrupted. "Look, I know you had this intense loyalty to Sera. And I know that something

I don't understand happened when we took you back to the orphanage and it messed with your head."

"You have no idea," she muttered. "I still feel like parts of me are missing. And I don't know what parts of me are even *me*."

"You're still you," Karlson helpfully interjected. Ama shot him a look. "What?" he teased. "Don't you think we would have noticed if you had changed too much?"

"Jenne wants that. That intensity. That absolute, unwavering devotion," Hendrick said. "The only other person she's had any sort of stability with is me, and I'm really not her type."

Ama supposed she could accept that. There would have to be a lot of talking to get past everything and she wasn't looking forward to that. What would she even say to Jenne, after leaving like that?

"I don't think you understand." Hendrick's stare was intense. "Jenne is… different. She hasn't been the same since you left. She isn't the same optimistic person she was. I think…I think you broke her heart."

"Fuck," Ama swore under her breath. A fresh wave of guilt washed over her. "It doesn't matter what I do, I always mess everything up."

"Now don't you start that again," Hendrick scolded. "You just have some work to do."

Ama arched an eyebrow. "This sounds like a ploy to get me back to the village."

"That would be amazing," he said, "but no. I'm actually more concerned with Jenne right now."

Ama's face was sceptical. "Really? You've been trying to…"

"Also," Hendrick interrupted again, "she's going to *melt* when she sees *this*." He gestured broadly over Ama's newfound style.

"Wait, what?" Ama said. "She's here?" Ama was not at all prepared for that.

Sensing her panic, Hendrick raised his hand palms outward. She remembered the gesture from when he had trapped her at the inn the first time they had met. "Not *here* here. She's outside of the city. She stayed to gather some rosemary while I went to find you."

Ama looked at Karlson. "Did you plan this?" Karlson shook his head.

Hendrick leaned in closer. "She knows you better than you think."

"She hardly knows me at all!" Ama protested.

"You and I both know that's not true," he said with an annoying certainty.

"Go!" Karlson shoed her out from behind the counter. "Porridge needs to move anyway. Tell yourself you're doing it for Porridge."

It was a surprisingly effective way of manipulating her. Ama's heart raced as she unhitched Porridge from the beam, but she turned quickly and ran back inside.

"What are you doing?" yelled Hendrick.

"I forgot something!" she yelled back. Ama grabbed a small pouch hanging from a nail at the back and looped it around her neck. She ran back out and mounted Porridge, turning to the two people who knew her best in this world, even though it had only been a few months. She would reflect on that later. Right now, she had other things to deal with.

"Thank you," she said quietly. And then she rode off.

"What was that?" Hendrick asked Karlson.

"She's been working on that for months. Mostly when she thought I couldn't see."

"But what is it?"

"I don't know if I'm allowed to say."

Chapter Thirty-One

Gaudium Celestis / Mundi Taedium

Jenne knelt in front of a particularly lush patch of rosemary. The best time to harvest it further south was a few weeks ago, but plants apparently matured a bit slower here. She would have plenty for her various hair oils, as well as enough for Pèire, assuming he would even be there by next winter.

The salt in the air was different too. It was cooler and humid. She wasn't sure if she liked the way the salt clung to her skin. On their way here, she had noticed that some fools had planted grapes. The folly of nobles, no doubt. And they'd work their peasants to the bone trying to make them grow. If her village disappeared, they might be forced to join them. Which is why she needed to make sure she gathered enough to sell.

Jenne knew she had not been herself lately. She knew that Hendrick was worried. He had spent the entirety of the trip assuring her that Ama was certain to be here. That Ama just needed some time to process what had happened to her. That Ama actually cared, even though she always said she didn't.

It was a strange role-reversal for her. Usually, it was Jenne who was always optimistic. It was her who rushed headlong into the next adventure, dragging Hendrick along. That was what he liked about her. That was what *everyone* liked about her. She knew she had enthusiasm in spades. Too much, if she was being honest. And she had even controlled herself as much as possible over the last year. Except for maybe killing her husband-to-be, that was maybe a bit too far, but even Hendrick had thought it was a good idea. At least, he didn't object too much.

But all of it was based on the assumption that the village would always be there. That Ama would *somehow* fall in love with her and stay. Hendrick was convinced of it, but Jenne, for the first time in a long while, began to feel the tendrils of doubt settle in. She felt like she couldn't just push the thoughts out of her mind anymore. She couldn't focus or *will* someone to like her.

And she wasn't sure she could recover from that.

As much as she admired Ama, she did not want to *be* practical. She did not want to *accept* that the world was a terrible place. She did not want to flow around the rocks like a gentle stream. She wanted to smash through them, to force the world to change rather than be changed by it. And up until now, the world had mostly let her.

Jenne stared toward the ocean. The bright sun glittering across the waves as it slowly crashed into the horizon. She had been so excited to come here and normally, that excitement would carry her through all obstacles, but as the days wore on and they got closer to Burdigila, she wondered if she had been making a mistake. It was only Hendrick who had urged her forward and kept her from turning around.

The cool breeze coming from the ocean contrasted with the hot breath of the horse breathing on her neck. It took only moments for her to register what was going on. She turned to see her favourite silly grey mare, waiting expectantly for pets.

"Porridge!" she squealed. Jenne wrapped her arms around her thick neck, hugging her tightly before obliging. Her eyes scanned the fields, trying to find Ama, but she wasn't there. "Where did you come from?" she teased, scritching behind her ears. The pit in Jenne's stomach grew. Maybe Ama wasn't coming and Porridge had followed them here. But no, Surgoi had said Karlson was here, and Karlson wouldn't be here without Ama.

And then she saw her. Sand-coloured hair, only in tight braids, like he had said. Her shift billowed and hung loose in the ocean breeze. For some reason, there were no sleeves on it. She looked absurd. But good. Really, *really* good. Her arms flexed as she walked and she stood upright, almost swaggering across the field. Like she knew she looked good.

Jenne found herself getting angry at her confidence. Had she found someone else? Is that why she was walking the way she was? That couldn't be it, because she had said she *couldn't* settle down. But the danger had passed, hadn't it? Why wouldn't Ama have settled down with *her* if that was the case? Was she still upset about what Jenne had said when she had asked her to leave? Is that why she had moved on?

Jenne scolded herself. Her thoughts were spiralling out of control again and that would make her do something rash. She was an adult, she reminded herself. Ama was coming toward her. She would hear what she had to say before making any decisions.

She watched as Ama's braids bounced around her neck. When she got close enough, she could make out the markings on her arms. She could only guess at what they meant, but she seemed to be covered in them. There were even some on her neck. She wondered if there were any others that she couldn't see. The thought made heat rise to her cheeks.

Ama slowed her pace as she got close enough to speak. She reached out and steadied herself against Porridge, who didn't mind the extra attention. They both petted her for several seconds before Ama managed to find the nerve to speak.

"Hendrick told me that you had changed."

Jenne wanted to lash out. Was she only here because Hendrick had told her he was concerned? But she saw Ama's contrition. She could be calm and collected. She could think things through. "It looks like you're the one who's changed." She decided to settle on teasing. She hoped her voice didn't carry too much playfulness because she was still very unsure where this was going.

Ama nodded, directing her attention to Porridge. She took a deep breath. "I'm sorry," she said at last. "You've been nothing but extremely kind. And I've seen how everyone in the village loves you and how far your friends are willing to go for you and I've seen how impulsive and joyful and wonderful you are and I hate that I might be the reason that changed."

Jenne's face softened, but Ama didn't see because she was still staring at Porridge and she couldn't bear to check.

"I hate," she continued, "that I don't understand what it's like to give of yourself so freely to so many people and to have them all love you in return. I can't be impulsive. I've been terrified of caring about people too much for the past eight years, and even then, I only cared about Sister Klara and Sera."

Jenne's eyebrows knit together. "But you do."

Ama finally brought herself to look at Jenne.

"You do care about people," Jenne repeated. "That's why you work so hard to be *useful*. That's why you always felt you had to leave. That's why you took in an eleven-year-old boy no-one else wanted."

"He's twelve now," Ama interrupted.

"Shut up," Jenne laughed. "No-one thinks you don't care. We all love that you care *so much*. Your problem is that you don't believe others care about you."

"It was you," Ama muttered, as though no-one was listening.

"What?" Jenne asked, confused.

"It was you." Ama looked directly at Jenne now. "You were the one who kept me here."

"I still don't understand."

"It's okay. I'll tell you about it someday."

"Does that mean there will be other days between now and *someday*?" Jenne smiled, bouncing on her toes.

Ama only swept her into a hug. Jenne had so missed the scent of linen and chamomile, along with the iron dust that always clung to her. She couldn't help the smile that split her face against Ama's neck. Ama released her, but it hadn't been enough. Jenne surged forward, crashing her lips into Ama's in a bruising kiss. Jenne reached up to tug at Ama's braids, pulling her in closer and preventing her from escaping, tongue darting across her teeth. "This is so much better," she said against her lips.

"I should keep the braids?" Ama tried to say, her lip still caught between Jenne's

"You should keep the braids."

Porridge sauntered up to the forge and nuzzled her sleeping friend, still curled up and absorbing the last of the sun's summer rays. Hendrick was still at the counter and Karlson was banging away, making nails. When Hendrick saw Jenne clasping Ama's hand and leaning against her arm as though she were several cups in, his smile extended from ear to ear.

"Now I hope you know you owe me for this," he said, pointing a meaty finger at Jenne.

"For what?" She wanted to sound annoyed, but she couldn't stop from grinning.

"I could have spent several days with Surgoi, but you had me rushing here!"

"I swear, I'll make it up to you," Jenne promised.

"Fine. For now, we need to decide something. Txomin is dead, the villa…"

"What? Ama interrupted. You didn't mention that."

"Right, I guess I skipped that part when I was telling you about the dragon." Hendrick pawed at the back of his neck. "So yeah, Txomin is dead, Danel took over the ovens, but Markel sold the mill, but then left and no-one is really running it, because the maltsters only need part of it, so we kind of need that if we're going to keep existing. Should we go back and try and find someone to run it, or should we cut our losses and stay here, knowing that we might have to leave quickly if people's attitudes toward us change?"

"I know how to run the mill," Karlson said.

All three adults looked at him in unison.

"I do. It's the same system my father used to build the blower in the forge, just attached to a water wheel. I was there when he built it."

"I thought Txomin built it," Hendrick said.

Karlson shook his head. "That's why Txomin took me in. To keep it running."

"Didn't Txomin hit you?" Ama asked.

"Yeah. He was angry that I couldn't fill flour sacks fast enough, but that's not what I spent most of my time doing there."

"That's why you didn't know enough about the forge not to touch black iron," Ama mused. "You never spent any time there."

"Still," Hendrick said, "You can't run it by yourself."

"If I can find some people to go with us, can we go back?" Karlson asked.

"I...don't see why not," Hendrick said.

"Alright!" Karlson shouted before bounding off.

"Uh... I'll take care of this, I guess." Ama ducked behind the forge to douse the coals and clean up.

"You," Jenne poked her finger into Hendrick's chest.

"What?" Hendrick protested.

"Are going to have to watch after him."

"Okay." He turned to leave. "I'll see you later at the inn."

"Absolutely not."

"What?"

Jenne thrust her coin pouch at him. "Ama is taking your spot. You'll have to find somewhere else."

Hendrick stood agape for a few moments before fully accepting what was going on. It was an inconvenience, certainly, but he was glad to have his friend back. Hendrick was about to make a crude joke, but decided it would have fallen on deaf ears. All of Jenne's attention was on Ama, bustling around the forge, picking up hammers and sweeping embers. He turned and lumbered off after Karlson.

The innkeeper was wary that Jenne had brought a strange looking woman back with her instead of the great hulking man she had been with previously.

"She's my cousin," Jenne said when the innkeeper gave them a side eye.

"Will you be needing food brought to your door?"

Ama slid a silver piece across the counter. "Don't you dare."

Jenne giggled and dragged her prize upstairs. Ama recalled the first time she had pulled her away. She had been reluctant then, wary and afraid that she would lose her heart, only for it to be crushed when she brought doom upon all of them. Now, though, all she could feel was a giddiness. It felt wrong to feel like this after so long. She had accepted that she could be wanted. She had accepted that the dangers had passed. It would take time to feel like she *deserved* to feel loved.

Jenne felt no such reservations. Jenne *needed* to show Ama exactly how much she deserved it. As soon as she had entered the room, Jenne pushed Ama's back against the door, pulling on her braids like a leash, leading her into her mouth. Ama gasped, breaking away, lips bruised and swollen. "Where's the key?" she panted.

"Sorry," Jenne said, chest heaving. She withdrew the large iron key handing it to Ama. Ama turned the key, locking them in and placed it on the small table next to them. "I was being impulsive again."

"Good," Ama said. "You be you, and let me be me."

Jenne grinned and threw herself again at Ama, lips colliding. She kissed her hungrily, tongue delving, sliding ravenous across Ama's. She took all of it, sinking backward into the door, allowing herself to be consumed. Jenne pulled herself up by Ama's neck. She had finally gotten what she had wanted for so long and she was now refusing to let go. Jenne bit at her lips, nipping, teasing, but greed overtook her and she drew blood. Ama pulled her head back, feeling the pulse in her lower lip as a trickle flowed lazily across her chin.

"I don't care," she said, eyes wide and dark.

Flecks of amber shone in Jenne's indigo irises. She surged forward again and caught Ama's lips. Ama spun them around and pulled Jenne toward the bed. It was heavy oak, simple, but overengineered and would likely last a century or more. Ama sat and sunk into the down mattress, frowning.

"How much did you pay for this room?" she asked.

"Not enough if I get to do what I've been wanting to for this long."

A spike of fear shot though Ama that quickly turned to adrenaline. She felt it pool at her core and quickly lamented wearing trousers, though, she thought, a skirt would not have fared much better sitting like this.

Jenne knelt between her legs, mouth open, practically drooling at her prize. She savoured pulling

Ama's shift free from her belt, skittering her nimble fingers across her sides. The tips of her fingers traced the outside curve of Ama's breasts and Ama, for once, sighed into it.

"Up." Jenne said, lips popping with the p sound. Ama couldn't help but obey. She lifted her arms, allowing Jenne to slip her shift over her head, over her arms, though she had to stand to do it. "You didn't braid any other hair?" Jenne teased.

"For you, I'll braid whatever you want," Ama said, slipping her hand around Jenne's curves. "Including your legs around me."

Jenne squealed as Ama pulled her onto the bed, wrapping her legs around her waist. She leaned in to kiss her, urgency fading as it felt like they had all the time in the world. Jenne braced herself against Ama's breasts, thumbing the inside curve, her hardened nipple that was somehow even softer than the rest of her. She ducked into her neck, nipping at the delicate skin of her throat, trying to kiss lower, beneath her collar bones, but couldn't reach. They swayed back and forth, jockeying for position, laughing and sighing against skin.

Jenne angled her hips against Ama, heat bursting from her centre against her bare stomach. At some point, Ama had untied her apron. Jenne felt Ama's calloused fingers dig into her thighs, slipping deliciously underneath the hem of her skirt, skating so close to where she needed them that it was pure torture. Her hands found the curve of Jenne's waist, held tightly by the fabric of her garments and then suddenly, in one fluid motion, Ama had lifted the entirety of what Jenne was wearing over her head.

Jenne's indigo eyes sparkled in surprise, the cool moonlight illuminating her nakedness. "You practiced this!" she accused, mouth in the shape of a perfect *o*, but still smiling. "It was a long time ago, I promise," Ama swore.

Jenne looked at her with scepticism, but decided she didn't care right now. "Well, you're *mine* from now on," her look growing darker as she leaned forward to capture Ama's lips again. She hummed against Ama, pushing her flat against the bed. Ama's fingers continued to glide around Jenne's thighs, maddeningly avoiding her core. Jenne moved her hips to try and capture Ama's fingers, but she kept moving just out of reach.

Jenne found Ama's throat and gave a gentle squeeze. "I swear to god, Ama, if you don't fuck me right now, I will end you like I did those men."

"After the shit I've been though, death threats aren't going to work on me," Ama rasped. Jenne squeezed tighter. Apparently, this was the wrong time to try and make jokes.

Ama slid her arms around Jenne's ass, pulling her forward. She squealed, losing her grip on Ama's neck, kneeling upright to avoid colliding with the headboard. Before she understood what was going on, she felt the warm wet heat of Ama's mouth where she needed it most. Jenne gasped, steadying herself against the wall.

Ama's tongue slipped wickedly across her opening. Tracing, delving just inside. Jenne's clit ached, counting burning heartbeats. This was absolute, delicious torture. Jenne thrust a hand down between her legs and took a fistful of Ama's braids, forcing her upward, forcing her clit into her devilish mouth and finally relieving her need for pressure. Jenne sang a full-throated note that echoed off of thick limestone walls.

Ama's eyes sparkled, but Jenne couldn't see. Hers were screwed shut, fingers firmly interlocked between Ama's braids, pulling her into her core. She dragged her hips across the flat of her molten tongue and it was all Ama could do to let her.

Ama drank her in. All of her, without reservation. She could happily drown in this inn, between Jenne's slick thighs, with Jenne's taste cascading across her cheeks in rivulets. She was only vaguely aware of the chorus of Jenne's moans bouncing between the walls as her ears were filled with the sound of blood rushing through Jenne's legs, echoed half a moment later by the pulse against her tongue.

At last, a scream tore through Jenne as she thrust her hips into Ama's mouth one last time. Ama held her hips fast to her face, swirling the flat of her tongue against Jenne's abused clit, draining every flicker of pleasure. Jenne continued to ring off the walls. Ama was kind of impressed at how long she could hold that note. When there wasn't a single puff of air left and her clit had become so sensitive she thought it would burst, Jenne finally released her grip on Ama, collapsing against the mattress.

Ama let her pant for a few moments before she wrapped her arms around her. It was summer and stones were really good at keeping the heat trapped inside. Even in the slight moonlight, Ama could see the beads of sweat pebbled on Jenne's skin. Despite the heat, Jenne nestled backwards, aligning their bodies to fit neatly against Ama.

"That was…" she started. "That was amazing."

"You rode my face like a saddle," Ama teased.

"Did you… was that… okay?" Jenne said nervously. She felt the rhythmic laughter Ama tried to keep inside ripple from her chest against her back. Ama bit gently down on Jenne's shoulder.

"I want you to do that every single day," she said low against her ear. Jenne grinned, her spark renewed. She squirmed free from Ama's grasp, pushing her on her side. Ama sank back into the mattress as Jenne practically leapt on top of her. Jenne attacked Ama's breasts, which, like the rest of her, were lean and compact, but Jenne found them to be the softest thing in the world. She snaked her tongue around one nipple, twisting the other between her fingers. The sensation of her hot mouth on one and the slight twinge of pain in the other caused a fluttering low in Ama's abdomen, followed closely by a warm liquid feeling further down.

Jenne's clever fingers chased it, slipping between her muscled thighs, coming away coated. She placed them carefully between swollen lips, pulling them clean before lowering herself to kiss Ama long and slow. It was still somewhat unnerving to Ama that another woman could find her attractive enough to want *this*. That *she* could be something someone *wants*. Jenne understood. And she vowed to prove it to her every day.

Mid-kiss, Ama felt Jenne's fingers slip between her lips. Her hand settled, cupping Ama's core, massaging the whole of her vulva. It was a comforting movement, one that told her Jenne had paid attention. That she *got* Ama. She could restrain her need to ravish Ama until Ama was ready for it.

And Ama *was* ready for it. She angled her hips toward Jenne's touch. Her deft finger slid into her centre. Jenne smiled against Ama's lips, pleased with how easily this had gone. How ready Ama was for her. *Her* smith. So strong and imposing to the world, but fragile as glass for her. There would be time for her violent delights another time, but for now, she would go slowly.

She settled into the rhythm provided by Ama's hips. And though it felt like the most natural and intuitive thing in the world, she knew she was still relatively new at this. She closed her eyes, even though the moon had passed their window and it was almost black. She wanted to feel where Ama's hips led her. In low. Out, slowly tracing along her front wall.

After several gentle thrusts, Jenne felt confident enough to add just a bit of extra pressure where she thought Ama might want it as she pulled out. She heard a deeper pant. She felt her hips slow, dragging that part of the movement out just a bit longer. She felt Ama relax and open to her. "Another," she whispered in the dark. Jenne grinned, giddy at how well she was doing, but contained herself and did as she was asked.

The pressure against her insides increased just enough. Ama could feel herself racing toward that tipping point. Jenne was letting her be in control, letting her fuck herself against her hand. She knew that Jenne wanted so badly to devour her, but she was being so patient right now. One day she would let her rip the orgasms from her body, but for now, this was the sweetest, most considerate thing in the world.

Ama felt the rush of that tipping point hit. The flood against her legs, the flutter against Jenne's fingers and that rush of heat. Only a few more. She angled her clit to grind against Jenne's palm and Jenne let her. Ama did not usually make a lot of noise, but when it came this time, she sang for Jenne. Ama's strong fingers flexed hard into Jenne's shoulders. She would probably have bruises, but Jenne didn't mind. She would wear the marks proudly.

They sank back into the bed, spent and exhausted. They had a long day of planning tomorrow, Ama thought as she drifted off to sleep, Jenne nuzzled close against her neck. Jenne drew lazy circles across Ama's chest, wondering if Hendrick would build them a bed like this.

Epilogue

News of the dragon had quickly been forgotten, as had plans of building a fort near the pass in the mountains. Ama was certain they would try again, but for now, no-one actually wanted to be lord of these lands. Some king would no-doubt grant these lands to someone he needed to reward, but it would be some low-level fool who would have to scrape and save in order to afford to do anything with it. She suspected that finding and hiring enough men to collect the taxes necessary would take longer than her lifetime. If they were lucky, their village would go unnoticed by the wider world of important people for most of that time.

In the meantime, Ama pounded metal.

Jenne watched her hand a stranger a small pouch. He had walked off by the time she got there.

"Who was that?" she asked.

"It's a secret," she teased.

Jenne rolled her eyes.

"It's what I do best." Ama flashed a smile at Jenne, who was now leaning against the counter with a loaf of bread and a piece of cheese. The tabby stirred and nosed at the cheese, before Jenne yanked it away. Karlson had convinced them to take her with them and somehow, she was still alive and just as content to sleep the days away next to this new forge.

"Second best," Jenne reminded her. Ama visibly blushed, despite the heat of the forge.

"You two are gross," Karlson whined, though the effect was lessened by the fact that his voice had dropped an octave.

"Right," Ama bit. "I'm pretty sure that gaggle of girls isn't here for me." She pointed her hammer at four girls huddled together just close enough to the forge to stare at Karlson. Karlson attempted to stammer out a response, but embarrassment overcame him.

"I have to go check on the mill," he managed to get out before quickly rushing away.

"You go and do that," Ama said, laughing.

"Don't be late for dinner," Jenne called.

"How long do you think he'll be gone?" Ama asked.

"Long enough. Douse it. Now." Jenne ordered. Ama complied and raced to catch up with her. She was already half way to the house.

After they had returned, Ama and Hendrick had finished fixing up Karlson's house. Hendrick had laughed when Jenne asked him to build her a bigger bed because the old herbalist's hut would in no way accommodate something so large, so it ended up in Ama's room. Jenne spent more and more nights there until they decided to ask Karlson if she should stay permanently. Karlson said that he thought she already was.

When Ama did catch up to Jenne, she was already in their room and already undressed. She was an absolutely stunning sight, even more so in full daylight. Her smooth brown sun-warmed skin positively glowed, like she was a saint in some stained-glass cathedral window. She remembered how it was the smoothness of her face that had initially caught her eye all those years ago.

"I have something for you," she said once she picked her jaw up off the floor.

"It had better be you. Naked." Jenne demanded.

"We'll get to that." Ama took a small bag off of a nail behind the door and handed it to her.

"What's this?" she asked.

"Just open it."

Jenne pulled open the drawstring. Inside was a small, long handled gold spoon.

"When did you get this?" she demanded, shocked.

"I made it in Burdigila."

"That was four years ago!"

Ama nodded.

"But why?"

"First of all, I still owed you for that ointment."

Jenne rolled her eyes. "That was a joke. How did you not know that was a joke?"

"Second," Ama continued, "I know there's no world where we could freely exist and be *normal* outside of this tiny settlement. I can't give you that. You could have had that with that man your father sent."

"I killed him, remember?"

"I do. It was a very eventful few days. But I can't help the feeling that while I've *always* been not normal, I feel like I took that from you."

Jenne smiled sympathetically. "None of that is true. You need to stop taking on responsibility for everyone else's feelings. Let me feel what I feel. I thought we'd talked about this? Why are you bringing this up again?"

Ama shuffled nervously. "We can't ever get married," she mumbled. "This is my dowry."

"What?" Jenne's look was confused.

"Girls at the orphanage were given a small amount of gold in case we needed to get married. If we didn't, the gold stayed at the orphanage. I had some with me because we were to go to the city to buy supplies when I was taken. I've had it ever since."

"And you made it into this?" Jenne whispered.

Ama nodded.

Jenne threw her arms around Ama, holding her so tightly she thought she might break. Her heart thundered loudly against her ribs as Jenne assaulted her with kisses. Her lips came away coated in iron dust, but she didn't care. At that moment, Ama was the sweetest thing she had ever tasted.

"Bed. Now!" Jenne ordered. Ama sat and Jenne raced to straddle her, pulling frantically at her shift. All gentleness had disappeared. She needed to show this woman how much she wanted her this instant.

Ama was pushed back against the wall, the cool stones contrasting against Jenne's hot tongue against her nipples. Ama had discovered that Jenne much preferred to use her mouth rather than her hands for pretty much everything. Somewhere along the way, her trousers had disappeared and her legs were wrapped around Jenne's torso. Jenne pulled her backward and Ama slid until she was flat on her back. Jenne pulled her knees to her shoulders and leaned forward to kiss Ama. The softness of her breasts against her hard hamstrings and so achingly close to where she needed to be touched was dizzying.

Jenne wasted no time slithering between her thighs, breathing hotly against Ama's core. She narrowed her lips and blew a shot of cool air against her clit. Ama inhaled sharply as she suddenly became aware of every burning nerve firing, every pulse of her heartbeat slamming against the hard nub. It was quickly replaced by the flat of Jenne's tongue and the temperature suddenly increased tenfold.

Ama was practically delirious when Jenne slipped a finger inside. It went in so easily that Ama almost didn't notice at first. Over the last four years, Jenne had learned to play Ama's body like a finely tuned instrument. The second finger, Ama felt, but the third pulled noises out of her that she wasn't aware she could make. Jenne settled into the rhythm she knew Ama's body liked and Ama's hips reciprocated. It only took moments for her to shudder and buck against Jenne's hands. She was fairly certain she had never gotten there so quickly.

Ama sat up on her elbows, but Jenne pulled her wrist, making her collapse back down on one side. Jenne used the momentum to flip Ama onto her stomach and twist her arm behind her back. Ama gasped in surprise. "Where did you learn that?" Ama said into the pillow.

"Hendrick taught me a few things years ago."

"Hendrick taught you bedroom tricks?"

"No, just about taking people by surprise if needed."

"And you thought you'd use them on me?"

Jenne nodded, but Ama couldn't see.

"You stay there. I didn't say I was done with you yet," Jenne ordered. Ama smirked against the pillow. Then she felt teeth on her ass and she yelped. A giggle was all she got in response. She felt Jenne splay her legs and then her molten tongue on her lips again. Her clit was still oversensitive, but the heat and pressure against her core was bringing her back around.

Jenne's tongue teased around her thighs, but her hot breath around her centre kept her just on the edge of arousal. She felt her pulse steadily increase. Steadily grow stronger against her clit. Ama angled her hips, grinding down against the bed to relieve the pressure. Which is when Jenne's tongue found a place she wasn't expecting. Ama's eyes flew open. Everything about this was wrong, but *my god*, it felt..., indescribable. *Good* was not an appropriate word for it. *Good* was a word for things like butterflies and rainbows and warm hugs. This felt like the distilled essence of everything the devil might tempt you with in exchange for your soul.

Her fingers dug into the pillow and two fingers filled her. Then three. Ama tried to relax, but it was so much. She was so full. Ama was afraid she would tear it in two in an explosion of down feathers. She felt like she contained the entire heat of the forge inside her. Like it had spread to every nerve and through every vein. She was certain she was screaming, but all she could hear was the pounding of her heartbeat and the rush of blood. It was so loud. She came completely undone.

When she came to, Jenne was kneeling over her, rubbing her chest. "Sorry, I should have asked," she said, wiping her mouth. The evening sunlight filtered through her dark hair, locks falling about her face. Why did she have to be so beautiful and how did Ama ever deserve her? Ama cupped her face and drew her in for a kiss. They were both sticky and dripping with the smell of sex. "I think we both need to bathe before dinner."

Jenne nodded and laughed.

They searched the house for Karlson, but he wasn't there. They found him waiting outside with Hendrick.

"You two need to close the shutters," Karlson sputtered as he walked into the house, lumbering past them, limbs far too long to look like they belonged to him.

Hendrick nodded. "Look, I knew what you were going to do when I built you that bed, but, uh, that was a bit much."

Ama looked bashful. Jenne told him he was just jealous.

"We should probably start planning a house for Karlson. It'll take a year just to gather enough stone and he might be ready for it sooner rather than later if you two don't behave."

"Isn't this house Karlson's?" Ama asked.

"Or your own house, I don't really care. I don't think he does either."

"Why don't we build it where the herbalist's hut is. It's mostly fallen down anyway. That way we won't have to be so careful about what we grow in the kitchen garden," Ama said.

"And the whole village won't have to hear us," Jenne added.

"I am bemoaning getting you two together right now," Hendrick whined.

"That's a big word. Did you learn it from Surgoi?" Ama asked. Hendrick pouted at her.

"Well come in for supper then. We'll make it up to you," Jenne said.

Ama rose with the sun. She carried a small candle outside and lit it with an ember from last night's fire. Jenne's hand slipped over her shoulder. Ama reached across her body to interlace their fingers.

"Happy birthday," Jenne whispered, kissing her ear.

Ama smiled sadly. "Do you know why I got these?" she asked, flexing her fingers.

"Your markings?"

Ama nodded.

"Tell me."

"After… what happened. My body didn't feel like my own. I kept seeing hands that weren't mine. Hearing a voice I had never spoken with. But I knew those hands and that voice. I felt like I had to make them different and then climb into that body. I'm not explaining it very well. I don't think I can."

Jenne laced her arms around Ama's neck. She listened.

"She would have liked you." Ama whispered. "You two would have gotten into so much trouble together as kids."

She felt Jenne smile against her neck. "Thankfully we both had you around to keep us in check."

"I'm doing a terrible job at that," Ama laughed. She pointed to a string of characters along her collarbone. "Do you know what this one is?" she asked. Jenne shook her head.

"It's your name. I had Astrid tell me what sounds the runes made."

"Who's Astrid?" Jenne asked. "Should I be jealous?"

"You have nothing to worry about," Ama teased and then grew serious. "I was told that it was impossible to separate two souls and that we would die together. But Sera left, or at least, as much of herself as she could separate. Astrid told me that I must have had someone here who held me so tightly that I wouldn't be able to leave."

"Me?" Jenne whispered.

Ama nodded. Tears came freely and unbidden.

"I love you," Jenne sniffed. "So, so much."

"I love you too," Ama wiped her tears across her arm. They sat for a few minutes in a comfortable silence.

"I have one more thing," she whispered, voice sore.

Jenne squeezed tighter. "What is it?"

"Do you remember that man?"

"No. There are lots of men."

"The one you saw me give money to a few months ago. He came back this morning."

She felt Jenne nod against her neck.

"He found her."

"Found who?"

"Your younger sister. She's in Narbo Maritus."

For once, Jenne had no words. All she could do was hold her smith as tight as her strength would allow. When she had finished, Jenne rested her head on Ama's lap and they sat, watching the smoke from Sera's candle drift upward to the heavens.

Together.

Need just a little bit more?

Check in on Jenne's sister in the short story Just A Kiss. Sign up for the newsletter at marinestjean.ca to receive it FREE.

About The Author

Marine lives in the wilds of Canada with her wife and cat. When not writing, she is riding her motorcycle, doing witchcraft in the woods or building a deck. Your mom probably told you to stay away from her at one point.
She was probably right.

This is an independently published book.
You can help me and all other independent publishers by leaving a review
Follow Marine on Bluesky @marinestjean.bsky.social
Sign up for the newsletter at
marinestjean.ca

www.ingramcontent.com/pod-product-compliance
Lightning Source LLC
Chambersburg PA
CBHW070217260626
47160CB00002B/585